THE
TELL-TALE
HORSE

**Center Point
Large Print**

**This Large Print Book carries the
Seal of Approval of N.A.V.H.**

THE
TELL-TALE
HORSE

RITA MAE BROWN

CENTER POINT PUBLISHING
THORNDIKE, MAINE

This Center Point Large Print edition
is published in the year 2007 by arrangement with
The Random House Publishing Group,
a division of Random House, Inc.

The text of this Large Print edition is unabridged. In other
aspects, this book may vary from the original edition.
Printed in the United States of America.
Set in 16-point Times New Roman type.

ISBN-10: 1-60285-082-8
ISBN-13: 978-1-60285-082-8

Library of Congress Cataloging-in-Publication Data

Brown, Rita Mae.
    The tell-tale horse / Rita Mae Brown.--Center Point large print ed.
        p. cm.
    ISBN-13: 978-1-60285-082-8 (lib. bdg. : alk. paper)
        1. Arnold, Jane (Fictitious character)--Fiction. 2. Women hunters--Fiction.
    3. Fox hunting--Fiction. 4. Virginia--Fiction. 5. Large type books. I. Title.

PS3552.R698T46 2007
813'.54--dc22

2007034528

*Dedicated to
Donna Gaerttner,
who loves foxhounds*

CAST OF CHARACTERS

THE HUMANS

Jane Arnold, Sister, is Master of Foxhounds of the Jefferson Hunt Club in central Virginia. She loves her hounds, her horses, and her house pets. Occasionally, she finds humans lovable too. Strong, healthy, vibrant at seventy-three, she's proof of the benefits of the outdoor life.

Shaker Crown is the huntsman. He's acquired the discipline of holding his tongue and his temper most times, and he's wonderful with hounds. In his early forties, he's finding his way back to love.

Crawford Howard, a self-made man, moved to Virginia from Indiana. He's egotistical and ambitious and thinks he knows more than he does about foxhunting. But he's also generous, intelligent, and fond of young people. His great disappointment is not being a father but he never speaks of this, especially to his wife.

Marty Howard loves her husband. They've had their ups and downs but they understand each other. She is accustomed to sweeping up after him, but she does this less than in the past. He's got to learn sometime. She's a better rider than her husband, which spurs him on.

Charlotte Norton is the young headmistress of Custis Hall, a prestigious prep school for young ladies. Dedicated to education, she's cool in a crisis.

Anne Harris, Tootie, is one of the brightest students Charlotte Norton has ever known. Taciturn, observant, yet capable of delivering a stinging barb, this senior shines with promise. She's beautiful, petite, African-American, and a strong rider.

Valentina Smith is the class president. Blonde, tall, lean, and drop-dead gorgeous, the kid is a natural politician. She and Tootie clash at times but they are good friends. Val loves foxhunting.

Felicity Porter seems overshadowed by Tootie and Val but she is highly intelligent and has a sturdy self-regard. She's the kind of person who is quietly competent. She too is a good rider.

Pamela Rene seems burdened by being African-American, whereas for Tootie it's a given. Pamela can't stand Val and feels tremendously competitive with Tootie, whom she accuses of being an Oreo cookie. Her family substituted money for love, which makes Pamela poor. Underneath it all she's basically a good person, but that can be hard to appreciate.

Betty Franklin is the long-serving honorary whipper-in at JHC. Her judgment, way with hounds, knowledge of territory, and ability to ride make her a standout. Many is the huntsman who would kill to have Betty Franklin whip in to him or her. She's in her midforties, a mother, happily married to *Bobby Franklin,* and a dear, dear friend to Sister.

Walter Lungrun, M.D., joint master of foxhounds, has held this position for a year. He's learning all he can. He adores Sister, and the feeling is mutual. Their only complaint is there's so much work to do they rarely have time for a good talk. Walter is in his late thirties. He is the result of an affair that Raymond Arnold, Sr., Jane's husband, Ray, had with Walter's mother. Mr. Lungrun never knew—or pretended he didn't—and Sister didn't know until a year ago.

Edward Bancroft, in his seventies, head of the Bancroft family, formerly ran a large corporation founded by his family in the mid-nineteenth century. His wife, *Tedi,* is one of Sister's oldest friends. Tedi rides splendid Thoroughbreds and is always impeccably turned out, as is her surviving daughter, *Sybil Fawkes,* who is in her second year as an honorary whipper-in. The Bancrofts are true givers in terms of money, time, and genuine caring.

Ben Sidell has been sheriff of the county for three years. Since he was hired from Ohio, he sometimes needs help in the labyrinthine ways of the South. He relies on Sister's knowledge and discretion.

Ilona Aldridge Merriman, in her fifties, rides well, lives well, but isn't truly happy. Sometimes she can get fussy and act like the fashion police. She has a secret from her college days that is not revealed in this book.

Ramsey Merriman, Ilona's husband, coasts along. He's pleasant, with enough money to be spoiled. He's also a skirt chaser, which he tries to hide from his wife.

Venita Cabel Harper, or Cabel, together with her

husband, Clayton, developed and built in the early eighties an aftermarket electronic business installing cell phones and high-end radio systems in cars. Today they can install GPS systems and even tracking devices. As Ilona's best friend, she knows her secret.

Clayton Harper, brilliant in business, has turned out to be a dud at the rest of life. He drinks like a fish, sleeps with any woman he can lay his hands on, and basically just tries to keep peace with Cabel.

Lakshmi Vajay, called High, dynamic and handsome, originally hails from a province in India at the base of the Himalayas. He made his fortune in Mumbai and then left for Virginia. He enjoys the occasional discreet affair.

Madhur Vajay, Mandy, is gorgeous in her middle years, a devoted mother at the stage where she is beginning to feel an inner power separate from her remarkable beauty. Unlike Ilona and Cabel, she's unaware of High's occasional forays.

Kasmir Barbhaiya is in his midforties, widowed, and a college classmate of High's. He falls in love with Virginia while visiting the Vajays. Eventually he will fall in love again, guided by his deceased wife's spirit, but not in this book. He has made over a billion dollars in pharmaceuticals but would give it all up if he could bring his wife back. He keeps this to himself and is fantastically generous.

Gray Lorillard is retired from a prestigious Washington, D.C., accounting firm. He is Sam's older brother, and he currently dates Sister Jane.

Marion Maggiolo owns Horse Country. She's a vital member of the horse and foxhunting community. She's known for her good works, her vision, and her marvelous sly humor.

Garvey Stokes owns Aluminum Manufacturing. He's a decent rider and hunts when he can.

Lorraine Rasmussen dates Shaker Crown. She's in her late thirties, quite attractive, and learning to ride.

THE AMERICAN FOXHOUNDS

Sister and Shaker have carefully bred a balanced pack. The American foxhound blends English, French, and Irish blood, the first identifiable pack having been brought here in 1650 by Robert de la Brooke of Maryland. Individual hounds were shipped over before that date, but Brooke brought an entire pack. In 1785, General Lafayette sent his mentor and hero, George Washington, a pack of French hounds whose voices were said to sound like the bells of Moscow.

Whatever the strain, the American foxhound is highly intelligent and beautifully built, with strong sloping shoulders, powerful hips and thighs, and a nice tight foot. The whole aspect of the hound in motion is one of grace and power in the effortless covering of ground. The American hound is racier than the English hound and stands perhaps two feet at the shoulder, although size is not nearly as important as nose, drive, cry, and biddability. The American hound is sensitive and extremely loving and has eyes that range from softest brown to gold to sky-blue. While one doesn't often see the sky-blue, there is a line that contains it. The hound lives to please its master and to chase foxes.

Cora is the strike hound, which means she often finds the scent first. She's the dominant female in the pack and is in her sixth season.

Diana is the anchor hound, and she's in her fourth season. All the other hounds trust her, and if they need direction she'll give it.

Dragon is her littermate. He possesses tremendous drive and a fabulous nose, but he's arrogant. He wants to be strike hound. Cora hates him.

Dasher is also Diana and Dragon's litter mate. He lacks his brother's brilliance, but he's steady and smart.

Asa is in his seventh season and is invaluable in teaching the younger hounds, which are the second A litter and the P litter. A hound's name usually begins with the first letter of his mother's name, so the D hounds are out of Delia.

THE HORSES

Sister's horses are *Keepsake,* a Thoroughbred/quarter-horse cross (written TB/QH by horsemen). He's an intelligent gelding of eight years.

Lafayette, a gray TB, is eleven now, fabulously athletic, talented, and eager to go.

Rickyroo is a seven-year-old TB gelding who shows great promise.

Aztec is a six-year-old gelding TB who is learning the ropes. He's also very athletic, with great stamina. He has a good mind.

Shaker's horses come from the steeplechase circuit, so they are TBs. *Showboat, Hojo,* and *Gunpowder* can all jump the moon, as you might expect.

Betty's two horses are *Outlaw,* a tough QH who has seen everything and can do it all, and *Magellan,* a TB given to her by club social director Sorrel Buruss. Magellan is a bigger and rangier horse than Betty was accustomed to riding, but she's now used to him.

Matador, a gray TB, six years old, sixteen hands, is a former steeplechaser. Sister buys him.

Sybil Bancroft Fawkes owns two TBs, *Postman* and *Bombadier,* a fellow with great good sense.

THE FOXES

The reds can reach a height of sixteen inches and a length of forty-one inches, and they can weigh up to fifteen pounds. Obviously, since these are wild animals who do not willingly come forth to be measured, there's more variation than the standard just cited. *Target;* his spouse, *Charlene;* his *Aunt Netty* and his *Uncle Yancy* are the reds. They can be haughty. A red fox has a white tip on its luxurious brush, except for Aunt Netty, who has only a wisp of white tip; her brush is tatty.

The grays may reach fifteen inches in height and forty-four inches in length and may weigh up to fourteen pounds. The common wisdom is that grays are smaller than reds, but there are some big ones out there. Sometimes people call them slab-sided grays, because they can be reddish. They do not have a white tip on their tail, but they may have a black one, as well as a black-tipped mane. Some grays are so dark as to be black.

The grays are *Comet, Inky,* and *Georgia.* Their dens are a bit more modest than those of the red foxes, who like to announce their abodes with a prominent pile of dirt and bones outside. Perhaps not all grays are modest or all reds full of themselves, but as a rule of thumb it's so.

THE BIRDS

Athena is a great horned owl. This type of owl can stand two and a half feet in height with a wingspread of four feet and can weigh up to five pounds.

Bitsy is a screech owl. She is eight and a half inches high with a twenty-inch wingspread. She weighs a whopping six ounces and she's reddish brown. Her considerable lungs make up for her stature.

St. Just, a crow, is a foot and a half in height, his wingspread is a surprising three feet, and he weighs one pound.

Raleigh is a Doberman who likes to be with Sister.

Rooster is a harrier and was willed to Sister by her old lover, Peter Wheeler.

Golliwog, or Golly, is a large calico cat and would hate being included with the dogs as a pet. She is the Queen of All She Surveys.

SOME USEFUL TERMS

Away. A fox has *gone away* when he has left the covert. Hounds are *away* when they have left the covert on the line of the fox.

Brush. The fox's tail.

Burning scent. Scent so strong or hot that hounds pursue the line without hesitation.

Bye day. A day not regularly on the fixture card.

Capper. Nonmember who pays a fee—a cap—to hunt for that day's sport.

Carry a good head. When horses run well together to a good scent, a scent spread wide enough for the whole pack to feel it.

Carry a line. When hounds follow the scent. This is also called *working a line.*

Cast. Hounds spread out in search of scent. They may cast themselves or be cast by the huntsman.

Charlie. A term for a fox. A fox may also be called *Reynard.*

Check. When hounds lose the scent and stop. The field must wait quietly while the hounds search for the scent.

Colors. A distinguishing color, usually worn on the collar but sometimes on the facings of a coat, that identifies a hunt. Colors can be awarded only by the master and can be worn only in the field, or with scarlet tails by men at a hunt ball, again on collar or facings.

Coop. A jump resembling a chicken coop.

Couple straps. Two-strap hound collars connected by a swivel link. Some members of staff will carry these on the right rear of the saddle. Hounds are always spoken of and counted in couples, and since the days of the pharaohs in ancient Egypt, hounds have been brought to meets coupled. Today, hounds walk or are driven to the meets. Rarely, if ever, are they coupled, but a whipper-in still carries couple straps should a hound need assistance.

Covert. Pronounced *cover.* A patch of woods or bushes where a fox might hide.

Cry. How one hound tells another what is happening. The sound will differ according to the various stages of the chase. It's also called *giving tongue* and should occur when a hound is working a line.

Cub hunting. The informal hunting of young foxes in the late summer and early fall, before formal hunting. The main purpose is to enter young hounds into the pack. Until recently only the most knowledgeable members were invited to cub hunt, since they would not interfere with young hounds.

Dog fox. The male fox.

Dog hound. The male hound.

Double. A series of short sharp notes blown on the horn to alert all that a fox is afoot. The *gone away* series of notes is a form of doubling the horn.

Draft. To acquire hounds from another hunt is to accept a draft.

Draw. The plan by which a fox is hunted or

searched for in a certain area, such as a covert.

Drive. The desire to push the fox, to get up with the line. It's a very desirable trait in hounds, as long as they remain obedient.

Dwell. To hunt without getting forward. A hound who dwells is a bit of a putterer.

Enter. Hounds are entered into the pack when they first hunt, usually during cubbing season.

Field. The group of people riding to hounds, exclusive of the master and hunt staff.

Field master. The person appointed by the master to control the field. Often it is the master him- or herself.

First flight. The riders following the hunt who jump and therefore go first.

Fixture. A card sent to all dues-paying members, stating when and where the hounds will meet. A fixture card properly received is an invitation to hunt. This means the card is mailed or handed to a member by the master.

Flea-bitten. Said of a horse whose coat is white or gray and flecked with darker spots.

Gone away. The call on the horn when the fox leaves the covert.

Gone to ground. A fox who has ducked into his den or some other refuge has gone to ground.

Good night. The traditional farewell to the master after the hunt, regardless of the time of day.

Gyp. A female hound.

Hilltopper. A rider who follows the hunt but does not jump. Hilltoppers are also called the *second field.*

Hoick. The huntsman's cheer to the hounds. It is derived from the Latin *hic haec hoc,* which means *here.*

Hold hard. To stop immediately.

Huntsman. The person in charge of the hounds, in the field and in the kennel.

Kennelman. A hunt staff member who feeds the hounds and cleans the kennels. In wealthy hunts there may be a number of kennelmen. In hunts with a modest budget, the huntsman or even the master will clean kennels and feed hounds.

Lark. To jump fences unnecessarily when hounds aren't running. Masters frown on this, since it is often an invitation to an accident.

Lieu in. Norman term for "go in." English hunting terms derive from Norman French after 1066. Most of those terms go back to Latin. The hunting vocabulary is literally thousands of years old. For Western people it starts with Greek.

Lift. To take the hounds from a lost scent in the hopes of finding a better scent farther on.

Line. The scent trail of the fox.

Livery. The uniform worn by the professional members of the hunt staff. Usually it is scarlet, but blue, yellow, brown, and gray are also used. The recent dominance of scarlet has to do with people buying coats off the rack as opposed to having tailors cut them. (When anything is mass-produced, the choices usually dwindle, and such is the case with livery.)

Mask. The fox's head.

Meet. The site where the day's hunting begins.

MFH. Short for master of foxhounds; the individual in charge of the hunt: hiring, firing, landowner relations, opening territory (in large hunts this is the job of the hunt secretary), developing the pack of hounds, determining the first cast of each meet. As in any leadership position, the master is also the lightning rod for criticism. The master may hunt the hounds, although this is usually done by a professional huntsman, who is also responsible for the hounds in the field and at the kennels. A long relationship between a master and a huntsman allows the hunt to develop and grow.

Music. The sound of hounds in full cry.

Nose. The scenting ability of a hound.

Override. To press hounds too closely.

Overrun. When hounds shoot past the line of a scent. Often the scent has been diverted or foiled by a clever fox.

Ratcatcher. Informal dress worn during cubbing season and bye days.

Rate. Slow down or speed up. Think of a car's clutch.

Second field. Those who follow the hunt but do not jump; hilltoppers.

Stern. A hound's tail.

Stiff-necked fox. One who runs in a straight line.

Strike hounds. A hound who, through keenness, nose, and often higher intelligence, finds the scent first and presses it.

Tail hounds. Those hounds running at the rear of the pack. This is not necessarily because they aren't keen; they may be older hounds.

Tally-ho. The cheer when the fox is viewed. Derived from the Norman *ty a hillaut,* thus coming into the English language in 1066.

Tongue. To vocally pursue a fox.

View halloo (halloa). The cry given by a staff member who sees a fox. Staff may also say *tally-ho* or, should the fox turn back, *tally back.* One reason a different cry may be used by staff, especially in territory where the huntsman can't see the staff, is that the field in their enthusiasm may cheer something other than a fox.

Vixen. The female fox.

Walk. Puppies are *walked out* in the summer and fall of their first year. It's part of their education and a delight for both puppies and staff.

Whippers-in. Also called whips, these are staff members who assist the huntsman, who make sure the hounds "do right."

THE
TELL-TALE
HORSE

CHAPTER 1

Dots of brightness sparkled in the night from electric fairy lights shaped like tiny candles on the denuded dogwoods lining the driveway. Slashes of yellow light spilled onto deep snow from the high windows in the ballroom. The brick Georgian building had settled into the landscape over the years, so that people viewing this scene from outside might have thought themselves in the eighteenth century. The faint music would have put an end to that reverie. No Mozart, but everything else a hunt ball could wish. The swirl of elegant people inside added to the beauty of the scene. It was Saturday night, February 16, and the Casanova Hunt Ball was in full swing. Only stars and tiny glittering lights offered relief from the blackness of a new moon, and it was bitterly cold. Perhaps that, too, fed the frenetic energy inside, for the moon always pulls on humans whether visible or not.

Jane "Sister" Arnold, Master of Foxhounds of the Jefferson Hunt, her escort, Gray Lorillard, and a large contingent of Jefferson members had come to the Casanova Hunt Ball. The two clubs enjoyed warm relations as well as a touch of competitiveness. The Jefferson Hunt members, whose own ball had been marred by a drunken scuffle and torn bodices, relaxed here. Surely nothing so tacky could happen at Casanova.

Seated at the master's table were Bill and Joyce Fendley, joint masters of Casanova; their daughter, Jeanne Clark, now also a joint master; and her husband, John. Sister and Gray, Marion Maggiolo, and the entire Bancroft clan filled out the rest. Every table on the ballroom floor hosted at least one couple from JHC. Libations flowed, the dance floor was jammed, and Sister danced every dance as the gentlemen in attendance lined up to squire the master. Being Virginians, they performed this duty without thinking about it. No lady should ever sit out a dance unless she chooses to do so. Age, looks, and bloodline certainly improve a lady's chances of further engagements, but all belles have to be treated as great beauties. It's the custom.

In Sister's case, the gentlemen truly enjoyed dancing with her. Seventy-three, a trim six feet, with shining silver hair and buoyant spirits, she had the gift of making a man feel like a man and she was a wonderful dancer.

Joyce Fendley, passing her on the floor, called over her partner's shoulder, "Don't you ever wear out?"

Sister laughed. "If I did, I wouldn't tell you."

As the music ended, High Vajay, head of the Vajay family and a stalwart of the Jefferson Hunt, held out his gloved hand for Sister. His family called him Lakshmi, but the Virginians, fearful of murdering his given name, had nicknamed him High. It suited him, for he was tall and reed-thin, with salt-and-pepper hair, a handsome man who reveled in the high life.

His wife, Madhur, now Mandy, had been Miss Cosmos in 1990; at thirty-nine, her stunning beauty had only intensified with age. Their children, eight and ten years old, were tucked in bed at home, two hours southwest of Fauquier County, where everyone was gathered.

"Master, you move like a panther," High purred.

"Means I have claws." She smiled up at him, a pleasure for her since she often looked a bit down at a fellow.

"I've seen them." He held her tighter.

He had, too; there were moments in the hunt field when she had to wield her power, lest a hound, horse, or human be endangered, usually in that order.

After their waltz, High walked Sister back to her table, where she and Gray sat down at the same moment. The band took a break.

"What a party." Gray grinned, his military mustache calling attention to his white teeth.

"Anytime I'm with you, darling, it's a celebration."

He kissed her on the cheek. For a year and a half they'd been keeping company, as Sister's generation politely called it. They drew closer each day, but neither one was prepared to say *I love you*.

But they did love each other. In fact, many of the people in this room loved each other, but they may not have recognized the feeling. Americans focus on romantic love, particularly the pursuit stage, glossing over the sustaining bonds of friendship, a condition Sister often thought of as love made bearable. She enjoyed the members of her club and loved a few with all her heart. There were Tedi and Edward Bancroft, friends for most of her life. She loved Betty Franklin, her first whipper-in, a prized position and sometimes a dangerous one. Betty Franklin, in her forties, stood talking to a group of people while Bobby, her husband, returned from the bar with her tonic water and lime.

Sister cast her eyes about the room and smiled, perhaps not realizing how very much she did care for many of those assembled but realizing she was happy: blissfully, rapturously happy.

Marion Maggiolo, owner of Horse Country, the premier emporium for foxhunting needs and other equestrian pursuits, swept back to the table, her thick gray hair, once liver chestnut, offsetting her perfect complexion. No woman could look at Marion without envying her incredibly creamy skin. The rest wasn't bad either, for she knew how to put herself together, displaying the creative eye so evident in her store displays. Ladies may wear only black or white gowns to a hunt ball. Marion's elegant white dress, clearly custom-made because it emphasized all of her best parts, was no exception tonight.

"This ball is a triumph," Marion told Casanova's masters, now back at the table.

Joyce, eyes sparkling, demurred. "We didn't do a bad job."

Bill, square-jawed, draped his arm over his wife's

back. "Joyce and the committee planned this better than the invasion of Iraq."

"I don't wonder." Sister raised an eyebrow and the others laughed.

Slinking under the weight of black bugle beads, Trudy Pontiakowski, chair of the ball, made her way to Sister's table.

Her face, tight around the eyes and mouth, bore testimony to her determination to look young; the plastic surgeon did the rest.

"Marion, no one is hopelessly inebriated. See?" She swept her hand to include the room.

"Not yet, Trudy." Marion noted that Trudy herself was one drink away from the state she had just described.

"You could have lent us Trigger. He would have been perfectly safe."

Trigger was the life-sized horse that Marion and her staff rolled out in front of the store each morning, usually reversing the process at night.

Joyce intervened. "Trudy, Trigger's got an abscess."

This made everyone laugh. Trudy, tipsy though she was, knew her master well enough to know this really meant, *Shut up and leave Marion alone,* so she left with a gracious nod.

Marion leaned toward Joyce. "Thanks."

Joyce waved her hand in dismissal. "She's a great social organizer, but not always as tactful as one might wish."

Sister laughed. "At least she's not a bulldozer."

"Oh, well, we have a few of those, too," Bill noted. "How can people open their mouths without thinking? The stuff that falls out!"

"Cost George Allen his Senate seat." Gray referred to a popular Republican Senator who lost his re-election bid in 2006 thanks to loose lips.

"How do you keep from blurting out, *You're too dumb to have been born*?" Sister asked Joyce.

"Count to ten. Ten again." She added quickly, "Failing that, I do multiplication tables."

"Wise." Sister sipped from her champagne flute. "I bite my tongue because I really want to say, *You ass-hole.*"

They all laughed.

High returned with a portly middle-aged gentleman from Pune, a city two hours southeast of Mumbai, set amid rolling green hills, and addressed Sister.

"Master Arnold, this is Kasmir Barbhaiya. He just arrived." He introduced Kasmir to Marion and the others.

"So sorry to be late." Kasmir bowed. In white tie and gloves, his gold foxhead studs with ruby eyes twinkled.

"Welcome to Casanova." Bill stood and shook hands. Kasmir, educated at Eton, Oxford, and finally MIT, spent a fortune on his clothes. Not only were they bespoke—specially made just for him—he patronized the same sartorial establishments as did the Prince of Wales. He and High had met at Oxford,

30

their friendship ripening over the years until now they were as close as brothers.

"I will repent of my tardiness by condensing pleasure in fewer hours." His dark eyes shone.

As they left the masters, High looked over his shoulder to wink at Sister.

"That High, he's cooking up something," Sister said, and winked back. Then she noticed Marion suddenly break into a forced social smile. Since Ilona Aldridge Merriman was approaching, she understood Marion's frozen countenance.

"Why, you Casanova darlin's have outshone us, yes, you have, and I am so pleased to be here." Ilona deposited the Cristal she'd been toting onto the center of the table.

"How extravagant," Joyce murmured appreciatively.

"Thank you, Ilona." Bill lost no time in motioning a waiter to uncork the liquid treasure.

Two incredibly expensive facelifts over the decades did give Ilona a youthful appearance. Looks mattered to her perhaps more than to most women. She dieted with pathological precision, exercised religiously, and, to her great credit, hunted with abandon with Jefferson Hunt.

Turning her light blue eyes to Marion, Ilona flashed her own false smile. "Those marvelous earrings set off your thick hair. I still can't believe you haven't started to color your tresses, darlin'. Your natural sorrel color drove men wild. It's harder to have that effect when one fades, so to speak. Not that you could fade, darlin'."

"Your taste is impeccable, Ilona. Cristal." Marion sidestepped the backhanded compliment.

"Master." Ilona beamed at Sister.

"The rest of us get older. You get younger. You must have a painting in your attic." Sister was alluding to that novel of psychological insight, *The Picture of Dorian Gray.*

"You flatter me."

"Someone has to." Marion fired a shot across the bow, enjoying Ilona's struggle to keep her false bonhomie.

A flicker, then a cold reply came from lips shining with fresh lipstick. "Ramsey does nicely on that account." She opened her arms to the table as the cork popped. "Enjoy your bubbly, and thank you, Masters Fendley, thank you."

She slid from their table to the next, making her rounds.

"Guess she didn't like your ball." Marion arched an eyebrow.

"Balls." Sister was fed up with Ilona, who showed up at meets behaving like the fashion police.

"Balls, said the queen. If I had two, I'd be king. If I had four I'd be a pinball machine." Bill poured the champagne into flutes the waiter brought.

They laughed at the old chestnut, touching glasses.

Joyce leaned toward Marion. "She will never forgive you."

"Balls." Marion echoed Sister, causing more laughter.

"Speaking of balls, Ramsey operates on the use-them-or-lose-them principle." Bill was in good form tonight, his broad smile accenting a strong masculine face.

Gray touched glasses again. "True enough, but if a man has taste and is fortunate enough to win the hand of the right woman, best to use them in one location."

"My philosophy exactly." Bill grinned.

"It was a good thing you said that, honey." Joyce smiled like the Cheshire cat.

"Here's what sets my teeth on edge." Marion delighted in the sensation of exquisite champagne sliding down her throat. "My affair—brief, mind you, brief—occurred before Ilona married Ramsey. Twenty-five years ago! Get over it, lady!"

"Then what would she do? Ilona is loyal to her tragedies—intensely loyal, since they're so small and she's so spoiled." Sister, among dear friends, could speak her mind. "But she is also loyal to her friends. She's remained devoted to Cabel Harper, so loyalty obviously cuts both ways."

Jeanne, in her thirties, the youngest at the table, looked at her husband, John, and asked, "Is this a generation thing? No one forgets anything?"

"Forget? Hell. They make half the stuff up to be important. A lot of people just love to suffer," Bill said to his daughter, while John laughed.

"Perhaps the example of the two Marys at the foot

of the cross inspired them." Gray's mustache twitched upward.

"I say give up the cross. Other people need the wood." Sister laughed, then stopped abruptly, whispering, "Here comes my Mary. Deliver me!"

"Too late."

Her Mary was Venita Cabel Harper, still hovering at forty-two although that age had been current for the last ten years.

Given the social catchet of Jefferson Hunt, she'd die before she'd resign but, like Ilona, Cabel had never forgiven Sister for a fling with Clayton Harper, her husband some eight years her senior. Sister and Clayton both considered it harmless, since it couldn't last, and they knew it.

Because Clayton was married, Sister was cast as the evil vixen, and not just in Cabel's mind either. Sex was Sister's Achilles' heel. Most times she could discipline herself, but every now and then she broke bad.

This being Virginia, discretion only went so far. Sooner or later you were found out. Some busybody, gender irrelevant, was forever scanning the horizon for gossip. But Sister had had ample time to repent her earlier indiscretions.

"Thank you for a lovely evening, Joyce . . . Bill. Clayton and I will take our leave." Cabel nodded pleasantly to Sister. "Beautiful gown, Master." The joke was that Cabel never rode with Clayton, given his fondness for drink. She'd make sure they left together, but she would drive her own car.

"You look splendid as always, Cabel."

"See you in the hunt field."

As the frosted-blonde lady returned to her table to pick up her purse and her husband, Sister said sarcastically, "Venita happens to be an unusual, even lovely name. But her grandmother was a Cabell. Have you ever known a Virginian, even if related to that family only by once delivering flour to them, who can resist parading the name front and center?"

Joyce considered this. "Come to think of it, no."

"Even the Randolphs don't do that. They allow you to discover their grandeur over time." Bill, like most state history buffs, appreciated the many advancements both Cabells and Randolphs had bequeathed to the state by their foresight and energy.

The surname *Cabell* contains two *l*'s but Cabel's mother, choosing it as her daughter's middle name, dropped one of them. Or so she said. Her enemies said she couldn't spell.

"You know what I am." Gray smiled conspiratorially.

"Famous for horsemen, beautiful women, a piercing mind, and a fondness for liquid refreshment." Joyce diplomatically refrained from saying the Lorillards produced drunks generation after generation.

"True," Gray agreed.

Marion's naturally high spirits rose with the champagne. "Well, the Maggiolos are Johnny-come-latelies on the paternal side. They came from Genoa.

Mother's family arrived on the *Mayflower*. Theirs is an interesting match. Dad moved us to Fauquier County in the sixties. Glad he did."

"We're lucky to have you. We WASPs can be"— Sister searched for the right word—"too restrained."

"Is it *re*strained or *con*strained?" asked Joyce, WASP herself.

"Constipated," Bill interjected.

"Ah, still too restrained." Gray laughed and then shrugged. "I should know. I'm a black WASP."

It sounded contradictory in that WASP, of course, stands for white Anglo-Saxon Protestant, but Gray had absorbed the Lorillard culture minus the color. What he had that the others did not were the stories of his great-grandmother's grandmother and grandfather, stories from another continent handed down along with a very large helping of grit.

"Retreating." Marion noted that Cabel, her arm through that of the unsteady Clayton, appeared to be led out the door, the time being ten thirty. Actually, Cabel was leading *him*.

"It's hard to believe, but once upon a time Clayton was gorgeous," Sister mused.

"Too much lasagna." Marion giggled.

"Do you think Cabel knows how to make lasagna?" Sister found this incongruous.

"Why not? She helped Clayton build his business. He had the idea; she had the energy. She can learn to do anything."

Clayton installed unbelievably expensive sound

and telephone systems in cars and trucks. The punch numbers for the radio, like a keyboard, also worked for the phone. A tiny speaker above the rearview mirror allowed the driver to talk while keeping both hands on the wheel.

"Exactly when did you favor Clayton with your person?" Bill put it delicately, knowing Sister wouldn't be angry with him.

"Nineteen ninety-eight," Gray answered.

For a moment, conversation stopped.

Finally Sister said, "You've done your homework."

He took her hand in his. "I want to learn everything there is to know about you."

"Not everything, please," she replied. She'd only sipped half a glass, but the champagne had put her one step from giddy, since she rarely drank.

"Oh?" Gray's eyebrows rose.

"A girl has to have some secrets."

"Here, here!" Joyce raised her glass, as did the other ladies.

"You could give us a hint," Bill said.

"Dad, then it wouldn't be a secret," Jeanne responded.

"One hint. I'll divulge one. No man in this room has any idea of the time it takes to remove the hair on your body, do the hair on your head, polish your nails, apply makeup, and so on." Sister lifted her hand.

"Shaving takes time," Gray said, "especially if you have a mustache."

"Hope I never do." Sister laughed.

The rest of the evening continued in this vein, laughter, dancing, marvelous food, good liquor, and Cuban cigars for those gentlemen and a few ladies who donned their coats, repairing to the pristine outdoors to puff contentedly away, all the while cursing an embargo in effect since the presidency of John F. Kennedy, who had humidors packed with Cuban cigars, enough to last decades if he'd lived, poor fellow.

Finally the clock struck twelve. The band played on, but Gray rose and kissed Sister's hand. "Honey, I'd better be going." He had a meeting in Washington, even though it was Sunday, with the number-two man in the IRS. Gray, retired from the most prestigious D.C. accounting firm, was often called quietly, away from prying eyes, to counsel on tax matters. Capital gains was his specialty. He didn't mind performing regular audits for businesses, though. Gray lacked haughtiness and, much as he had flourished among the powerful, he was equally happy sifting through the records of a small local company, working with the owner. He truly loved accounting, hard as it was for many people to understand, because it gave him insight into different types of businesses. It also made him an extremely shrewd investor. There was a time when a rich and powerful African-American excited comment. These days, fortunately, success was becoming more evenly distributed.

After Gray left, Marion touched Sister's shoulder. "Ready?"

"Of course."

Not wishing to drive the whole way back to her farm, Sister had accepted Marion's invitation to spend the night in Warrenton. Marion lifted her spirits, making her laugh until the tears rolled down her cheeks. Also, she liked seeing Marion's house. Whatever Marion touched became colorful, dramatic, splashed with a hint of flamboyance like Marion herself. Sister's house, by contrast, was subdued, anchored in the eighteenth century.

Driving back to town, roads packed hard with snow despite the snowplows' steady work, the two chattered about the ball and about politics.

"You should run for office," Sister counseled.

"Never," came the swift one-word reply.

"Marion, you have uncommon good sense. You'd never squander the taxpayers' money."

"That's not what people want these days. They want false glamour, a smooth liar, and, above all, a pious hypocrite."

"There are a few good people in the game."

"I know, but I couldn't do it. Could you?"

"Actually, I think I could. Would I enjoy it? No."

"You know what? I forgot to bring Trigger in. Do you mind if we swing by the store? Won't take but two minutes. I didn't want to say anything in front of Trudy when I realized I'd left him outside. She would have run her mouth all over the ballroom. And I did say I was worried he'd be damaged. Got so busy trying to get out of the store on time that Trigger slipped my mind."

"Let's put Trigger in his stall," Sister agreed.

"It's not hard for two of us to move him inside."

"It will be a treat, in high heels and snow." The older woman laughed, although she didn't mind getting her feet wet. It wouldn't take long.

Driving in from the west, they turned onto Main Street, then right onto Alexandria Pike, moving slowly down the steep grade. There were two parking lots, one larger than the other; Marion pulled into the smaller one out front.

Both women stepped out, heels sinking into the packed snow, and did a double take.

"Those damn kids! This is what happens when I forget to take Trigger in."

A beautiful naked model sat astride the life-sized statue.

Sister paused before wrenching her heel from the snow. "Looks real."

"Trigger's been saddled with gorillas and with witches for Halloween. And it always makes the newspaper, the photograph. They're so slick, those kids. They do it right under my nose when the store's open."

The snow made a small popping sound as the two begowned women worked their way toward the horse statue, now burdened by the naked woman.

Sister grabbed Marion's arm just as she was about to unlock the chain that anchored Trigger to the building. "Marion, don't touch anything!"

"Why?"

"This isn't a model."

"What?"

The rider, ravishingly beautiful, jet-black hair and dark eyes, had her hands on Trigger's neck as though holding his mane. Her mouth was slightly open. A tiny hole was visible over her left bosom, where her heart would be. Sister walked behind the dead woman to behold a small exit wound.

"She's real!"

Marion followed Sister's finger. "Oh, my God!"

"Whoever did this had plenty of time." With the sangfroid that was typical of her in dangerous and difficult situations, Sister had already quickly absorbed the details.

"What makes you say that?"

"When a person dies they void themselves. She's clean as a whistle." Sister stepped back to study the body. "What a beautiful, beautiful woman, in the first flower of life."

Marion, voice low, whispered, "Lady Godiva."

CHAPTER 2

Marion called on her cell phone, and the two women waited for the sheriff in front of the store. The door was still locked.

"That's one good thing. At least nothing is stolen." Sister wrapped her arms around herself and kicked snow off her shoes.

"I hope not. There's a downstairs door that the public doesn't use but we do. It's storage."

Without another word, the two women carefully negotiated the steep steps down to the lower level. Despite being plowed two days ago, the area was packed hard again, thanks to the recent snowfall. The February sky glittered with stars so bright some shone blue-white.

Marion fetched her car keys from her pocket, pressing the tiny LED light on the chain. A narrow bright-white beam illuminated the doorknob.

Relief filled Sister's voice. "Nothing is smashed."

Marion placed the key in the lock, but the door swung open without a click. "That's odd."

Sister knelt down. "It's cut clean through. The tongue of the lock is in the door."

Marion, face ashen now, grabbed Sister's forearm. "Maybe he's still in the store."

"Do you have a gun in there?"

"No."

Sister spied a box of twitches, a device used on the lip to make horses stand still for things they might not like, such as getting their mane pulled. A small loop of chain was embedded in a three-foot heavy wooden dowel. She grabbed one. "I'll go first. If he's in there, I want to get him."

"It's my store. I should go first." Marion plucked a twitch out of the box too.

"I'm six feet tall and a master. I'm used to phys-ical . . ." Sister's voice trailed off as her foot touched the first stair. She flicked on the light, feeling incredibly alive. Danger was her element.

Marion recognized the truth in Sister's words. Sister Jane Arnold was tough as nails and surprisingly quick on her feet. Marion figured if Sister did whack someone, she could then help bring him down. Prudent and wise, not a woman to take an unnecessary chance, Marion was no coward. She thought Sister was reckless, heedless, but then most foxhunters are.

Sister hesitated at the top of the stairs that emerged into the tack and equipment room. The only sound was the slight *whir* of the heating system, set at sixty at night to keep pipes from freezing. Marion reached up behind her to click on the lights for the first floor. Nothing seemed disturbed at first glance, but if the killer was also a savvy thief, he or she would head for the saddles, some of them $4,000 a pop.

They stepped into the next room, which contained liniments and other odds and ends crucial to horse people. In the distance Marion heard a siren. "Thank God," she whispered.

Sister nodded.

They moved to the north wall, where the gorgeous English leather bridles hung, the saddles on racks before them. Not one had been moved. Carefully, they inspected every inch of the store, including the two dressing rooms and the smaller storage room next door. Everything was in order, except that the phone lines had been sliced through.

Marion checked the locked case where antique jewelry, Essex crystals, and foxhunting china was kept.

Again, untouched. So were the cases by the cash register, which housed specially cast hunting horns, the size of whose bells helped to determine the tone. They could cost $300, give or take; a specially ordered silver one was truly expensive. All was in order here as well.

Red lights reflected through the windows at the front door.

"Why would someone go to all the trouble to cut that lock and leave this place intact?" Marion sank to the front counter.

"I don't know."

Both women instinctively scanned the long shelves right above the cash register, where items of extraordinary value were often displayed. These shelves ran at a right angle to each other, the longer of the two terminating not far from the front door. The bronze sculpture of a fox above the register stood, gorgeous as ever, awaiting a buyer with very deep pockets. Just as the sheriff reached the front door, Marion and Sister gasped.

"It's gone!"

The John Barton Payne silver bowl, weighing thirty-five pounds with a two-foot diameter and engraved with past winners of the Warrenton Horse Show, had vanished along with the companion thirty-pound silver tray and the close to two-pound silver ladle. Its value was unmeasurable. The Warrenton Horse Show, owner of this impressive perpetual memorial trophy, would be disconsolate. Donated to the show in 1935, the sentimental value exceeded its monetary value.

It was two-thirty in the morning before Sister and Marion, finally in pajamas, collapsed in the living room, a fire roaring near their warmed feet. Though exhausted, neither could sleep.

During the ordeal, Sister had noted that Marion did not cry, whine, or complain about how awful this was. The younger woman had kept to the facts and answered the sheriff's questions clearly. She showed him the cut lock and even had the presence of mind to hand him a detailed photograph pulled off the computer showing all sides of the punch bowl.

Given the hour, no one from the local paper was monitoring the sheriff's calls, so they were spared the press, at least for now. No one recognized the slain beauty. The forensic crew and the ambulance struggled to remove her, tearing some skin in the process. Using warm water from the store bathroom, they carefully soaked the leftover patches until they could put the unstuck flesh into little plastic bags. Somehow, this process upset the two friends as much as discovering the body in the first place. The initial shock had been wearing off, but now the terrible event was becoming more real.

"Odd that a woman so stunning is a cipher. Beautiful women are generally noticed," Sister mused.

"She could have been murdered somewhere else and then brought here by whoever killed her and cleaned her up," Marion replied.

"But why would the murderer want to steal a punch bowl? You know there's a photograph of me in the punch bowl, age two, along with a foxhound puppy?"

"All the more reason to find it." Marion stared into the fire, every fiber of her body tired, her mind overwhelmed but still functioning. "Why my store?"

"Your store is central in town. Most everyone goes past it."

"What if this is meant for me in some way?"

"Unfortunately, Marion, we can only wait and see."

"I need to warn Wendy. This will blast her right out of bed, but she'll forgive me." Wendy Saunders had worked in the store with Marion for years. "I suppose I should call my brother too, even though it's closing in on the hour of the wolf." She meant between three and four in the morning.

"The Romans had a saying, 'Man is wolf to man.'"

"In this case, woman." Marion punched in the numbers, then listened with a flash of disgust. "Damn these things. They never work when you need them." She hurled the cell phone into the fire, where it began popping within seconds.

It was the one outburst of emotion she had allowed herself.

Sister nodded approvingly. "God, I wish I'd done that. Half the time my damn cell phone doesn't work either."

A bit of tension ebbed away as the plastic cell phone melted, taking all the information Marion had encoded there into the fire.

CHAPTER 3

Leg-breaking weather, Sister thought to herself. Just a few inches of slick mud masked frozen ground underneath.

The bite in the air kept hounds, horses, foxes, and humans alert. It was Tuesday, February 19, three days after the Casanova Hunt Ball, and the victim remained unidentified. Marion's store had closed one day to accommodate further forensics but was now open. When Sister went home Sunday afternoon, her friends had rallied around, the bizarre circumstances of the murder having made the news stations. The corpse stayed cold and covered at the morgue, so there were no photos of her, but Trigger flashed across local television screens and made the newspapers.

Foxhunting, thank the gods, swept away the cares of this world, even cares as disgusting as murder. A lapse in concentration could mean missing the fox or, worse, the jump. A fall on this greasy mud meant a cleaning bill at the very least and perhaps a broken bone. It was called leg-breaking weather for good reason.

The fox cared little for this. A stout field of twenty-five people was gathered on a hill overlooking old Tattenhall Station, an abandoned white board-and-batten building still exuding a forlorn charm. Hounds had picked up the perfume of a young red dog fox looking for a girlfriend behind the abandoned station.

Courting season usually started in mid-January for gray foxes, while reds took up the siren call of love in February. This bright, cheerful youngster, new to romance, was still learning the ways of the female. He'd run a beautiful six-mile loop, leading them right back to their starting point. Sister reflected impishly that all the higher vertebrates took their time with this process, and some males never did figure it out.

Shaker Crown, huntsman, dropped his feet out of the stirrups and wiggled his toes, praying for circulation. Sister, observing her longtime hunt servant and friend, kicked her feet out of the stirrups as well, a tingle occurring in her toes immediately, followed by mild pain. Cold took its toll but hunting is a cold-weather sport. They were used to it, even if they did sometimes shiver. She couldn't feel her fingers. Sister believed foxhunting toughened you up. Rarely did she or other club members suffer the full effects of flus or colds; their immune systems were cast iron.

Horses stamped their feet, splatters of mud and snow squishing out from shod hooves. Tedi and Edward Bancroft rode immediately behind Sister. Four talented high school seniors from Custis Hall, a private girls' academy, rode in the rear as was proper. Joining first flight, the jumpers, as a capper was Kasmir Barbhaiya in black tails (also called a weasel-belly coat), top hat, white cords, and custom-made boots. Riding one of the Vajays' Thoroughbreds, Kasmir proved impressive. Behind them, grateful for the check and breathing time, stood second field, Bobby Franklin in charge. Everyone's cheeks glowed with high color.

Dragon, a bold fourth-year hound ever impatient of leisure—and he considered a check leisure—grumbled. *"There's a fox behind the church at the crossroads. Why doesn't Shaker take us there?"*

Asa didn't bother to look at the upstart hound. *"Trust the huntsman."*

"We've only run for an hour." Dragon stood.

"Shut your trap," Cora, strike hound and leader growled. *"Shaker will think we're babbling."*

Dragon's littermate Diana wondered how her brother could be so blockheaded when her other brother, Dasher, overflowed with good sense.

Even the first-year entry, taken out two at a time so as not to overload the pack with youngsters, displayed more good manners than Dragon.

A light breeze had picked up since first cast at nine o'clock. It blew from the west with a bite and the riders, sweating from the long hard run, felt a slow chill seep in.

Sister turned around. "Scent will hold, don't you think, Tedi?"

"Stick like glue." Tedi and Ed were perfectly turned out, as usual. Sister scanned the horses. None looked blown. While it is the riders' responsibility to see to their mounts, an awful lot of riders were not horsemen. They really didn't know when a horse had had enough and should be taken in. Sister would politely tell such persons that their horses were tucked up and they should return to the trailers. While she never rejoiced in a human being hurt, the mistreatment, even through ignorance, of a horse upset her more.

A trickle of sweat rolled down her backbone. She'd half turned from the wind. Her undershirt now felt like a cold compress against her skin.

The layers of clothing a foxhunter wears, tested by centuries of use, protects the rider, but sooner or later, a wet cold will creep in. The mercury, hanging at 40 degrees Fahrenheit, intensified the dampness. A snow, even though the temperature would be 32 degrees or colder, often felt warmer than these conditions.

Thick pewter clouds hung low. It surely was a good scenting day.

Flanking Shaker on the left was Betty Franklin on Magellan, tested and tried as a whipper-in; Sybil Bancroft Fawkes was on the right, riding Postman, still as a statue. Sybil, owner of two thoroughbreds, loved the breed for their heart and stamina.

Horses adore this kind of weather. Since they originated in cool savannahs, forty to the low fifties feels like heaven to them. Humans prefer the low seventies, which feels too warm to horses, but they manage it.

Shaker, Betty, and Sybil counted heads.

"All on," Shaker said, which meant all the hounds were together. "Let's walk down toward Chapel

Cross. We might pick up something along the way, and we'll be heading cross wind."

Both whippers-in nodded and moved a bit farther away from the pack. There was no need to speak, since a whipper-in does not question the judgment of the huntsman or the master. Oh, they may do so in private, but when hunting the protocol is much like that in battle: You obey your superior officer and get the job done.

Sister smiled when she observed Shaker turning the beautiful pack, a balanced and level pack, north toward Chapel Cross. It had taken her decades to create a level pack. Whatever some blowhard may say to the contrary, there is no shortcut to a great pack of hounds. A master breeds for nose, cry, biddability, good conformation, and, of course, drive. What's the point of having a fabulous-looking pack of hounds, with voices like the bells of Moscow, if they don't want to hunt?

Dragon was a smart-ass but his drive was exhilarating. He shot ahead of the pack.

"Back to 'em." Betty spoke sharply to him, her crop held on the pack side of Magellan so hounds could see it.

"He's a lot of work, that twit." Magellan snorted, two streams of air shooting out from his flared nostrils.

Betty, somewhat understanding her fellow, patted him on the neck. After two years, they'd finally become a team, trusting each other.

The board-and-batten of the railroad buildings, white with Charleston-green trim, stood out from the muddy background, streaks of snow gleaming in crevices and the north sides of hills. Norfolk and Southern, the railroad company, had provided the point as a courtesy to local residents. Although Tattenhall Station had been abandoned in the 1960s, the locals maintained it and even decorated it for the holidays.

The pack had reached the railroad track and crossed it, with the small station, a little gingerbread on the eaves, now behind them, when Cora opened, *"Here!"*

The other hounds, noses down, honored her, and the whole pack, in full cry, flew over the lower meadow on the eastern side of the station and turned northward, again cross wind.

Sister, on Aztec, a young horse but quick to learn, kept at an easy gallop, behind the pack but not close enough to crowd them. They crossed the tertiary two-lane road and vaulted over a row of trimmed hedges, which made for a lovely jump, slippery on the other side.

The pace quickened. Aztec lengthened his stride and took a long three-foot-six-inch coop, which sagged a bit in the middle; perhaps it was only three-two there. His hind end skidded on the other side, but he quickly got his hooves under him and pushed off. Behind her, Sister could hear the *splat* of hooves as they sank into the mud and then gathered steam to surge forward.

The fox, whom no one could see, since he had a considerable head start, ran a huge serpentine S. Hounds had to work very hard to stick to his line, thanks to the wind changes, and in one low swale the wind swirled. Sister could see the little wind devil, small snow sparkles in the air, which then disappeared as she rode straight through it.

The fox headed toward Chapel Cross, no evasions now. A neck-or-nothing run saw hounds stretched flat out, sterns behind them, long sloping powerful shoulders illustrating the wisdom of good conformation, as the animals could reach far out with their front legs. Deep chests allowed plenty of heart girth and, behind, powerful loins and quarters, like a big engine in a Porsche, pushed them seemingly effortlessly forward.

The music filled the countryside. In the far distance, Sister saw Faye Spencer hurry out onto her front porch, pulling on a parka. Faye, widowed young when her husband was killed in the second Iraq War, waved. Sister took off her cap, two short ribbons streaming, and waved back. She made a mental note to stop by Faye's for a visit; she hadn't seen her since the hunt Christmas party. Where did the time go?

Faye, quite good-looking, hadn't lacked for suitors once a year passed after Gregory's death. She appeared in no hurry to favor anyone.

Valentina "Val" Smith, one of the students from Custis Hall, caught Cabel Harper shooting Faye the bird and raised her eyebrows.

A double fence line between two pastures loomed

ahead, a coop in each fence and a bounce in between which meant no stride; the horse must clear one coop and then immediately launch to clear the second. Sister liked bounce jumps so long as she remembered to keep her leg on her horse. Sometimes she would become so enthralled with the hound work that she took a jump without realizing it. Thank God, her horses were fabulous and loved to hunt. They could think for her.

Aztec, a bit younger than her other hunters, did need more attention, so as he launched smoothly over the first coop she clucked when he landed, giving him a hard squeeze, hands forward, and if he thought to hesitate he gave no sign of it. He took the second coop a little big; she lost her right stirrup iron on the muddy landing. No matter. Foxhunters learn to pick up stirrup irons on the run, and it's a poor trainer who doesn't teach his or her charges such valuable lessons. This isn't dressage at Devon. This is survival. Ride without if you must.

Fishing for the stirrup iron longer than she would have wished, Sister finally slipped her boot into it—couldn't feel her toes anyway—and turned her head for a moment to see how her field was negotiating the bounce jump.

Ilona Merriman, riding a half-Thoroughbred half-warmblood mix, hit it perfectly. Behind her, Cabel Harper bobbled on the second jump but hung on, laughing when she righted herself. Saturdays their husbands hunted too. Good thing this was a Tuesday, because neither Ramsey nor Clayton were good riders. Chances are the bounce jump would have unhorsed them.

Interesting as the sight was, Sister turned away from the spectacle as hounds now roared like an organ, full throttle.

The pack ran close together, Cora and Dragon fighting for the lead, Diana, anchor hound, steady in the middle front. If hounds overran the line, Diana usually brought them back. If she failed, the tail hounds, older, a touch slower but very wise, called the pack back to rights. All young entry—Peanut and Parson of the P litter, Ammo and Allie of the A litter—acquitted themselves with honor.

No overrunning today for this young red. Tricks exhausted, or too young to know more, he now flew for all he was worth. Well, he sure was worth a great run. Fifteen minutes later, the pack dug into his den behind the tidy Episcopal Church at Chapel Cross. Shaker dismounted, blew "Gone to Ground," and got back up. He couldn't feel his feet either. It was a happy huntsman that turned for home. Sister, too, felt exhilarated at how beautifully her hounds had worked.

Wind at their backs made the twenty-minute ride a trifle more pleasant. Close to Tattenhall Station, the tertiary state road, stone and crushed stone now mud, made the going slower.

A field master can ride in front alone when the hunt is done or allow people to come up and chat. Three years ago, an old lover of Sister's, who had long become a precious friend, passed away. She and Peter Wheeler had so often ridden back together that she'd spent the first half of the season after his death holding back her tears and riding alone. She'd gotten herself together a bit by the second half and begun chatting with folks again on the ride home. She could now remember Peter with warmth and gratitude for his gifts to her.

Today Tedi, Edward, and Gray all came alongside.

Bunny Taliaferro, riding coach at Custis Hall, rode right behind. Anne "Tootie" Harris, Val Smith, Felicity Porter, and Pamela Rene, all students, had earned the privilege to go out with Jefferson Hunt. After each ride they were required to write about their experiences, bringing in geography, topography, plants, animals, weather conditions, and history. They'd be able to fill pages today, since Tattenhall Station mirrored the history of America's railroads, particularly the spur lines.

Back at the trailers, most people checked their horses, removed bridles and martingales, took off saddles, and threw rugs in their stable colors over their horses' backs. Sister loosened the girth of her saddle but didn't take it off. She worried about the cold on that big sweaty spot even with a nice heavy blanket on the horse.

Tootie came up. "Master, Val's taking care of Iota"—she named her horse—"so I can take care of Aztec."

Sister handed her Aztec's bridle, squeezing Tootie's shoulder. She just loved this kid. "Thanks, honey."

Jennifer Schneider, a new member, already had the table set up, and people brought their dishes to it. Jefferson Hunt tailgates flourished in sleet, snow, or rain. Occasionally they had the use of a building, but no matter what this group could eat.

High Vajay, talking to Garvey Stokes, owner of Aluminum Manufacturing, nodded when Sister approached them.

"Master, what a wonderful hunt. Thank you." High's manners added to his considerable appeal. "I want you to have a chance to talk to my college friend. Once Garvey and I resolve the economy, I'll bring Kasmir to you."

Sister didn't even try to untangle the caste system of India, but she knew whatever High was it was at the top. He'd started out in the diplomatic service but quickly realized he'd be at the whim of changing administrations, so he took a job at Craig and Abrams, a large multilayered electronics corporation. Intelligent and driven, he had steered his division toward wireless phones twenty years ago and retired at forty-five. He'd learned to love Virginia when working in Washington, D.C., for half a year for the company. He'd vowed to return, and two years ago, a free man, he did. Once nestled in the Blue Ridge foothills, none of the Vajays ever looked back.

"How are you doing?" Garvey took Sister's gloved hand in his.

She'd been his master when he was a child, and earlier this year she had helped him through a dreadful time. He thought of her as a second mother but wisely did not say so. Most women in the company of handsome younger men do not wish to be considered motherly.

"I'm all right, but what a jolt."

"How's Marion?" High inquired.

"Watchful but okay. Obviously, we're all worried for her. The sheriff still doesn't know who the woman is—I mean, was."

"He's thorough. He called my wife and then me. I guess he figured anyone from India would know someone else from India."

"Doesn't India have over a billion people?" Garvey asked, his thick eyebrows rising upward. "And six million of them have AIDS?"

"True." High couldn't resist reaching for a tiny cinnamon bun, although he resisted commenting on the AIDS explosion, which could undermine, in time, much of India's recent gains. "But that wasn't as naïve as it might seem, because expatriates in any country often find one another. He e-mailed me photos. I didn't recognize her."

"It's possible she's an American citizen of Indian descent," Sister opined.

Garvey smiled. "We have everything here."

"You have us." High slapped him on the back.

Valentina and Felicity waited for Sister to leave the men.

"Girls."

"No one fell off. With this footing. A miracle." Val got to the point, part of her direct character. "No bottles."

If someone came off, a bottle was owed to the club.

As senior class president, the tall lovely blonde exuded a natural air of authority. She was one inch taller than Sister, which made Sister smile, since rarely was she topped by another woman.

"You didn't get one bottle." Felicity smiled shyly, a young lady of unforced reserve yet warm.

"I know, and the bar is getting low."

"If we come off you only get a six-pack of soda." Val turned. "Here comes the African queen."

She teased Tootie, diminutive at five foot four and lavishly gorgeous. Tootie was African-American, hence "African queen." Tootie was high yellow, a term only old folks, black and white, would have used. Tootie's skin, creamy, shimmering like light café au lait, signified someone of high blood from way back. Tootie didn't give a damn about any of that in any case; her generation hadn't suffered from racism to the degree that their parents had. Good as this was, it didn't mean there wasn't a reservoir of stupidity out there for which these youngsters were often unprepared.

"If I were Tootie, I'd hit you in the mouth," Felicity said quietly.

"Ef you."

"Val, one dollar. Actually two. That was ugly."

The three girls had made a pact at the beginning of

their senior year that when any one of them swore they had to give Felicity, the banker, one dollar. At the end of their senior year, this ever-growing sum would go to a party.

Pamela Rene, also African-American, walked with Tootie. The two didn't much like each other, but most times they managed a truce.

Pamela smiled at Sister. "Thank you, Master."

"You're most welcome." Sister was pleased that Pamela's hunting manners were up to form, for one should thank the master.

"The pack"—Tootie paused, eyes shining—"you could have thrown a blanket over them."

One of the many reasons Sister so loved this seventeen-year-old was the girl loved hounds. She rode to hunt as opposed to hunting to ride.

"I was proud of them. The four young ones in there ran like old pros," Sister agreed.

She'd seen these girls grow up in their years at Custis Hall as she'd seen so many juniors in her over thirty years as master. All people under twenty-one were usually styled juniors for foxhunting clubs and the dues were much lower than for those of voting age. When a young person came back after college, more likely returning to hunting in their early thirties, she was wildly happy. She hoped these girls would find their way back to her or, if not to her, then to another master at another hunt.

"Sister, I've gotten an early acceptance at Ol' Miss." Pamela beamed.

"You didn't tell me." Val shot her mouth off before Sister could reply. "Oops, sorry."

"Congratulations, Pamela. I know you Custis Hall ladies will receive other acceptances. Any college would be fortunate to have you."

"I really want to go to Ol' Miss." Pamela truly was excited.

Anything to put distance between her super-rich magnate father and her critical former-model mother. Oxford, Mississippi, was a long whistle from Chicago, where the Renes lived.

"Her mother will kill her," Val said offhandedly.

"Well, Pamela, you'll make the right decision." Sister considered her words carefully. "No one wants to disappoint her parents, but you have to follow your heart, you know." She winked. "Takes a Yankee girl with guts to go down into the Delta."

Pamela's face registered the compliment. "Thank you, Master."

Val giggled and said to Sister in a low voice. "Mrs. Harper shot the bird at Mrs. Spencer."

Sister's eyebrows raised. "Whatever for?"

Val shrugged, and Sister shook her head at this odd deed.

Ronnie Haslip, club treasurer, a boyhood friend of Sister's deceased son, called out, "Master, we need you."

She turned to see Ronnie, her joint master Walter Lungrun, Betty, Bobby, and Sybil and wondered what it could be. Well, they were smiling so it couldn't be too bad.

"Excuse me, girls." As she walked toward the adults she wondered what she could do to help Felicity, two months pregnant. Her parents didn't know; Charlotte Norton, headmistress at Custis Hall, didn't know. The hunt season would be over in less than a month. Sister had the feeling that a lot was going to happen between now and then, and not just to Felicity.

"Are you all ganging up on me?" Sister put one hand on Ronnie's shoulder, another on Walter's, drawing the two men near her.

They slipped their arms around her small waist.

Betty, hand on hip, shook her head. "You are shameless with men."

Ronnie, who adored Betty as most members did, said, "She's tall, gorgeous, and rides us all into the ground. You're shorter, pretty as a peach, but so-o-o married. All that virtue"—he clucked—"so dull, darling."

Betty laughed. "It's true. Should I have an affair just to prove I can do it?" She paused, glancing at her husband, overweight and suffering on another diet. "Can't do it. I'm still crazy about the guy."

Walter, still on an adrenaline high from the chase, squeezed Sister closer to him. "Ronnie, let her go. She's mine."

"Never," Ronnie replied. "Let me cut to the chase, Master. As you know, Kilowatt is available."

Kilowatt, a fantastic Thoroughbred, was formerly owned by a physician now deceased. His estate evidenced little desire to pay board bills. The executor, Cookie Finn, a lawyer of unimpeachable reputation, had approached Walter.

Sister nodded. "I see. He's a fine horse."

"Your bench is deep enough, but Shaker has only Showboat, Hojo, and Gunpowder." Ronnie pushed on. "Showboat is fourteen. Hojo is eight, plenty of good years there, but Gunpowder, great as he is, is eighteen. We should buy Kilowatt for Shaker."

"Ronnie, I can't believe you're suggesting we dip into the treasury. You're usually tight as a tick, plus we've lost the wonderful monetary gifts Crawford used to make. That really hurts."

Crawford Howard was a wealthy member who had resigned from the club in a huff.

"I know, I know." Ronnie let go of her waist and held up his hand to stay protest. "What I would like to do, with your permission, is pass the hat. It is the responsibility of the club to mount professional staff. We aren't rich enough to perform this service via our much-called-upon treasury, but if I can canvass the elected"—he used the word Calvinists use for those with a ticket straight to heaven—"might could."

Betty put in her two cents. "Sister, everyone knows we took a big hit when Crawford pissed off. Forgive my French."

"Guess they do," the older woman agreed.

"I'll put up five hundred. I'm sure Mom and Dad will be generous," Sybil volunteered.

"Honey, your mother and father give so much to

this club I'd be embarrassed to ask for more."

"I'm not." Ronnie smiled.

"We know that." Sister smiled back at him. She looked to Walter.

"I don't see any other way." Walter slid his hand from her waist to hold her right hand.

"Before I say yes, how much?"

"Fifteen thousand. He's been vetted sound, by the way," Ronnie added. "Cookie started at twenty-five. Really, Kilowatt would be snapped up at that price if he were shown at the northern Virginia hunts."

"That's the truth." Sister acknowledged the deep pockets riding in those fabled hunts, as well as the fact that Kilowatt was supremely talented as well as beautiful.

"I give my blessing with one caveat: Go to the Bancrofts last. See if you can't secure the sum before leaning on Tedi and Edward."

"I promise." Ronnie inclined his head, a polite bow to his superior.

"All right, then. Let's do the shake-and-howdy." Sister kissed Ronnie on the cheek, then Walter.

"What about me?" Betty pretended to pout.

"All right." Sister made a face, then kissed Betty. "Sybil, I have enough for all." She kissed the much younger woman's cold cheek. "Now come on, we've got to mix and mingle. We have cappers."

Cappers were guests, people who joined the hunt for the day, paying a cap fee. They always added a little dash of paprika to the stew.

Ben Sidell, sheriff, drove up in his squad car slowly, the road being slick.

"You missed a good one," Sister said in greeting him.

"I'll be out Saturday. I was in the neighborhood so I thought I'd drop by."

"Trouble?"

"Someone shot out Faye Spencer's barn light. Nothing major." He waved to Val, who noticed him.

"Give everyone the benefit of your personality," Sister teased him.

High Vajay bounded up, wearing his dark navy frock coat, top hat, and cream string gloves, then slipped on the ice, going down on one knee.

"That's how you should address your master." Sister made light of his predicament and reached out her hand, which he grasped for balance to stand.

"Mandy looked out the window this morning and declined to brave the elements. She'll be sorry when she hears how good it was. I'm delighted I came out." He paused. "People think India is hot, but we come from the north by the mountains. Snow and ice descend upon us, but I must confess I never hunted in cold weather before moving here."

"High, it was a lucky day when your family came on board." She meant it; their buoyant spirits and natural warmth lifted everyone up.

Kasmir, stepping much more carefully, joined them. "A most delightful day. Thank you, Master."

"Mr. Barbhaiya,"—she breathed an inward sigh of

relief that she had remembered his name correctly—
"we are honored to have you. Your turnout is perfect
and, sir, you can ride!"

Pleased, he smiled, his teeth sparkling under his
bushy mustache. "I find myself in London often. I do
believe the best tailors for gentlemen are on Jermyn
Street." Indeed, the street he named was famous for
such establishments.

"No doubt, although should you ever find yourself
in Lexington, Kentucky, there is a tailor on Red Mile
Road, Le Cheval, who does a credible job. I have my
vests and coats made there. And you must go to Horse
Country. That's where I buy everything else, plus the
really heavy winter frock coats are just the warmest.
The clothing is ready-made but alterations can be
effected."

"Ah, yes, I stopped into that enticing establish-
ment."

High laughed. "He made Marion very happy. Three
thousand dollars happy."

Kasmir lifted his eyes to heaven. "Ah, I am a weak
mortal. When Miss Maggiolo took me under her wing
I became distracted by her skin, her mane of steel-
gray hair, her very graciousness."

Bemused, Sister asked, "Did you convey these sentiments to my dear friend?"

"I conveyed a bottle of Mumm de Crémant via mes-
senger after I left the store. This was the Saturday
morning of the ball. I was favored by two dances that
evening and a tête-à-tête stroll down the hall." He

paused. "I am not a handsome fellow like High here. I am middle-aged, portly, and a widower. It will take a long siege, I think, to gain favor with Maid Marion."

"Mr. Barbhaiya, Marion is not superficial, I can promise you. A good kind heart will count heavily in your favor. And, sir, you underrate your looks." She thought to herself how subtle he had been to send Mumm de Crémant and not a flashy brand.

This especially delighted him. For all his sparkling personality, he was a lonely man in the small hours and wondered if he would ever again find a woman to truly love him and not his money. "Please call me Kasmir. I would be honored."

"Kasmir, the honor is mutual."

"He's going to settle here," High declared matter-of-factly. "Leave Mumbai forever. Kasmir says his late wife came to him in a dream and told him he would find happiness here."

Kasmir blushed. "It is true."

"If there is anything I can do to help you, please allow me to do so." Sister genuinely meant this. She understood how it felt to lose your spouse and force yourself to go on.

"I am most obliged. Good evening, Master." He bid her farewell correctly, even though it was just noon.

Sister was thrilled Kasmir gave the proper address of "Good evening, Master." As the two men started to walk away, she stepped forward. "Kasmir, excuse me." The two men stopped. "Norfolk and Southern

67

will sell Tattenhall Station, three hundred acres surrounded by commanding views and some gorgeous building sites." She paused. "And as High owns Chapel Cross"—this was the estate named for the crossroads—"you would be country neighbors. I can give you the number of the person to call. The company has at long last decided to sell these small stations, while still retaining rights to the spur lines, the actual tracks. The only reason I know this is because the decision was made just last week. A friend of mine is a corporate officer and knows how much Tattenhall Station means to us. It will be publicly offered next month."

After writing out the number, Sister made her way to the tailgate but was waylaid by Cabel Harper. "I was so sorry to hear what happened to you and Marion after the ball. It must have been a terrible shock."

"It was."

"Makes you wonder."

"Does," Sister agreed. "By the way, Ilona mentioned how wonderful she thought the Casanova Ball was."

Both women looked to Ilona, now conversing with Kasmir and High.

"The decorations exceeded my expectations. Did Trudy Pontiakowski come up with the theme? She was the chair, you know." Cabel rubbed her cold hands together.

"Trudy never does anything halfway. I expect the

theme was voted on by the ball committee and passed by the masters."

"Why don't we try a theme next year? Our decorations are too predictable."

"That's a good idea." Sister waited a moment, smiled, and then sprang, just like a fox leaping on an unsuspecting mouse. "Please accept the honor and the hard labor of being next year's ball chairman. You're so creative."

Cabel, knowing she was caught but rising to the challenge, said, "I will. And I know beforehand it will be one long agony with Ronnie over the budget."

"That's possible, but given your persuasive powers I'm sure you can get things donated. You have a wealth of contacts."

"I'm going to start right this minute. Ilona doesn't know it, but she's donating a winter's supply of bottled gas for the auction."

The Merrimans owned a local gas company, selling natural gas and oil to heat houses. Their reputation for service was spotless. Ramsey ran the company, the third generation of Merrimans to do so, while Ilona successfully played the stock market.

Sister watched as Cabel spoke to Ilona, who seemed to brighten during the conversation. *Praise a fool,* Sister thought to herself.

Later, back in the kennels, horses put up, rubbed down, and very happy, Sister went over the list of hounds who had hunted that day.

Shaker fed everyone, checked them for cuts and soreness, and then put the girls back with the girls, the boys with the boys.

Both humans were grateful for the quiet time together in the functional office, filled with photos of Jefferson Hunt dating back to 1887.

"Good idea today, swooping down to Chapel Cross."

Shaker rubbed some cream into his hands, now sore and chapped. "Thanks, but on fine scenting days any huntsman looks good."

"True, it's the in-between days that show up a good huntsman. On the bad days, Jesus H. Christ himself couldn't get a fox up."

Shaker smiled. "Maybe he could."

"Well, all right. Say, I heard they got the roof on Crawford's chapel. St. Swithin will be pleased."

"Asshole."

"St. Swithin? He's a good saint."

"Crawford." Shaker laughed. "Good he got it under roof, though. He must have three crews working there."

"Sam says he's possessed."

Sam Lorillard was Gray's brother, a talented horseman and recovering alcoholic.

"Whose day is it today?" Shaker asked.

"Empty."

"Really?"

"According to my *Oxford Dictionary of Saints* it is," Sister replied.

She possessed an odd talent for dates and kept the

saints' days for herself, feeling those former figures deserved to be remembered. She'd consult her saints' book if she couldn't recall whose feast day it was. February 19 was the day Henry the Fourth defeated the rebels at Bramham Moor in 1408, and the beginning of the battle of Iwo Jima in 1945, which lasted until March 17.

"Hmm," was his reply. "I've been thinking."

"I'm scared." She tapped him with the clipboard with the hound names on it.

"No, really. About what happened in Warrenton." His craggy face, serious, briefly made him look older than his forty years. "Do you think that woman was put there for Marion to see as a warning?"

"I don't know. She was meant as some kind of warning. Whether it was for Marion or not, who knows?"

"And that huge punch bowl was stolen, right?"

"Yes. That thing is heavy. I lifted it once to help Marion clean it."

"You and Cabel keep competing for it in the Corinthian Hunter Class. Actually, a lot of our members want their names inscribed on that bowl. Worth a fortune."

"Worth a lot, that's for sure. But you know, Shaker, it doesn't add up."

"No, it's like one of those in-between days you mentioned for scenting. You have to find a line, and even when you do, it breaks. Hounds cast and find again. The day is like that, hard close work between huntsmen and hounds, but you can turn it into reasonably good sport if you and hounds keep thinking, keep feeling temperature changes and wind currents. Why am I telling you this? You know."

"True." She nodded.

"Well, what crossed my mind is maybe Lady Godiva is a clue."

A car pulled up outside. They heard the door slam.

Ronnie Haslip burst through the kennel office door, waving a check. "Kasmir paid for the whole thing!" He slapped the check on the big square schoolteacher's desk.

Sister, eyes wide, stared at it, picked it up, and uttered the old expression: "Jesus H. Christ on a raft."

Shaker looked at Ronnie, then Sister. "What's up?"

"Kasmir Barbhaiya bought Kilowatt for you. Gunpowder's getting age on him, Showboat's no spring chicken." Ronnie glowed.

"That's a great horse!" Shaker clapped his hands together.

Sister hugged Ronnie. "How'd you do it?"

"I didn't do anything. High and Kasmir came up to me. Kasmir said, his exact words, *Please allow me the pleasure to help your most excellent and beautiful master.*"

"He said *beautiful?*" Sister felt a flush.

"He did!" Ronnie puffed out his chest, his victory making him giddy.

Sister smiled. "From now on, February nineteenth is St. Kasmir Day."

CHAPTER 4

Crawford Howard slapped down his copy of *Barron's*, which he read cover to cover, as he did the *London Financial Times*, *The Wall Street Journal*, and a host of specialized financial reports. Not that he swallowed whole what was written therein, but he liked to have an overview of world markets. He invested prudently in stocks, bonds, and land. Once he'd tried platinum but found that metals, like corn futures, demanded highly specialized knowledge as well as impeccable timing.

His waistline had expanded in his middle years, as had his concept of himself. Crawford, who unlike Edward Bancroft did not start this life with a silver spoon in his mouth, made his first fortune building strip malls in Indiana and Iowa. After that, he steam-rolled his fortune with brilliant land acquisitions and deep forays into blue chip stocks. Moving to Virginia thirteen years ago appeared to be retirement. Instead, he began purchasing small pharmacies and medical supply companies, and just last week a company that disposed of biohazardous waste from hospitals and doctors' offices. He invested in a few high-tech stocks, not many. But he did invest in a local start-up company, Warp Speed, run by Faye Spencer.

Crawford irritated people. Sam Lorillard, Gray's brother, ran his steeplechase barn. Rory Ackerman, another recovering alcoholic and friend of Sam's, also worked there. Crawford treated them well. He also treated his wife well. Marty truly loved him, something he learned only after she forgave his affair with a young tart whose breasts were so enhanced she struggled to remain upright. The bimbo with the big rack had only loved his money.

Perhaps his greatest vanity was when he lost face at the last Jefferson Hunt Ball. Earlier in the season, he had deserted Jefferson Hunt Club and bought a pack of hounds just like you'd buy a loaf of bread. He couldn't hunt a hair of them. Big English hounds, Dumfriesshire, black and tan and good-looking. He made a fool of himself among the foxhunting community. This tormented him like a thorn that breaks off in the lip. Determined to show up Sister Jane at her own game, he'd been casting about for a huntsman. Marty soothed his ego by saying he didn't have the time to hunt hounds. He really should be field master. That was a joke too, but one step at a time.

Marty hoped she could eventually lead her proud, bullheaded, but adoring husband back into Jefferson Hunt. She missed her friends, and she missed the bracing runs too. Knowing Crawford, she guessed about two years would do it if she was patient and careful.

She stood behind him in the den he had paneled in rich deep rosewood as he pointed to his enormous computer screen. "See, I can follow the market in Japan"—he hit a button—"or Germany or London."

He inhaled. "London always bears watching, you know."

As London is the financial epicenter of the world, this was an understatement.

"Well, what little I've learned about money moving around the world, I've learned from you," Marty said. She placed her hand on his shoulder, and he reached up with his left hand to cover hers.

"Honey, this computer does everything but go to the bathroom for you." He smiled. "I know, don't say it. I can't resist toys. What I'm studying now is how a surgeon in, say, Edinburgh can operate while a surgeon at Johns Hopkins in Maryland consults with him. Actually, the surgeon from Johns Hopkins could be fishing out in Chesapeake Bay, watching the operation on the latest incarnation of a cell phone."

"Amazing, isn't it? Do you ever wish you'd hopped on the dot-com bandwagon?" She knew the answer, but he never tired of telling his story.

"Sure I do, but now is a better time to invest in technology. Okay, maybe not nanotechnology because that hasn't shaken out. I mean, scientists can figure out molecular engineering. The trick is profit. Just because something is high tech doesn't mean it will turn a dollar."

"I know you." She ran a finger over the back of his neck. "Buying these small pharmacy companies and Sanifirm; you're working up to something. You're learning the business side of medicine. Once you see where the holes are, you'll plug them and hit another big home run right out of the park. You have a genius for reading the tea leaves."

He beamed. "It's what I learned after I knew it all that gave me the edge."

She laughed. "Me too." She looked out the tall paned windows. "Looks like another front coming in."

He ducked his head around the big screen. "Does look nasty. Three fifteen. Hmm."

"I was so hoping we could take the hounds out tomorrow." Marty had discovered she liked being around the hounds. She'd been spending two to three hours a day in the makeshift kennel.

Crawford planned to build a true kennel come spring, once the heaving and thawing stopped. Fortunately, St. Swithin's was framed up so the workmen could continue despite weather. The stone chapel, another vanity but an appealing one, was dedicated to the very late Bishop of Winchester, who died in 862. Those early Wessex Christians believed heavy rainfall was a manifestation of his power.

"We'll just see when we wake up. That's what's great about having our own pack of hounds. We go when we please."

He neglected to say that his was an outlaw pack, since he refused to have truck with the MFHA, the Master of Foxhounds Association of America. This meant that no recognized hunt could draft him a hound, and no members of a recognized hunt could hunt with him without getting suspended from their own hunt. At this juncture, that helped him. No one would see what a dreadful mess he made of it. Although once his pack ran right through the Jefferson pack, and he'd likely never live it down.

"Heard they had a good one today."

"Who told you that?" A flicker of irritation crept into his voice, a rather nice baritone.

"Sam. Gray called him about one thing or another."

"Oh." He paused and looked over at his wife, now standing at the window, the sky darkening. "Bizarre about Lady Godiva."

"Still don't know a thing."

"Even though she sets my teeth on edge, if anyone can handle that situation, it would be Sister."

"Actually, honey, you could have handled it. I thought you and Sister got on quite well. She valued your every word when you sat on the board. She told everyone you brought a rigorous approach to projects, and your financial acuity was amazing."

"Well. . . ." His voice trailed off. "You know the legend of Lady Godiva."

"It's true. It's not a legend. I looked it up."

He smiled sheepishly. "I did too."

"Funny, isn't it, how the past keeps grabbing us around the ankles?"

"The past is prologue." He was a keen student of history. "She was a Saxon lady married to Leofric, earl of Mercia. He taxed his people mercilessly and she pleaded for them for years. One day I guess he got tired of the nagging. He told her he'd lift the taxes

77

if she'd ride through Coventry naked. That was about 1040, give or take a year. Anyway, she did it and he kept his word."

"He must have loved her."

"Perhaps. He certainly loved his reputation. How would it appear if he broke a vow after her sacrifice?"

"And that's where we get *Peeping Tom*." She laughed.

"Not much wick in *his* candle, stupid oaf."

The townspeople, knowing full well how great an act this was for such a grand lady, withdrew, shutting all their windows. Tom, a tailor, drilled a hole in his shutter so he could see the beautiful woman, her body shielded only by her long hair. Some folks said back then he was struck blind. Others said that one of the two soldiers walking with the lady to guard her thrust his sword in the hole when he saw the white of Tom's eye. However it happened, the name *Peeping Tom* has stuck in the English language to this day.

Godiva had a good heart, for she convinced her husband, a rich and powerful man, to found a monastery at Stow, Lincolnshire. In 1043 Leofric built and endowed a Benedictine monastery at Coventry, thanks to her urging. She became a benefactress of monasteries at Leominster, Chester, Wenlock, Worcester, and Evesham. Surely she possessed energy as well as beauty.

"Her brother, Thorold of Bucknall, was sheriff of Lincolnshire." Crawford stood up, stretching. "Seems the family were all doers, for lack of a better word."

He walked up to her, standing next to her at the window. "When you hear of something like that murder at Horse Country, you can't help running scenarios through your mind."

"Such as?"

"Was this a sex killing?"

"Wouldn't we know by now? I mean, that would show up during the autopsy. The papers said nothing about it."

"You're right." He inhaled deeply. "Unless the police are withholding information. Sometimes they'll hold something back to provoke the killer." He paused. "I wonder if this has something to do with taxation?"

"Or some unjust practice. But Crawford, why make a beautiful innocent pay for it?"

"Maybe she wasn't innocent."

CHAPTER 5

The old apple orchard rested a quarter of a mile from the kennels located on Sister Jane's Roughneck Farm. Many hunt clubs purchase land for a clubhouse and kennels, but in the early sixties Sister and her husband, Ray, joint masters of the Jefferson Hunt, thought to save money by refurbishing the old kennels first built in 1887 that were standing on the land.

The financial effort of JHC focused entirely on hunting, so land for a clubhouse was never purchased, although the club did own show grounds on land donated by the Bancrofts. Since other organizations would rent the attractive venue, it provided about seven thousand a year in income, a help to be sure. Occasionally, not having a clubhouse proved a burden, since any indoor activity needed a host willing to allow throngs, sometimes in muddy boots, to tramp through their house. Sister vowed to herself that the day would come when she would find or build a clubhouse. She began to hope this would happen before her century if God would grant her one hundred years.

In spring, when the gnarled apple trees blossomed, the fragrance wafted through the kennels and through Sister's wonderful unpretentious house, centuries old and centuries loved. A clubhouse in the apple orchard would raise spirits, but somehow it seemed the wrong location for Sister's secret dream.

This evening, the twilight shrouded in low clouds cast a gloom over the orchard. Georgia, a young gray fox, nearly black, lived there in a tidy den. The setting pleased her. Water was close by, thanks to the kennels and barns, if she wished to walk in that direction. If she headed east, a tiny stream crisscrossed the end of the orchard, as well as the farm road that divided the pastures on the eastern side. Broad Creek, a swift-running rock-strewn stream, lovely to behold in any season though occasionally difficult to cross, was on the far side of those pastures running into the Bancroft place, After All Farm.

Sleet rattled against the tree bark. Georgia, cozy in

her den, some corncobs and treasures with her, lifted her head sharply as her mother, Inky, a jet-black fox, entered.

"Going to be a night of it." Inky sat down on the sweet-smelling hay that Georgia changed often, being so close to the barn.

Inky's den, farther down the farm road in a pasture north of the apple orchard, was in an old ruin under a powerful walnut tree. Fox families often stay close to one another, and Inky and Georgia were no exception. Many times a young female won't breed in her first season but will help her parents. The boys usually move farther away from the home den, but foxes have a family feeling, one that most humans never seem to notice. Sister and Shaker were exceptions.

"I came in early."

Inky pushed an orange golf ball toward her daughter. *"You're going to get as bad as Target."* She named a red fox who collected things, the shinier the better.

"Uncle Yancy is worse." Georgia smiled, naming an old fox whose mate, Aunt Netty, nagged at him constantly. Uncle Yancy, fed up, would move out. She'd find him and move in, to the amusement of the others. He'd left Pattypan Forge on After All Farm just a few weeks ago to return to his old den half a mile west of Georgia's den in the apple orchard. Aunt Netty declared she loved Pattypan Forge, built in 1792, so roomy now that she'd cleaned out Yancy's

mess. How long would that last before she bedeviled him again?

"Far as I know among our neighbors, only Charlene bred. It's going to be a bad spring and summer. Funny, how the humans can't tell. They keep on breeding regardless."

"You know, Georgia, I often wonder if they used to know things as we know them and somehow, way back when they started living in cities, they began to lose the ability. Now it's gone. I mean, they can hardly tell what the weather will be from one day to the next. On their own, I mean. It's sad and dangerous."

"Why is it dangerous?" Georgia asked.

"An animal that violates or forgets its own nature eventually dies, I think. Trouble is, they'll take a lot of us down with them. Well, I won't be solving that giant problem anytime soon." Inky batted the orange golf ball back to Georgia. *"At least Sister Jane is more like us. More animal."*

"I like her scent. Piney."

"Oh, that's her perfume," Inky smiled. *"She's never smelled any other way, whereas you'll notice the other humans change perfumes and colognes. I mean, we still know who they are, but they must like changing odors kind of like changing clothes. It's peculiar."* She paused. *"Bitsy bred."*

"No!" Georgia's whiskers drooped.

"Maybe Golly will kill some little owlets." Inky named Sister's grand calico cat, brimming with overweening pride.

82

"Bitsy will peck her eyes out."

"Well, we can hope." Inky laughed.

"Mom, more screech owls? It would be one thing if Athena bred." The great horned owl, the Queen of the Night, was a creature to be feared and obeyed. *"Her voice is beautiful, but Bitsy?"* Georgia grimaced.

"Maybe we can steal some earplugs out of the barn." Inky laughed. *"Or maybe we can leave a note for Sister to buy some. Ha. Wouldn't that be the day, when a fox writes a note!"*

"But we do." Georgia was confused.

"No, I mean write like them—you know, scribble on paper. They can't read our messages. Even Sister misses the subtle ones. She gets the scat, the urine markings, and even the little caches, but she misses other things. If I rub against a tree with smooth bark, she won't smell it. If it's rough bark, maybe she'll see some fur, but they can't read us like we can read them. Actually, they can't read one another too well, either. I mean, without writing."

"Must be truly awful to live with such poor senses, apart from their eyes, which are only good in day-time. I mean, really good."

"Ignorance is bliss, dear. They don't know what they don't have." Inky circled, then lay down grace-fully. *"Sister's upset."*

"That outlaw pack again?" Georgia knew about the Dumfriesshire hounds.

"That's not going to go away. He won't hunt our territory, but since he can't control the pack that

doesn't mean they won't run our way sometimes, and we don't know them. We'll have to be very alert." She flicked her tail, no white tip on the end like a red fox. *"No, she and a friend found a murdered woman Saturday night—well, I guess it was Sunday morning by then."*

"How do you know?"

"She brought some turkey over to my den and sat outside. She gets a little chatty sometimes if she smells me in there."

"Turkey? You got turkey?" Georgia, like all Jefferson foxes, had recourse to a five-gallon bucket filled about once every three weeks with kibble drizzled with corn oil.

Sometimes the kibble had Ivermectin in it to clean out the parasite loads, except when vixens were bred. No more Ivermectin until August then, because it's too dangerous for fox cubs to ingest. It took two days to feed at all the fixtures. People, even foxhunters, rarely know what it takes to manage wildlife properly: the territory, the kennels, the horses, and, of course, the vital landowners, without whose support there would be no foxhunting. One had to manage hunt staff too, if you were a master. Fortunately, Sister had an easy time there.

"You didn't get turkey?"

"Got my kibble with cheese. But I would have liked turkey."

"She probably ran out. She's good about passing around the treats." Inky loved Sister; it was mutual.

"Well, what about the murder?" Georgia's curiosity was pricked.

Inky told her all she knew. Sister's account had been graphic. The two foxes curled up in silence for a while after the story.

Finally Georgia said, *"Pretty stupid to kill a beautiful female at the height of her breeding powers."*

"Could have bred to the wrong person. Humans are funny about that." Inky thought out loud. *"Or refused to breed."*

"Did Sister have any ideas?" Georgia found most human behavior extraordinary, and being young she had much to learn.

"No. That's what worries her—well, that and the shock of seeing a naked body on horseback right in front of her friend's store."

"But you said a silver punch bowl had been stolen, big enough for us and a litter of cubs. So maybe the woman got in the way or maybe she was part of it and then got in the way."

"Could be, although wouldn't it be easier just to kill a person and leave her? That horse stuff was elaborate."

"I'm sorry Sister's upset. I think it's crazy, but it really has nothing to do with us."

As Inky and Georgia caught up on events, Sister and Gray, in bed under the covers, watched a basketball game. Sister kept nodding off even though she liked college basketball.

Gray, his arm around her, smiled.

Golly, flopped on Sister's legs, purred slightly as she slept. Raleigh, the Doberman, and Rooster, the harrier, snored on the rug alongside. Each had a thick fake fleece dog bed but they liked being right by Sister.

Sister was awakened by the beep of her cell phone on the nightstand. She reached for the phone, looked at the caller ID, and punched the button.

"Betty."

"Hey, girl. Did I wake you up? It's nine. You must be worn out."

"Well, I dozed off watching Kentucky."

"Bobby's watching that too." Betty liked football much better than basketball. "Forgot to tell you that X"—she used the nickname for Henry Xavier, forty-six, a club member and another of Sister's son's childhood friends—"will bring the liquor to Mill Ruins on Saturday."

"If we can hunt. This sleet could mess up everything if we get a deep freeze with it."

"Well, it looks that way. God, remember five years ago when just about every hunt in Virginia lost the last half of the season because it was one ice storm after another?"

"I'd rather not."

"This *has* been a long winter, though; it started early in November. Doubt that spring will arrive on time this year."

"It's been a hard winter. We've been lucky to get

hounds out. The snow's not bad, but a day like today—well, you know."

Before Betty could reply the line went dead.

Sister punched the button to redial and got a busy signal. "What's the point of paying a monthly bill if these phones cut out every time there's a little bit of weather?"

"I know." Enthralled by the game, a close one, Gray replied blandly.

The cell rang back and Betty started talking. "Lost you. I'll make it fast. News bulletin on Channel Twenty-nine. The woman's been identified."

"Why didn't you tell me that first?"

"Because it just came across the bottom of the screen. She's Aashi Mehra, twenty-two, from Bombay. Wait, now we call it Mumbai."

"It's a long way from Mumbai to Warrenton."

CHAPTER 6

At six in the morning on Wednesday, February 20, Sister stepped outside, having gulped a cup of Colombian coffee liberally laced with half-and-half. Golly, fed first, refused to follow, but Raleigh and Rooster tagged at her heels, their claws clicking on the thin veneer of ice.

The frozen grass, coated with ice, awaited sunrise to glitter. Each time Sister took a careful step, the ice cracked under her work boots. A jet of vapor escaped from her mouth, and steam poured from

Raleigh's and Rooster's mouths too. The mercury at 22 degrees Fahrenheit might climb, but how much? If it nudged over 32 degrees, the ruts in the old farm road would thaw and driving would test a person's reflexes.

Gray, asleep upstairs, would awaken at seven. He rose early on hunt mornings but, like most people of a certain age, he was set in his habits. She didn't mind that by her standards he was a sleep-in. He more than made up for it the rest of the day, for Gray, active in mind and body, liked projects. They were alike that way, yet she had found herself thinking of Big Ray lately. They had kept the same rhythm. Sure, they had had their various discreet affairs, but they were two people deeply in tune. Her lover, Peter Wheeler, older than she by close to seventeen years, while not close in the diurnal sense, had inflamed her mind like no one else she ever met. Sister had been well served by the men she loved. Wise in the ways of the world, she kept her mouth shut, allowing other people to mouth the hollow pieties that seemed to ward off whatever fears gnawed deep inside. The human animal is not monogamous, although men, at least before DNA testing, desperately tried to imprison a woman's sexuality to ensure that her offspring were theirs. She knew this subject caused explosions even in simple discussions so she shut up about it, but Jane Arnold had always taken her pleasure where she found it, and she would march under that banner for the remainder of her days.

She loved Gray but hadn't told him. Why? Words always came back to haunt her. But she knew she loved him, and she felt he loved her. Different from Big Ray or Peter Wheeler, both of them robust, extroverted, physical men, Gray soothed her but kept her alert mentally too. Handsome, descended from Lorillard slaves and therefore taking the Lorillard name, Gray possessed all the brilliance of that line, which ran in both white and black pedigrees. Of course, every true Virginian knew there was no such thing as an all-white or all-black pedigree, but that was another subject best left on the table. People could be wildly irrational about race from all quarters. Race and sex set up more shrieking and flying feathers than a cockfight.

On a cold crackling morning like today, Big Ray would have been walking with her, both of them with arms outstretched for balance, hands touching, trying not to fall on their keisters and laughing; God, how she could laugh with that man! A stream of ideas about hounds, horses, territory, and whippers-in, liberally spiced with both invective and praise, would awaken the birds, who would grumble about it. She would laugh to hear a disgruntled cheep from a hole high inside a tree or the censorious click of a beak from the owl in the barn. Owls make so many different sounds. She'd learned to recognize them; Sister had a rudimentary sense of most animal communication. People often wondered how she knew where the fox was or when a storm was coming.

She'd say, "The red-tailed hawk told me" and they'd laugh, never realizing she meant it.

This morning, all silent except for her breathing and the ice crackling, her eyes lifted to the east. A thin light-gray line gave hope the sun would rise eventually, and perhaps the cloud cover would disperse too.

The lights were on in the kennels. Shaker, like Sister, kept to his routine. He loved his work.

"How's Delia today?" she asked, as she walked into the large feeding room, nodding at the boys with their noses in the trough.

"She's gaining weight, but her hunting days are over, boss. She's slowed down, and it's hard to keep weight on her. I can see it melting off during a hard run."

"You're right. She can stay in the Big Girls pen until the day comes when they start to roll her. Won't be for a year or two. I'll take her up to the house then."

A master from Maryland had once upbraided Sister with the taunt, "You don't live in the real world," because Sister refused to put an old hound down as long as it was healthy. The other master was right in that this kept expenses higher. But damned if Sister would put down a hound who had served her well. She was the same about horses. Okay, it did run up the bill, but let them live out their final days in peace, comfort, and love. It was the least she could do for the devotion they accorded her.

Once a hound was rolled in the kennel by the

younger ones, she'd see if a member would have it for a house pet or she'd move it up to her own house. It pained her that people didn't understand what good pets foxhounds make. The longest it ever took her to potty train an older hound was two weeks. Most get it before then. Whip-smart, those hounds are fanatically clean. Perhaps it was vanity, for they knew how majestic they were.

She left Shaker and walked to the special run for hounds who needed extra attention or who had been injured during hunting. Now it was just sweet Delia, eating a warmed mash of kibble and canned food.

"Aren't you the lucky girl?"

"*I am,*" Delia replied, and stuck her nose back in the aluminum bowl.

"Love you, baby girl." Sister smiled at her old friend and returned to the feeding room.

"Boss, what saint's day is it?"

"Wulfric and Eustochium Calafato."

He laughed. "Those teachers at your Episcopal girls school certainly drilled information into your head."

"Latin too." She grinned.

"Okay, what did Wulfric and Eusto—you know—what did they do?"

"Wulfric was from Somerset, a contemporary of Lady Godiva, actually." They'd both done their Godiva research. "He hunted with hounds and hawks, so he should be dear to us. Maybe not as dear as St. Hubert, the patron saint of hunters, but important nonetheless. We can use all the celestial help there is.

He lived as an anchorite and supposedly possessed second sight. He healed a knight with paralysis. Mmm, bound books. Visited by Henry I and then his son, Stephen, when king. That's about all I know."

"I'll read up on him. What about the other guy?"

"Girl. Abbess of Messina, Franciscan order. She seems to have been strict and devout and died at thirty-five. Her body did not decay. She died in 1468, and when she was dug up from her grave in Monte-vergine in 1690 she was fresh as a daisy." Sister shrugged. "Nonetheless, dead as a doornail."

Shaker laughed. "Do you believe this stuff?"

"I take it with a grain of salt. Do I believe these people were extraordinary? Sure. A lot of saints behaved miserably before seeing the light. Just the fact that they redeemed themselves is worth emulating."

"So there's hope for me?"

"Hope for both of us."

"Must I vow poverty and chastity? I'm not good at either." His lopsided grin was infectious.

"Me neither. Both are overrated; I doubt they're really virtues. Getting someone to give up their worldly goods was an early form of income redistribution. Of course, the communists raised it to new heights."

"Another kind of religion gone bust."

"I'll say, and think of the millions that died because of it on both sides of the fence. Don't you think it odd that human beings will die for ideas? I'd die for a living creature but not for an idea. Too cold for me."

"Yep. Come on, boys. Look at how those coats gleam. That corn oil in the winter just works a treat."

"It does, and I don't care what the analysis is on the back of those big feed bags, nothing puts a shine on their coats like corn oil."

Shaker, wellies squishing on the concrete floor, which he washed obsessively, opened the door to the Big Boys' run, a quarter of an acre.

All the hounds enjoyed huge runs with grass, trees, and boulders as well as condos to supplement the beds inside the kennels. They liked being out and about. It certainly cut down on bad behavior, since everyone had plenty of room.

Once the boys trotted out, door closing behind them, Shaker refilled the troughs, poured corn oil over the high-protein kibble, and set the gallon jug high up on a shelf, along with the twenty-four others stored there. They bought in big lots to save money. Sister might carry hounds longer than another master, but with her practical mind she saved in all other areas.

"All right, my fast ladies," Shaker called, and the bitches shot into the feed room, tails high.

"We're excited this morning." Sister smiled at the hounds. "Shaker, I've been thinking about Dragon. When he was in sick bay after being torn up by that coyote early in the season, the pack was more cohesive."

"Yeah, I've been thinking about that too. He's only

been back in for the last three hunts, and I can feel the difference. For one thing, he distracts Cora."

"He challenges her. We can't have two strike hounds, and Diddy might develop into a good one when we most need her, when Cora retires. But Dragon is ready now."

"Draft him?"

"No. Not yet. What if we use Dragon on Tuesdays, Cora on Thursdays, and toss a coin for Saturdays? We'll see how the pack performs. If they go equally well, no need to change anything or draft him out. If not, then we should draft him to a hunt needing a good fast strike hound."

"We've got plenty of the blood," Shaker replied.

"Yes, but you know how that goes."

He did. A hunt might have a litter of six really good hounds. One would get stolen, another lost in some fashion. One might develop an unexpected illness. Before you knew it, not much of that blood was left. "It's a strong line, that D line. Delia put some wonderful puppies on the ground over the years. Cross with Asa was the best, I think."

"Archie." She named a hound killed by a bear, a hound dipped in gold, he was so superb.

"Right. Tell you what, we'd better never lose that Archie blood."

"You know it goes all the way back to Piedmont blood through old Middleburg. Quite a journey through time, those bloodlines." She cited two great northern Virginia hunts, each having made contributions to the upgrading of hounds and each still hunting outstanding packs of hounds to this day over some of the most beautiful country in the world.

One of the great things about Virginia was the depth of the hunting bench. Old Dominion, Fairfax, Loudoun, Warrenton, Casanova, Orange with their ring necks of Talbot tan, Deep Run, Farmington, Keswick, Rockbridge, Bull Run, to name a few ripping good hunts. A person could fall out of bed and land near a thunderous hunt.

"Plan's a good one. Try tomorrow."

"You bet." She left the kennels and looked in at the stables where Tootie, Val, and Felicity worked.

"Good morning, Master," all three sang out.

"Good morning, ladies." She closed the barn doors behind her. "Aren't you glad your father bought you that Jeep?" She addressed this to Valentina.

"Yes, ma'am. Otherwise we'd have to walk and it's a hike."

"We could hitch rides." Tootie winked.

"Sure." Felicity was filling the water buckets.

After a brief chat there, Sister walked back to the house. She invited the girls up for breakfast each day specifically, because they would not come on their own. Charlotte Norton drilled manners into her students. And many of them had endured the drill at home too. It would be presumptuous simply to arrive in Sister's kitchen—although their presence was a daily delight to her.

"Good morning, darling." Gray beamed at her.

"Back at you. A fresh pot."

She poured her second cup. "The girls will be up in about forty minutes. I'll start on cream of wheat now. I'm assuming you'll want some."

"Yes, ma'am. With orange-blossom honey."

He continued to read the paper. No need to pull out honey and jams just yet. He'd set the table too. Gray liked small chores as well as big ones, and he wasn't fussy about what was supposed to be women's work or men's. Work was work.

"I've been thinking."

"Oh?" She ran water in a large saucepan.

"I'm not cut out for retirement."

"You're hardly retired, honey. You ran a special audit at Aluminum Manufacturing last month, and you just had a meeting with the Number Two guy at the IRS, most hated government agency in America."

"For a while the Defense Department was running neck and neck," he remarked. "I'll always do consulting. But you know, accounting is what I've done all my life."

"You're the best. Why else would you receive the calls you do?"

He shrugged. "Thanks." He paused. "I thought I'd start a small restoration business. Since Sam and I have been working on the old home place, I'm reminded of how much I love construction, especially historical places. Even one as simple as ours. The work is outstanding. Those heavy hand-hewn beams, does anyone do that anymore?"

"Well." She considered this as she set the flame underneath the cream of wheat. "You have an eye. I guess finding a crew of artisans—I mean, they'd have to be more than construction workers—will be critical."

"Will."

"What about Sam?"

"What do you mean?"

"Would you go into business with him?"

"No." The reply was swift but not loud.

"Oh."

He folded the paper in quarters, longways. "He's a horseman. He should stick to horses." He picked up his coffee cup, then put it back down. "He's been really good at the house. We're doing okay but, but Janie, I don't know as I will ever trust my brother one hundred percent."

"He's been sober a year and a half—"

"I know." Gray ran his forefinger over his salt-and-pepper military mustache. "He's my brother. I love him but he's an alcoholic. They slip back."

"Gray, he drank Sterno down at the railroad station when he couldn't get Thunderbird. He hit bottom. Showing him the way to Fellowship Hall was a great kindness on your part. He came through. Like many in recovery, he'll probably never touch another drop."

"I know."

"Why am I standing up for him?" Sister pulled homemade bread from the breadbox. "He might not want to run a business."

"That's the other thing. I don't know how much stress Sam can handle. Trying to make payroll during a lean month or two makes you sweat. I wouldn't want to put him in a position where he might weaken."

"Makes sense. So you'd do this by yourself?"

"Right now that's my plan, but I'm still thinking it through. Tell you one thing. I've been researching software, cell phone contracts, and the like; my God, how does anyone cut through the bullshit?"

"I stick to my iMac and Alltel, which works except for some pockets and some days."

"That works for you, but for a business I need something more sophisticated. Something different from what I use for accounting jobs. For reconstruction I need to see things in three dimensions; I need graphic capabilities as well as engineering."

"Don't look at me." She laughed, then stopped herself. "You know who might know? Marion. She has a store computer system, but she bought a different one at home. She's arty, you know, so I bet she can draw and do everything on her home system. Just an idea."

"Good one." He plucked out the news section. He'd been reading the sports page. "Look at this."

A photo of our beautiful Lady Godiva was in the middle column. "My God, she was stunning." Gray whistled. "She worked for Craig and Abrams, Washington office."

Sister put her hand on his shoulder. "Craig and Abrams. That's High Vajay's old firm."

"Wonder if he knew her. He'd be upset." Gray continued to read the column.

"Does the paper say what her job was?"

"Research."

"That covers a multitude of sins."

"That's just it, isn't it?"

CHAPTER 7

No." Felicity clamped her lips tight.

Val, irritated, scrubbed harder at the bit, fine English steel, with a toothbrush. "You think they won't find out."

Tootie, weary of Val's badgering, answered for Felicity. "She won't see them until spring break. By then she'll have it figured out."

"By then she'll look like she swallowed a pumpkin," Val shot back.

"Shows what you know." Felicity smiled slightly. "I'll have a little bulge, but it won't be bad. I need time to think."

"You need to get to the doctor in the first trimester, I know that." Val thought having a baby at seventeen was the most ridiculous, stupid, backward act in the world.

Tootie thought otherwise, although what mattered was what Felicity thought. "She'd need parental consent for an abortion."

"We can forge their names. Show me a letter from your mother and father and I'll start practicing. I'm good at art; this can't be so different."

"Val, you can't mean that." Felicity was scandalized.

"Of course I mean it. We're all three going to Princeton together, and that's that."

"We have to get in first," Tootie replied dryly.

"We will. With our grade point averages, athletic points, and extracurricular stuff? Zip." She swooped her hand flat and away like something flying.

"Who knows?" Felicity shrugged. "Pamela is going to Ol' Miss. Speaking of parents, bet she hasn't told hers yet."

"Her mother will go mental." Tootie giggled.

Pamela's mother harbored exalted dreams for her daughter even while she upbraided her for not being as beautiful as she herself was and thought she had remained. This lethal combination made Pamela wary, sullen, and even overweight in defiance of her mother's constant harping on looks, looks, looks.

"Early admission cuts the anxiety." Felicity side-stepped the abortion discussion. "Maybe we should have asked for it with Princeton."

"Some colleges are ending early admissions after this year." Tootie refilled a small water bucket to continue cleaning tack, her fingers aching a bit when the warm water hit them, for the barn was cold. "They're making a mistake."

"Look." Val rounded on Felicity again. "Talk to your parents. They'll agree to an abortion. Don't tell Howie." This was Felicity's boyfriend, star quarterback at the Miller School. "Just get it over with. Go to Princeton. Graduate. Do what comes next, probably graduate school, then marry well. Get it? The children follow."

"That's your path, not mine." Felicity, though mild-mannered, was proving stronger than Val had anticipated.

"Felicity, be reasonable. Your mind is so good. I mean, you have such a business brain. You're the only one in our class who ever makes money when we have projects, plus you come up with the ideas in the first place. Who would have thought to sell bandannas in school colors?"

"Or Mardi Gras beads in school colors before the big day, Fat Tuesday. Don't you love that name? It's like Boca Raton. Sounds good until you remember it's *mouth of the rat*." Tootie complimented Felicity but wisely did not tell her what to do. After all, it wasn't her body. "We're finished. Let's go to breakfast." Tootie hung up the bridle, neatly making a figure eight around the headband, noseband, and cheek pieces with the throat latch. "We'll turn out horses after breakfast."

"Gives everyone time to eat and relax. I've learned more about horses from Sister than from Bunny," Val said.

"Different things to learn. Bunny's good about basics—barn management stuff—but as a riding coach her main job is to win at horse shows. Alums like ribbons and trophies. The more silver the team brings home the more checks the alumnae write."

"True," Val agreed. "Our soccer team helps too."

"Some of our alumnae foxhunt. Hey, why don't we ask Sister about that?" Felicity brightened.

Sister had been keeping an eye on the stable, every now and then stepping into the cold mudroom to glance out the backdoor window. When she saw them close the big double doors behind them, she poured the coffee.

"Felicity has this great idea!" Val, first through the door, walked to the pantry without being told, returning with four bowls.

Tootie followed, bringing jams and honey. Felicity brought the daily silverware.

"I'm all ears."

"Let's have a Custis Hall alumnae-and-student fox-hunt." Felicity smiled.

"That's the best idea I've heard all year."

"It's only February twenty-first, there's time for more ideas." Val sat down at the sturdy farmer's table.

Sister ladled the cream of wheat into five bowls. Felicity and Tootie carried four to the table. Tootie placed Gray's in front of him, then put down Sister's. Before sitting down, Tootie scooted back for the fifth bowl, hers.

The brass teapot whistled. Sister poured herself hot water, flipped in a plain old Lipton's teabag, and joined the girls. If she drank one more cup of coffee she'd levitate.

"Master, may I have apple butter?" Felicity asked.

"Of course, honey, you know where it is."

"Girls," Sister said quietly, as they finally sat together.

"Oops." Val, starved, had just dipped her large spoon in the bowl.

They held hands and Sister prayed. "Heavenly Mother, for this which we are about to receive, we thank you. Amen."

"Amen," the girls echoed.

"Heavenly Mother. When did you start saying that?" Tootie smiled.

"Wanted to see if you were listening."

"We were." Val, grateful, picked up her loaded spoon.

"What do you think, ma'am?" Felicity hoped Sister would like her idea.

"Splendid, that's what I think. You're very creative in your way. Takes time to organize something like this. You all will have to come back as alumnae next fall. There's only a month left, give or take a day, for this season."

"I'll be here," Felicity replied, without fanfare.

Val deliberately put down her spoon. "You'll be coming back with Tootie and me from Princeton."

"I'm going to stay here and find a job. Howie will go to Piedmont Community College for two years, and then if he can pull his grades up he'll go to UVA or somewhere."

Face red, Val opened her mouth but Sister, next to her, put her hand on Val's hand. "Sweetheart, she has to find her own way. You can't live everyone's life for them no matter how intelligent you are."

"But Sister, she's throwing her life away! And furthermore, Howie Lindquist is dumb as a box of rocks. If anyone goes to UVA it should be Felicity."

"He's not dumb!" Felicity flashed anger, rare in her.

"Ladies, we have to support Felicity, no matter what. Is she throwing her life away? I don't know. What I do know is that it's her life. I also know that love is rare. She loves Howie."

Felicity melted in gratitude.

"But she's so young." Never having experienced even a twinge of love, Val couldn't grasp any choice not involving progress on a social, material, or intellectual level.

"Yes," was Sister's one-word reply.

They sat in silence for a minute; then Tootie, God knows why because it was so unlike her, just as Felicity's anger was a surprise, blurted out, "How do you know when you're in love?"

"Anne Harris!" Felicity laughed, calling Tootie by her full name. "You just know."

Val rolled her eyes. "Spare me. I'm eating."

Gray, amused, said, "You can't stop thinking about the person. Your heart beats faster when you see her. Sometimes you feel dizzy. You've never felt such energy, like electricity in your veins."

"Sounds like the flu." Val grimaced.

"Chills and fever. It's a good flu." Sister smiled at Gray.

"Can you avoid it?" Tootie asked.

"No," Gray responded firmly. "You can refuse to engage but you can't really avoid it."

"I am never falling in love," Val declared.

"Of course not. You're too in love with yourself." Felicity shocked everyone; normally she was so mild.

The statuesque blonde's face reddened. Then she, too, surprised everyone. "I *am* pretty self-centered."

Everyone put their spoons on their plate at the same time to stare at Val.

Finally Sister lifted her spoon. "You're at the time of life when one is relatively self-centered. The real sin is not outgrowing it."

"Like Crawford Howard?" Felicity asked.

"Mmm, he's egotistical, but I've seen worse." She paused. "Anyone ready for seconds?"

They were, so she refilled all the bowls.

Felicity devoured her second bowl. She was eating a lot these days.

Sister smiled at Felicity. "You're very young. You and Howie will grow up together, should you marry."

"We will. We have to tell both our parents. I thought I'd wait until spring break so I could do it face-to-face."

"On the one hand, I do understand your wanting to sit down with them. On the other hand, Felicity, you might want to tell them now and give them time to adjust. I'm assuming you and Howie don't wish to wait too terribly long before you marry, and I think you need parental consent for that," Sister said.

"He's eighteen."

"You're not," Val said, a hint of rancor. "Furthermore, has he asked you to marry him?"

"I'll be eighteen in June." Felicity ignored Val's question.

"Honey, time's a-flying." Sister gently prodded her.

Felicity looked down at her empty bowl. "You're right."

"Does Mrs. Norton know?" Sister felt Charlotte Norton was an excellent headmistress.

"No," Felicity answered.

"Sit down with her first. She has a good head on her shoulders. She cares deeply for her students, especially you three."

"I won't get thrown out?"

"No. However, you might want to keep this between the three of you. Sometimes girls can—well, dramatize. You're not that way, of course, but who is to say some freshman won't take a fit? Graduate, then tell the world; at least that's what I would do." Sister paused. "But you really must talk to Charlotte—Mrs. Norton. You can trust her."

"Yes, ma'am." Felicity's shoulder squared.

"If you're here, if you don't go off to college, will you organize the alumnae foxhunt?" Tootie was curious.

"She has to go to college!" Val tossed her blonde ponytail, unable to contain herself.

"I agree with you, Val, I do. Felicity may have to take some time off or—" Sister turned to her—"you could take night courses. Mary Baldwin offers very good ones. Actually, all the schools do."

"I've thought about that." Felicity had been thinking about a lot of things, one being how she could afford her beloved horse, Parson. "Sometimes"—she chose her words carefully—"I wonder if I can do all that needs to be done. Howie really has to go to college."

"He can be a coach." Val had no time for the well-built likable Howard.

"He still has to get his degree." Felicity had steel in her backbone when her beloved was criticized. "And I hope he has the chance to play football at a big college. He just has to get his grades up, that's all. He's not stupid, despite what you think, Val. It takes him longer to learn than it does for us but once he knows something it's in his head forever. He's not stupid." Her voice raised slightly.

"He was smart enough to fall in love with Felicity." Sister lightened the moment.

Tootie liked soaking up everything about hunting. "Not to change the subject, but when we were coming up over the hill at the old Lorillard place the other day—you know, graveyard at our backs—I smelled a fox but hounds didn't."

"Oh, Tootie, when we can smell it, hounds can't. It's over their heads." Val actually had learned about hounds, scent, and foxes, unlike many who hunt.

"I know that." Tootie continued patiently as if talking to a child, which she often considered Valentina. "But the ground was frozen. I didn't think scent would lift until it warmed a bit."

"You're right, Tootie. I'm impressed you noticed."

"What did happen then, Sister?" Felicity, with a good mind, lacked game sense and hound sense, but she was willing to learn as best she could.

Nature gives each of us various gifts. Some things can't be learned; you're born with the knowledge, but a reasonably intelligent person can still learn the fundamentals of any activity.

"Well, only the fox understands scent. Right?" Sister looked around at the girls.

"Right," they replied.

"Therefore, I can only make intelligent guesses. This is my guess: The ground was tight as a tick. Have you noticed how some horses almost wince when they land on the other side of a jump? Stings when it's this frozen. Any scent that hounds might find would have to be fresh, hot. If the scent was, say, an hour old or more, the ground would need to warm a bit, perhaps in sunlight, to lift it. I'm not saying hounds can't smell a frozen line, but I don't think they can run it very efficiently. Again, this is guesswork. You might find another master or huntsman who would contradict me. But I think what you smelled, Tootie, was a hot line, fresh as could be, but the bit of wind lifted it up, moved it, and it rose as well. By the time we reached the old Lorillard graveyard, hounds began to feather." Sister mentioned how hounds move their tails a bit when finding a light line, the feathering seeming to increase with intensity of scent. "As we moved on, though, heading west, the wind already had done its work." She held up her hand, palm outward. "Again, guesswork. And some spots carry warm air currents that help lift the air."

"Do grays and reds ever live close to one another? You know, like neighbors talking over a fence?" Val wondered.

"For years I thought not. That's what I'd been told as a child, and I saw no reason to disbelieve it. But I have noticed, when there's plenty to eat, they occasionally do live near one another. The problems always come during the lean years. That's when coyotes become especially lethal."

"Shoot 'em." Val felt no affection for this predator.

"You do and it helps until you kill the head bitch." Sister sighed. "Then all the females go into heat and you have more coyotes. They're here to stay. The issue is, can we manage them and protect our foxes?"

"Why not?" Felicity leaned forward, reaching for toast.

"I don't know. The coyote is relatively new to Virginia. We don't know the animal the way someone from Wyoming does, nor do we know how this efficient predator will affect our balance of nature. Coyotes adapt. Conditions here are different from the West. All I know is, I mean to protect my foxes."

"They're fun to chase." Val loved riding hard.

"Not for me." Sister smiled so as not to sound critical of Val. "It's a straight shot. I love the fox, all the ruses, doubling back, walking on top of fence lines, all the incredible things a fox does to fool us. I enjoy being pitted against God's most intelligent creation."

"Don't you think coyotes will change? It won't just be us." Tootie, ever thoughtful, was miles ahead of the other girls on this.

"Lynn Lloyd"—Sister named the master of Red Rock Hounds in Reno, Nevada—"says she has observed coyote running more like foxes with the population pressure out there in the high desert. She can see for fifty miles and, on a ridge, one hundred. We can't watch our quarry like Lynn can, so I believe she's observed a crucial adjustment in the coyote, proof that the animal is flexible. We know they're smart."

The phone rang.

"I'll get it, ma'am." Tootie hopped up. "Hello, Arnold residence. This is Anne Harris speaking."

"Tootie, how are you?" Marion Maggiolo's lilting voice rang out.

"I'm fine, Miss Maggiolo. How are you?"

"Recovering."

"Yes, ma'am. That must have been horrible."

"It was. When are you coming up to see me?"

"When I get some money." Tootie laughed.

"You don't have to buy a thing to visit. I'm always glad to see you. Is Sister there?"

"Yes, ma'am," Tootie said. "Sister, it's Miss Maggiolo."

"Ah." Sister put her napkin on the table and rose to take the receiver from Tootie. "Marion, darlin', how good to hear your voice."

"I called you the minute the sheriff called me."

Marion's voice dropped a few notes. "Did you know that the woman we found was High Vajay's mistress?"

"What?"

"Her first job at Craig and Adams was as High's secretary."

"That doesn't mean the affair continued when he retired."

"Doesn't mean it didn't either," Marion replied.

"Mandy will kill him." Sister put her hand on her hip.

"Unless he kills her first."

"Marion, how can you say that?"

"How do we know he didn't kill Aashi? Maybe she was blackmailing him. Maybe she was in love with him and pressuring him to leave Mandy. Happens every day."

"Marion, I just thought of something. High said your sheriff sent him a photograph of Aashi over the computer. He said he didn't recognize her."

"What?"

"That's what he said."

"Liar," Marion breathed out. "I'll tell the sheriff."

"Could be it wasn't a good picture. High's smart, he'd know they'd find out she was once his secretary."

"Could be High Vajay had a strong reason to kill her too." Marion felt no need to find reasons why High *didn't* kill Aashi. As far as she was concerned, he was the prime suspect. Having a prime suspect gave her some comfort, no matter how illusory.

Thursdays, after two thirty, Sister ran her feed store errands. Her friends and hunt club members knew her schedule. If you wanted to see her at the stable or kennels you didn't drop by Thursday afternoons.

She returned by five, happy to miss what passed for traffic in their part of the world. After dropping off specialty feed bags, body builder for the older horses, in the stable, she walked in the mudroom back door, dogs at her feet since they'd made the journey too.

There on a shelf sat a dozen pure-white roses with drops of blood on them. The symbolism gave her a shudder.

She searched for a card, not expecting to find one.

"Kids," she spoke to Raleigh and Rooster, "I'm in the crosshairs."

She decided not to mention this to anyone, not Shaker, Betty, even Gray. Word can get around and her instincts told her that whoever did this wanted to shake her up. Sister wasn't going to act like prey. Yes, she might be in the crosshairs but she was a hunter to her core. She'd sniff this wretch out, somehow, someway.

CHAPTER 8

The sky, a brilliant blue, glittered overhead. Crawford Howard, spirits rising, drove his big S Mercedes just for the fun of driving. He needed a break. Not that things weren't clipping along, but sometimes he'd let small problems nag him and spoil his day. Although he had come a long way in developing his foxhunting sense, he was only beginning to appreciate Sister's and Shaker's gifts with hounds, horses, and foxes. Exercising, feeding, breeding, maintaining a pack of hounds proved far more difficult than he had anticipated.

Foxhunting is art, instinct, and a dash of science.

He cruised past the stately home-fired brick country club. In the long slanting last rays of sunset, the faithful whacked away on the driving range. It was February 22, and the light was moving closer to the equinox.

He parked his car and waited until High Vajay finished his swing. "What are you doing out here in the cold? You'll tear a muscle."

High, one of the few who actually liked Crawford, nudged the bucket of balls with his Number Four driver. "I'll get better at this game if it kills me."

As it was not public knowledge that High was under suspicion for murder, he thought it best to keep cool and stick to his routine.

"It just might." Crawford peered down into the bucket, counting eight left. "When I saw you out here I had to stop. These other people are as crazy as you, I guess."

"Look who's talking," Cindy Chandler, a stalwart Jefferson Hunt member and a good golfer, called out to him. She said this with good humor so he smiled back.

"She's right." High needled him. "Any man who buys his own pack of outlaw hounds defies convention."

Crawford smiled. He liked that he was the talk of the town. He just wished he hadn't lost his pack at Paradise—a humiliating consequence of his fragile ego, and the result of his having deserted the JHC.

"Crawford, come back. We miss you." Cindy was sincere. "Surely there's a way to patch this up. Your Dumfriesshire hounds would flourish, and you'd save the money of building a kennel."

"Shaker has to apologize first."

Shaker had decked him at the last hunt ball.

"Unusual circumstances."

Crawford, on the dance floor, had collided with Shaker and Lorraine Rasmussen, which somehow pulled down Lorraine's strapless top, her glories exposed.

"Well-built woman." Crawford had lived long enough in Virginia to know understatement worked better than overstatement.

Cindy shook her club at him. "You men!"

High bowed slightly to her. "As a beautiful woman, you know exactly how we are."

She shook her head, returning to address the golf ball, which said not a word in return.

"I've had enough." High picked up the bucket and walked back to his mud-splattered Range Rover. He prized all things British, and in truth the hideously expensive SUV could go through anything.

Out of earshot, Crawford asked, "You knew the Craig and Abrams woman who was killed, didn't you?" Crawford had no way of knowing that High had denied such knowledge to the sheriff when first queried.

High lowered his voice as he opened the back door of the Rover. "Ben Sidell called on me, once they knew who she was and where she worked. Yes, I knew her. She was very sweet."

"Sorry."

"Me too. Her whole life was in front of her."

Satisfied, Crawford switched to his favorite subject, business. "Do you still own Craig and Abrams stock?"

"I do. I bought Hutchinson Essar stock too. That's how much I believe in the industry. Eventually one or both of those companies, currently in competition, will build WiFi systems to blanket all of India. It's happening here; it will happen there. WiFi is the real golden pot at the end of the rainbow."

"Vodofone wanted to take a controlling interest in Hutchinson Essar?"

Vodofone, a British mobile-phone company, realizing that the European market was stagnating, had bid for a controlling interest in Hutchinson Essar, India's fourth largest mobile operation.

The street value hovered at $13.5 million. Vodofone wanted a 67 percent stake. India's mobile phone market was booming, with customers signing up at the rate of 6.6 million subscribers a month.

This pushed Reliance Communications Ltd., the

Mumbai-based second largest operator, and Blackstone, a private equity group, into bed to see if they couldn't buy 100 percent of Hutchinson Essar. A dollop of national pride also sparked this effort, since the Indians wanted to keep the British out, having been rid of them only for about sixty years.

"Vodofone is well managed, has foresight." High pulled off his skin-tight golf gloves.

Warp Speed, Faye Spencer's company in town, was working on a device that would translate basic language. So an English speaker could understand a German, a Chinese, and vice versa. At present the circuitry had proved complicated and unreliable. The goal was to reduce the complexity, get to market first. This device could revolutionize business worldwide.

Warp Speed had the wisdom to concentrate on English, German, Chinese, Japanese, Spanish, and "government Indian" as there were so many dialects. They'd add French, Russian, and Portuguese later.

"What I'm really excited about is Warp Speed," High said. "I'm not really an entrepreneur but I couldn't resist the concept. Faye's too smart to get sucked into the vortex of pie-in-the-sky research. She's practical. The company has good management and accounting practices. If she can pull it off, triple digit millions will be hers, maybe more."

"And ours." Crawford smiled. "You talked me into investing in Warp Speed, remember?"

"I do. Talked Sister into a much smaller investment than ours, but she's naturally conservative. The

volatility in the electronics market, in software, esca-
lates. That worries me."

"What about this murder, though?" Crawford could
be bold.

High frowned. "I doubt Aashi's murder has to do
with the market."

"You're right. When they start killing men, I'll
worry." Crawford didn't consider himself sexist, but
in his mind, if men were killed, it might be more than
some form of sexual revenge or release.

"Ah." High leaned against his Rover.

"We might suggest that Faye Spencer hire security."

"She's pretty tough. I wouldn't worry too much,"
High countered.

"Maybe," Crawford said, unconvinced.

High smiled. "I do allow myself to dream of future
profits there."

"Down the road. If it ever happens," Crawford
remarked. "Faye's built a good team. She was smart
enough to take on a real businessperson, since she's
not. Her mind is full of wires, chips, dots of platinum,
and dreams, too, I guess."

"Once people thought computers in the home were
decades away." High crossed his arms over his chest.
"Everything happens so fast."

"High, you believe in conspiracies?"

"Like I said, this sector of the market is highly
volatile. Volatility can transform into violence. What
difference does it make if it's a conspiracy or one
genius nutcase?"

CHAPTER 9

Long days rarely bothered Sister, although long nights could get her. This Friday night, Washington's birthday, she leaned against the arm of the big sofa, legs outstretched. After taking a shower and double-checking her draw list for tomorrow's hunt at Tedi and Edward's After All Farm, she was grateful to relax.

The den, warmed by a strong fire in the simple but lovely fireplace, was Sister's favorite room. Much as she loved her huge kitchen, the original part of the 1788 house, she loved the den more, possibly because there, surrounded by photos of her family in silver frames, she basked in remembered love.

Before the kitchen was built, the original landowners had lived in a two-room log cabin a half mile away. The cabin had long since fallen down, but the ruins provided Inky with a spectacular den.

Jane Arnold had not led a particularly hard life. Like most she keenly felt the passing of her grandparents and then her mother and father. The death of her son in 1974, the hardest blow she'd ever been dealt, also taught her to appreciate every moment and to cherish the young. Big Ray died in 1991, although his snotty mother Lucinda, Mrs. Amos Arnold, was in her nineties, still holding sway in Richmond. So many friends had passed on. Each year she heard the wings of time beating more loudly. Her own death was out there somewhere, but then so was everyone else's. The difference was that when one is older you can't deny your chances of dying are one for one. RayRay, snatched from life at fourteen, never had the chance to feel life's deepened quickening, but in the fourteen years God gave him he spread happiness like pine pollen in early spring.

Golly, snuggled in the needlepoint pillows at the other end of the sofa, snored lightly. Raleigh and Rooster, both on their sides, dreamed, paws twitching.

Spread over Sister's lap were stock offerings and bond quotes. She picked up a prospectus for a company mining copper in China. Big Ray had taught her how to read these siren calls to profit and how to sift through an annual report. As to "hot news" on Wall Street, his advice still rang in her ears. "Don't follow the lemmings. It may take awhile, but you'll go over the cliff."

After he died, she managed her own portfolio with the help of their stockbroker and flourished. She'd lose money sometimes but mostly her mix of high risk, medium risk, and low risk, along with about 30 percent of her investments in bonds, gained annually. She shied away from metals but was interested in the China offering only because her mistrust of China ran—well, all the way to China. She felt investors were digging themselves into the proverbial hole.

She picked up a shiny pamphlet on a drug company developing an ultrasound machine to screen for breast cancer, making biopsies obsolete, and put it in the "consider" pile.

Her tiny little cell phone beeped. She leaned over to reach it with her left hand as it rested on the rectangular coffee table.

"Hello, Sister here."

"Sister, it's High Vajay."

"Good to hear your voice."

"I didn't want to have this conversation where others might overhear us so I thought I'd call. I hope I'm not disturbing you."

"Not in the least."

"I had a spontaneous eruption with Crawford."

"How interesting."

"Well, yes. We started talking business, finally retreating to the nineteenth hole for a drink. I'll get to the point: He's in over his head with those hounds and he knows it."

"That's a step in the right direction."

"He's looking for a professional huntsman. That won't really work either, ultimately."

"I suspect you're right. Creating and sustaining a hunt takes years to learn. You can't pick it up out of a book, although books help. And smart though he is, he has a difficult time taking advice."

"This is occurring to him slowly." High breathed deeply. "I have two ideas. One was to ask if you could send a huntsman his way, someone you trusted who might steer him away from this destructive path. An outlaw pack in the area hurts everyone."

"Are you suggesting this individual—and, yes, there are some candidates—might gently lead him to register with the MFHA?"

"That's one route. The problem is he'll have to hunt another county if he does that, because he's poaching on your territory. He wants the glory of being a master, but he's not truly a hunter."

"I agree, but he had made some progress with us. He actually watched hounds work on a few occasions."

"The Russians have also made progress, but would you want to bet on their government?"

Sister laughed. "What's your other idea?"

"Have a long lunch with Marty. See if you two beautiful ladies can't prevail on him to come back to Jefferson Hunt. It will be better for everyone."

A long, long pause followed. "High, you're right. Damage was done. Repairing relationships has to come from him and I don't know if Crawford is a big enough man to do it. As for me, I would take him back. When Crawford sat on the board and then became president—and as you know we had to slip him in with a shoehorn because the election was so tight—he created a business plan together with Ronnie Haslip that was sound. Of course, the economy can change with one disaster or political mess but, still, his five-year blueprint impressed me."

She did not mention that she had worked behind the scenes to elect Crawford to assuage his vanity. Desperately wanting to be master but lacking some of the key qualities that an MFH requires, Crawford became president and received attention and respect. In return, he was a decisive, motivated leader. The good offices of his wife didn't hurt either.

"It's worth a thought. The rub is, he insists that Shaker apologize first."

Sister breathed deeply. "That's going to take a lot of work on this end." She paused. "Lunch with Marty will be a pleasure regardless of the outcome. I miss her terribly."

"We all do."

"If nothing else, her politics, so far to the left by my standards, make me think. Hundreds of thousands, if not millions, of Americans think as she does. And Marty will roll her sleeves up and work."

"That's all I have to say."

"You're good to call me, and you're quite right, High. This shouldn't be overheard. I truly appreciate your concern. Also, it takes me away from these boring stock offerings I'm reading."

"Me too."

"Coincidence."

"What else can you do on a long February night?"

"With your gorgeous wife, I could think of alternatives."

His voice was warm. "She's visiting her sister in Phoenix. Be home next Saturday."

"Well, then, we'll both return to the siren call to spend money in hopes of making it. On the same subject, I still can't believe Kasmir bought Kilowatt for the club. We pick him up Sunday. Exactly how did Kasmir make his money?"

"The short version is he became president of a small pharmaceuticals company and rolled it into a national giant. He left two years ago when his wife died. Some men find solace in work but not Kasmir. He'd worked to create a fortune so that he and Geeta could retire relatively young. He's still a bit lost."

After hanging up, Sister thought how fortunate she was to have members that kept the club in their thoughts. And she determined to keep Kasmir here. She'd move heaven and earth for him to wind up with Tattenhall Station. She also noted that Vajay made no mention of what Marion had told her concerning his relationship with his former secretary. But then why would he? It was in his best interests to keep his mouth shut. She wondered how long Ben Sidell would give him to prepare his wife. Sooner or later, Mandy would have to be questioned.

A paper slithered to the floor onto Raleigh's back. He didn't move.

"Dead to the world," she said out loud, stopped herself, then dialed Ben Sidell, also a hunt club member. "Ben, forgive me if I'm calling at an inopportune time."

"Polishing my boots."

"Lay out the silk underwear. Supposed to be in the low twenties at first cast."

"Might be a two-layer day."

"I'm asking for information. Have there ever been other Godiva murders?"

"I've been researching past murders of young women for the last twenty years to see if any are similar."

"You're hooked too?"

"My profession, even if it didn't happen on my beat." His voice rose in register. "I can't help but get hooked. I told the sheriff up in Fauquier I'd poke around a little."

"Found anything?"

"No. There's nothing like this anywhere."

"Do you know if the girl in Warrenton was sexually molested? It wasn't in the papers, but I gather that law enforcement officials will withhold a piece of information to be able to identify the killer if he calls to brag or promise another killing."

"She wasn't. Given her extraordinary beauty, I find that odd. I guess that shows how jaundiced I've become."

"Most of us would agree with you. It isn't you, it's the times in which we live. Okay, here's my next question. Marion called and told me, thanks to the sheriff there, that they had learned the victim had been or still was Vajay's mistress. So I assume you know."

"Do." He paused. "I questioned him. Gave him a day to talk to Mandy."

"He's going to have a long phone conversation. She's in Phoenix."

"I know, but I can't wait until next Saturday when she returns to question her. So he's got twenty-four hours."

"Do you think a woman could have lifted the corpse up on Trigger?"

"Yes, if the body was still warm and pliable and not particularly heavy. It's not so much the weight as the unwieldiness of a fresh corpse. But two people could manage it without too much trouble. It's a hell of a lot easier to dump a body and run. That's why I come back to the ritual aspect."

"Even though the victim wasn't sexually molested, that doesn't mean sex isn't part of the motivation. Revenge?"

"Possible." Ben had been sheriff for three years, and in that time he had learned to trust the older woman. "What do you think?"

"Well"—she drew out a long breath—"we all know the legend of Lady Godiva. My first thought is there's some connection we don't yet see. My second thought is the victim is possibly in a highly sensitive position, in high-tech industry. My third thought is, given the manner of her murder, I think there will be more. When and where, I don't know, and I don't know why I feel that but I do."

"I do too. Instinct's a funny thing. You've got to go with it, but you can't really tell most other people, because they want logic. Logic is a small god. There's something so peculiar about this it makes my skin crawl. I've seen sights that will haunt me all my life but this is—I don't know, it's just so different. Almost gleeful. Really. Lady Godiva in front of Horse Country. There's a kind of dark humor at work."

"I'm so glad I called you." She sighed.

"If anything comes up, I'll let you know." He tapped the side of the phone absentmindedly, which Sister could hear. "How long have you known Margaret DuCharme?"

Margaret DuCharme, M.D., specialized in sports medicine. Good-looking, slightly introverted, the situation between her father and uncle sometimes wearied her as Paradise, the home place, fell down over the decades. The landholdings totaled about five thousand acres, give or take, and Alfred, her uncle, had kept them in good shape.

"All her life. She's bright, driven, fundamentally kind, and fundamentally lonesome." Sister encouraged him. "She needs you whether she knows it or not, and you need her."

This surprised him. "How do you know that?"

"The whole mess at Paradise last month brought you together, right?"

"We've had a few dates—well, the first one was lunch because it's not so, so—"

"Wise to start with lunch."

"Well, why did you say what you said?"

"Because I'm an old woman who can see around corners. And because you glow, you radiate excitement, when she walks into a room."

"God, am I that obvious?"

"To me. Probably not to others," she fibbed. "Make her laugh. Margaret needs to laugh."

When that conversation ended, Sister remembered

that this day was the feast day of another Margaret, Margaret of Cortona, a Franciscan penitent who lived from 1247 to 1297 and sounded like a wack job because of the way she mortifed herself, mistreated her son for a time, and attacked anything she considered a vice.

Sister shook her head, musing on what constitutes holiness. Seemed to her, given Lady Godiva's bravery and subsequent good works, that she deserved to be a saint far more than Margaret of Cortona, with her hair shirts and self-inflicted starvation.

CHAPTER 10

A sharp dry wind from the west sliced through boots and gloves. Hunters could keep their bodies warm, but feet and hands usually suffered—as did noses, which tended to run at inauspicious occasions.

Once mounted, Sister wanted to move off, but first cast, at ten, couldn't be pushed upward. Once people receive a fixture card with place and time for the hunt, you can't fool with it. People, many still on the ground, rooted for girths, searched for hairnets, struggled with stock pins.

Why don't they tie their stock pins at home when their fingers are warm? Sister thought to herself. She wore the titanium stock pin Garvey Stokes had made for her. As far as she knew, she had the only titanium stock pin in the world. The slender dull silver pin was fantastic.

Ilona Merriman, hairnet in place, derby correctly placed on her head—which is to say, straight across the brow—rode up to Sister, reined in Tom Tiger, her handy small Thoroughbred, gave a pregnant pause, and then tattled. "Jennifer Schneider—granted she's a new member—but she's not wearing a hairnet, her gloves are black, and her stock pin has a fox's head on it. She might as well learn sooner as later."

Sister wanted to slap Ilona, whom she'd always tolerated but never liked, not that Ilona deliberately crossed her. Of course, turnout should be proper. *Face danger with elegance* is the foxhunter's creed. But Jennifer, riding with Bobby Franklin, was green as grass. Sister gave each new member a copy of correct attire for JHC. She also gave them a year to pull it together.

"I'll have a word with her."

"I'll do it, if you like. Then the onus is on me." Like so many people, Ilona reveled in small displays of power.

"Thank you. It's better that I do it because you ride in the field. In time, Jennifer may move up to first flight. Sometimes a correcting word, no matter how kindly given, can spoil a relationship. I wouldn't want that to happen to you and Jennifer." Before Ilona could indicate that Jennifer was beneath her, Sister adroitly mentioned, "She's a Valentine on her mother's side."

The Valentine blood, an old Virginia family and one with steeplechase connections, would appeal to

Ilona's snobbery. She possessed little old Virginia blood but what she had had been magnified to gargantuan proportions.

"I didn't know that." Her cute little mouth became an O.

"Blood always tells." Sister couldn't resist. "Thank you for the heads-up. We do want our people to look perfect."

Ilona, now in possession of news, made a beeline for Cabel, who was getting a leg up from Clayton.

Ilona heard him chide her. "Go to the doctor. You haven't been to a doctor in twenty years, Cabel. There's no reason your legs should be weak."

Sister watched as Clayton huffed and puffed to lift Cabel, not particularly heavy. *God,* she thought to herself, *he's even fatter than he was two weeks ago.*

Seeing her staring in his direction, Clayton winked, which made Sister laugh. Fat he might be, but he hadn't lost his spark.

After a few welcoming words to guests from Sister and Walter, they moved off, hounds following, northward along Broad Creek. The wind buffeted them until they reached an area one mile from the Bancrofts' covered bridge, where the ground began to fall away. Shaker knew sooner or later they'd pick up a line, faint perhaps, but something to run, since this portion of Broad Creek sank low, providing protection from the wind. Any fox worth his or her salt, if picked up, would scamper to high ground where their signature perfume would be blown away.

February 23, being a Saturday, meant a large field. Today, sixty-seven hardy souls rode forward. Jefferson Hunt could count on big Saturdays even after New Year's, when fair-weather hunters kept to their fireplaces. Most of the Jefferson Hunt members truly wanted to hunt and took pride in facing conditions that would deter others.

Rickyroo, Sister's seven-year-old Thoroughbred, dark coat glistening, enjoyed the brisk weather. A quick study, he'd learned so much last season that Sister felt he was made and could handle any possibility—and they were out there, from mountain lions to wild boar, the worst of the worst.

Walter Lungrun, in his second year as joint master, rode right behind Tedi and Edward Bancroft, who usually rode in Sister's pocket. These two, always perfectly turned out, on beautiful horses, made Sister smile. They had more money than God, but even Ben Sidell, who made a modest salary as sheriff, looked perfect next to Bobby Franklin and the hilltoppers.

She prided herself on her field, their turnout, their hunting manners, and their hospitality to visitors. With the exception of Crawford, who had always been too flashy, she was rarely disappointed.

High Vajay was out, as was Kasmir, this time in a heavy frock coat, thicker gloves, and a sturdy derby attached to his back collar with a black hat cord.

Sister's coat had faded to a hue admired by newcomers because it meant you'd been hunting a long time. Her coat, black, lined in wool tattersall, cut the cold. Her cap, ribbons down, had faded also.

Non-staff members, those wearing caps, wore the ribbons up.

She sighed as they walked along. High-pressure systems meant tough hunting although a fox could pop out at any time, its scent then red hot. Anything could happen. She fretted since she wanted to show good sport, but as yet Sister had not figured out how to control the weather.

She glanced over her shoulder. The Custis Hall girls rode at the rear as usual. Juniors ride at the rear, as do grooms. When the pace quickens and people drop back, often not having a fast-enough horse or enough horse, then a junior may move up. A groom should assist those falling behind if they need it. These days a groom often helped only his or her employer, but they were there to serve. Few true grooms existed anymore; pony clubbers often fulfilled those duties at various barns, but they had much to learn about protocol. Even Tedi and Edward didn't take a groom out, although they did have stable help whereas Sister did not. She was so grateful to the Custis Hall girls for turning out her horses and cleaning staff tack on the days they rode that she had given each girl soft leather mustard gloves for Christmas presents. She was already wondering what to give them for graduation.

She stopped wondering when Cora spoke with high excitement. A large gray streak shot out to her left.

"Come!" Cora sang out.

The entire pack, honoring their strike hound and head bitch, closed in on the line and ran single file until they burst out of the woods, now running south-westerly. In three minutes, flat out amid the trees, the path narrow, Sister happily spied the old hog's back jump, thrilled her knees had survived the close quarters. She could clearly see Comet, the gray fox, ahead now bursting through the wildflower field, the whole pack bunched together.

Bitsy, the screech owl, flew silently overhead. She must have followed them from the covered bridge at the Bancrofts. Bitsy, living in Sister's stable, led an extremely active social life, enlivened by intense curiosity about everyone and everything. Sister was fine with that, so long as she kept her mouth shut, for her cry could wake the dead.

Comet faced into the wind, his scent streaming into flared hound nostrils. He zigzagged to break the flow but the scent was so hot the pack zigzagged with him. He'd run at a good clip but now he had to hit top speed. He'd been caught unawares, trying to court a new gray vixen living about a half mile from the small graveyard by the covered bridge. Romance clouded his senses.

He cut sharply right, leapt over the old fence setting off the wildflower field, some patches of snow still encrusted in small furrows here and there, like hard vanilla icing, then cut straight up toward Hangman's Ridge.

Sister sailed over the jump in the old fence line, Rickyroo's ears forward. He jumped a trifle flat, which helped old bones. A horse with a large bascule, the rounding of the back so prized in the show ring, could wear out even the Custis Hall girls after four hours of hunting. Better a horse that powered off hindquarters, reached out with forelegs, and then folded them up and kept that back just a little flat. A long pastern—the short bone just above the hoof—made the landing smoother too, but Sister didn't worry too much about that. Many horsemen declared a horse with a long pastern would break down sooner than one with upright pasterns. After a lifetime with horses, Sister thought it was six of one, half a dozen of the other.

Hounds pounded down the frozen farm road, although sections were getting greasy as the sun rose higher. It was already ten thirty.

Behind her Sister heard a loud rap on the coop. Someone had rubbed it. Footing in front of it was getting cut up. Well, if someone endured an involuntary dismount, another bottle for the club traveling bar. She collected these bottles assiduously, though she was not much of a drinker herself. Single-malt scotch on a wickedly cold day would pass her lips and that was about it, or maybe a cold beer on a stinky hot day. But alcohol rarely figured into Sister's socializing. She'd witnessed too many good people go down like Sam Lorillard.

Another rap followed. Yes, the ground was getting

cut up but the smart riders would rate, slow down a little, then squeeze hard at the takeoff spot to compensate, or not rate their horse's stride and leave early. So often, and not on purpose, people would follow too closely at the jumps. Some plain couldn't hold their horses. One of the great things about the Custis Hall girls riding in the rear was that Sister received a full report. As field master, her job was to stay behind the hounds without crowding them. What happened behind her, in a sense, was not her concern.

"He's going to Hangman's Ridge," Dasher called out.

"Damn," Asa growled.

Damn was right, because the moment Comet reached that high flat expanse exposed to fierce winds, even in summer, he knew he could relax. He crossed the long axis of the ridge and paused at the hanging tree, haunted by those who died there, earning their dispatch thanks to severe transgressions. Comet didn't like hearing their whispers. Occasionally he could see one of the hanged. Under the circumstances, let the hounds deal with it. He waited. They came onto the ridge and he slipped down the back side toward Roughneck Farm. His den was not far from that of his sister Inky. His scent would be long gone by the time the hounds reached the tree, so he just ambled on home.

"I hate this place," Diddy, a young female hound, whispered.

"Me too," Tinsel, another young hound, agreed.

"Drat!" Cora circled the tree, ignoring the whispers from the large branch formerly used to secure the rope.

Hounds milled about. Shaker rode up. He too disliked this spot. He urged them to cast themselves wider, which they did, but the damage was done, as was the day. He considered going down the narrow path to the farm road in hopes of rousing another fox, but he figured this was it. Couldn't complain. It had been a bracing run.

The fifteen-minute walk down the trail to the farm road produced squabbling in the bushes from two male cardinals who had been squabbling anyway. The goldfinches, chirpy as always, turned their backs to the redbirds, wishing the cardinals would fly up to tree limbs and stay out of their bushes. Cardinals pretty much did as they pleased, but at least they weren't as offensive as the blue jays, who would walk right up to a goldfinch on the ground to utter a stream of avian obscenities.

Returning to the coop, Sister paused. "Shaker, let's take hounds back to their kennels. Then we can drive back to After All and pick up the trailer and the party wagon. No point in walking all the way back there when the kennels are ten minutes away."

"Fine."

She turned to the field. "Folks, we're walking hounds back to the kennels and we'll meet you at After All. Walter will lead the field."

Walter nodded, happy that he was chosen by the

senior master to do this. His riding was improving, as was his hunting knowledge. Usually Tedi or Edward led the field when Sister, for whatever reason, did not.

Tedi smiled at Sister. She liked seeing Walter move up.

The two whippers-in rode beside the pack at ten o'clock and two o'clock. Shaker rode at six o'clock, and in this way the pack was kept together. Their discipline was good. They wouldn't bolt, but both Sister and Shaker thought better safe than sorry.

Back at the kennels, hounds cheerfully walked in, eager to discuss the day's hunt and to lord it over those not drawn to go out today, Dragon being one.

"Pretty good day in difficult conditions," Cora called out, as she went into the kennel.

Dragon, face pressed against the chain link fence around the boys' run, heard her loud and clear before she disappeared into the kennels for warm water to drink, a check over, and some kibble warmed with heated-up gravy, a special mix of Sister's.

Sybil helped Shaker with the hounds. Dragon growled with envy.

Sister and Betty led the four horses back to the barn. Both Betty and Sybil would drive over later to pick up their horses. In the meantime, each animal would be wiped down, checked, a blanket thrown over, put in a stall with fresh water and flakes of sweet hay.

Since the Custis Hall girls needed to ride back to

After All, the two old friends happily performed the after-hunt horse chores alone.

"Should we clean the tack?" Betty asked, after putting up Outlaw and Bombardier, her horse and Sybil's.

"We can do it after breakfast. Don't want to show up too late. I'll put up the coffeepot. Might as well get warmed from the inside out." Sister walked into the small but pretty office to make coffee. A hot plate and a small under-counter refrigerator were in the room. Sister thought someday, if she ever got ahead with money, she'd extend the office outward so she could build a proper kitchen and make a nice sitting room, since she spent more time in the barn than in the house.

She stopped. "Betty, Betty, come here!"

Betty opened the door, then stopped cold. "What in the hell?"

"That's what I say."

Before them on the desk gleamed the great silver John Barton Payne punch bowl from Marion Maggiolo's store.

Sister called Ben Sidell on his cell but it was turned off. He hadn't reached his trailer yet most likely.

She called Marion at Horse Country.

"Marion, your punch bowl is here."

"What?"

"On my office desk in the stable. Looks fine. I'll notify the sheriff here; you notify yours."

Marion paused, trying to eradicate the worry from her voice. "Why you?"

"I don't know, but I don't like it."

"It's possible whoever stole the punch bowl didn't kill that girl."

"I don't think so."

"I'm glad you have it, but"—Marion switched her thoughts—"where are your dogs?"

"In the house. I suspect whoever put this here knew not to put it in the house. Raleigh and Rooster would have taken down anyone they didn't know well." Anger infiltrated her voice. "I don't like being played with."

"*Play* may not be the right word. I wouldn't go out without those dogs or a thirty-eight. This is too weird."

After hanging up the phone, Sister turned to Betty, who was admiring the magnificent silver bowl.

Betty looked up. "Not good. Not good at all."

"Well, I hardly think I'm going to be the next Lady Godiva."

Betty tilted her head upward to the taller woman. "Jane, none of us has any idea what's going on, and that includes the authorities. Assume nothing. I don't think you should be in the house alone at night. One of us should be with you. We can take turns."

"Now, Betty, that's a little extreme." Sister felt a little shaky and tried to make light of it by changing the subject. "Funny, today is the Roman festival of Terminalia, celebrates the god Terminus."

"The things that pop into your mind." Betty put her hand on Sister's shoulder.

"He's the god of boundaries." She looked into Betty's quiet brown eyes. "Someone is crossing our boundaries, even those of life and death."

CHAPTER 11

Sister never made it to the breakfast at Tedi and Edward's. She called Walter and explained the situation, informing him she needed to wait for Ben Sidell. Ben left his horse in the Bancroft stables and drove right over. He, too, strongly advised she have someone with her at night until they knew more about the case.

By eight that evening, she'd had it; her patience was thin. Instead of admitting she was a bit scared, she became crabby. Gray babied her, which irritated her even more although part of her liked it.

"Go sit in the den. I'll be there in a minute," he commanded her.

Not accustomed to taking orders, Sister shot him a jaundiced look. She did, however, do as he said since she felt guilty about being moody.

She leaned against the arm of the sofa, her legs stretched out, her old cashmere robe soft against her freshly showered skin.

Golly immediately pounced on her toes. *"Tiny sausages."*

"She's in a bad mood. Leave her alone," Raleigh counseled the cat, an exercise in futility.

"The time to torture humans is when they're low."

Golly's extremely long, white whiskers swept forward, her pupils now large with anticipation.

"Golly!" Sister laughed, she couldn't help herself, because the cat jumped on her bosoms, sat upright on those pillows, and patted her face, pretending to be ferocious.

"Suck it up!" Golly enjoyed herself.

Rooster, curled up on the club chair across from the sofa, said laconically, *"Mental."*

Golly launched off Sister's chest and skidded across the coffee table, knocking a clean glass ashtray to the floor. Barely stopping herself from falling off the table, she bunched up and leapt onto Rooster with a heavy hit, then leapt right off. *"I'm the queen! You're a peasant."*

"Like I said, mental." Rooster burrowed his nose deeper in his paws, just in case Golly returned, claws unleashed.

Gray walked in as Golly touched the floor.

"You missed my very own Flying Wallenda." Sister's mood improved.

"That cat has a secret life. Probably works for the CIA." He put two hot toddies on coasters and stooped to pick up the ashtray, hand-painted on the bottom side with a hunting scene. "You know, I was reading somewhere, maybe the *Manchester Guardian*, where scientists discovered bees can detect explosives. CIA will put them to work. I figure Golly's on the payroll. Fresh kidneys must be her salary."

"Tuna!" Golly returned to Sister's feet but didn't bite.

Gray handed Sister the enticing mug. "Can't remember the proper glass for a toddy, but I figure it's hot whiskey so a mug will suffice." He sat on the sofa next to Golly, who turned her pretty head to allow him to admire her.

"Gray, I can't drink all of this."

"A sip or two. No harm in relaxing." He stroked Golly's head and was rewarded with a deep purr.

Golly threw in a few trills for variety, which made Sister laugh some more. "She's a complete lunatic and I couldn't live without her."

"I could," Rooster grumbled.

"Lowly rabbit runner." Golly interrupted a stream of high-pitched notes.

Rooster lifted his handsome head. *"You huge fur ball. I can run fox, bear, or coyote. I can run anything because my nose is good, but I'm trained to run rabbit and hare. That's my job. I don't go off on the wrong quarry. You shut up."*

"Seems to be a conversational evening." Gray took a long draft.

"Ignore her, Rooster." Raleigh climbed up on the wing chair, which had a throw over it for this purpose.

"Ray used to make a hot brick." Sister mused on her husband's favorite. "If the day had been nasty cold, after the horses were put up and hounds checked, he'd head for the kitchen. I can never remember the difference between a toddy and a brick."

"A brick is one-third an ounce of whiskey—you can

substitute rye if you like—a pinch of cinnamon, pinch sugar, a third an ounce of hot water, and a small pat of butter."

"I remember the butter. Made me think of yak butter. I drank it, though." She grimaced.

"Don't much like butter in a drink myself."

"What's your recipe for a toddy?"

He shifted, leaning against the arm after another long sip, placing his legs alongside Sister. Even though he showered, he wore knee-high Filson wool socks because his feet got cold so easily. "Standard. One ounce of bourbon, four ounces of boiling water, one teaspoon of sugar, three whole cloves, one cinnamon stick, and one lemon slice, medium thick. Most people slice the lemon paper thin. In this case, I substituted scotch for bourbon. I'm not much for bourbon. The drink is sweet anyway."

"Bourbon's okay if good but I prefer scotch if I'm going to drink." She paused. "And I like rye, but a good rye is hard to find. It fell out of favor. The younger generations don't much like hard liquor. Wine, beer, and mixes I don't even recognize seem to be their standard. My daddy always said, *Takes a man to drink rye;* then he'd hand me a little. I'm not sure what the message was." She smiled, for she loved her father; mother too.

"Toughening you up, your dad." Gray snuggled into the pillows by the arm.

"Get settled, will you?" Golly complained, as was her wont.

"Golly, if you'd drink a toddy it would improve your mood."

"If I drank a toddy I'd be in The Guinness Book of World Records. *"*

"You probably are. " Raleigh baited her vanity.

She bit. *"For what? "*

"Cat with the flabbiest belly. Swings when you walk. " Raleigh chortled, a breathy sound that dogs make when laughing.

Golly considered flaying him but was comfortable. *"I'll have my revenge. "*

"Did you know there's a drink called a Huntress Cocktail?" Gray stroked Golly more, her fur soft.

"I did not."

"Three-fourths ounce of bourbon, three-fourths ounce of cherry liqueur, one teaspoon of triple sec, and one ounce of heavy cream. Sounds awful."

"Does. Is there a Hunter's Cocktail? What's good for the goose is good for the gander."

"One and one-half ounces of rye and one-half ounce of cherry brandy. Stir and serve over ice. The other one you shake up with ice or ice shavings, then strain into a chilled cocktail glass."

"How did you learn so much about mixing drinks?"

"Alcoholism runs in the Lorillard family." He didn't smile, saying this as a matter of fact, which it was. "I can remember uncles, grandparents—white uncles too—gleefully sharing the mysteries of potions, mixed drinks, you name it. For a while there when I was young I drank a lot, but then I caught

143

myself. Obviously, Sam didn't." He stopped and lifted his glass. "To my pickled kin, regardless of the color of their skin."

Sister reached for her drink with a slight grunt and toasted. "At least Sam's back from the precipice."

"He works at it. That man is religious about his AA meetings. I guess you substitute one addiction for another. Ever notice how alcoholics always have a glass in their hand, water or soda or something?"

"I have, actually. What is it Alcoholics Anonymous says? *Alcohol is a craving of the body and an obsession of the mind.*" She shrugged. "What people do is their business as long as they don't wipe me out on the road. But there are still cultures or enclaves where drinking is important. Parliament in England, for one. Still seen as a real test of balls. Can a man hold his liquor? No wonder Tony Blair has hung on to power for so long. Hell, they're all too loaded to mount an effective ouster."

"Used to be that way here. I still think young men go through the phase, some of them." Gray thought about it. "What's the difference? If it's not drink, someone will hand you a pill and tell you life will be rosy. There's something in humans that can't accept reality."

At this, the animals lifted their ears. They'd been saying this for years to one another.

"True. It has to be prettied up or denied. But don't you think alcohol was one of the few ways to deaden physical pain before the advent of huge drug companies and the billions of profits from pills?"

"I do." Gray shrugged. "I'm not going to solve the alcohol problem." He took another gulp. "You know, I can't drink all this either." He laughed. "It's good, though, if I do say so myself."

"Yes, it is. We'll consider this as alcohol used for its proper purpose, a medicinal application."

"I've been thinking about the silver punch bowl."

"Yes." Her voice lowered again.

"It's pretty obvious. You've thought of it too. This person either knows you well or knows about you. The thing is, why do they want to implicate you?"

"For theft?"

"Murder."

She remained quiet while she took a long, long sip herself. "Why me?"

CHAPTER 12

The creamy English leather of the high-quality bridles hanging on the wall distracted Sister for a moment. It was noon on Sunday, February 24, and Marion had met Gray and Sister at Horse Country, which remained closed on the Sabbath, so the three of them could go through without being disturbed.

Aga, Marion's female Scottish terrier, led Raleigh and Rooster upstairs. Aga proved a gracious host, showing them her special ceramic food dish and matching water bowl.

"I had to repair the downstairs lock immediately," Marion said, leading them to the housing for the security system. She flipped open the heavy plastic box, exposing tiny colored wires and computer chips.

Gray, using the button LED flashlight on Marion's key chain, directed the thin bright beam into the box. Even though the overhead light shone brightly in the utility room, which housed the water heater, the furnace, and the water filter, he needed more light.

The two women peered behind him.

"All those tiny computer chips." Sister sighed. "No bigger than half your little fingernail."

"Airplanes are full of them too. Just think what would happen if one melted?" Marion tilted her head upward toward the colored entanglement in the box.

"How often do you revamp your security system?" Gray asked.

"I haven't. I mean, I remodeled seven years ago when I acquired the bottom of the building, but I haven't bought another system."

"Yes, it was state of the art. This isn't my field, ladies, but you'd be surprised what you learn when you defend a client in front of the IRS."

"What do you mean?" Marion wondered, ever curious.

"If a client had been robbed and his records destroyed, our firm—well, my old firm—investigates independently. I've stuck my nose in all kinds of security systems. The most troubling are the infrared ones."

"You mean where little red beams crisscross a room?" Sister knew that much anyway.

"Sounds like a great system. Anything moves and the system calls the satellite, which bounces to the police. However, in a store like this, what if, for whatever reason, an object falls off a shelf and sets off the alarm. You can see the problems."

"That's why I chose this system."

"It was good in its day, but I suspect whoever came into the store knew it depended on your phone lines, ground lines. Cutting them was easy. They all emerge from the building."

"Didn't you have a fruit loop—um—about seven years ago?" Sister recalled a somewhat odd employee.

"Well, more lazy than crazy." Marion frowned. "But he wasn't a thief."

"No ugly parting?" Gray glanced from the box to Marion.

"Firing someone is upsetting. He lost his temper, but it all worked out. He just wasn't meant to be inside. He's working on a farm west of town."

"A decent relationship?" Sister didn't need to elaborate.

"Socially"—Marion searched for the right word—"superficially pleasant, I'd say."

Gray pressed the button, the beam cut off, and he shut the box, handing Marion her keys. "I assume you're purchasing a new system?"

"Installed tomorrow to the tune of eighteen thousand dollars." Marion sighed.

The three of them repaired to her office, where she

turned on a light, the store remaining dark lest someone think it was open. "Aga, aren't you generous."

Aga, in the office, had allowed Raleigh and Rooster to play with her special nylabone.

Rooster grunted. *"Can't crack this thing."*

"All right, out," Sister ordered her two. "There isn't room for all of us."

Reluctantly, her two dogs left to flop down hard outside the door; the flop indicated canine sulking. Aga picked up her bone and joined them.

"Would you like coffee? A drink perhaps?"

"No, thanks." Gray was glad to sit down. His legs still ached from yesterday's riding.

"Me neither."

Gray leaned forward. "Marion, has the sheriff talked about your security system to you?"

"Only to ask who knows how to disarm it to open the store and how to set it to close it at night." She paused. "He did say I could put the punch bowl back up, since your sheriff dusted it. I don't think they have room for anything that big at the station." She leaned back.

"I'll bring it in." Gray started to get up.

"Not now, honey. We can do that in a minute." Sister leaned forward too. "Marion, is there a customer who knows about your security system?"

"I don't think so."

"If they're in the security or electronic business it wouldn't be too hard to figure out, especially on a day when you're really busy," Gray said.

"I hadn't thought of that." Marion frowned.

"Christmas," Sister suggested.

Marion paused. "That's a possibility. There are so many people in here from Thanksgiving to Christmas, a customer could easily slip into the furnace room undetected."

"Or check outside for the wire outlet," Gray added.

Gray rose. "I'll get the punch bowl. I won't set the alarm off, will I?"

"No." Marion smiled at him, then called out, "Wait, Gray. Let's put it in my car. I can put it back on the shelf once I'm sure the new security system works. And I have a system at home. I'll keep the bowl there."

He returned and leaned against the office door, glad to keep his knees straight for a moment.

"I can't think of anyone who would want to kill someone, steal a punch bowl, and then leave it in my barn." Sister folded her hands together. "I'm dizzy from thinking."

"Goes around faster and faster. We need to slow down." Marion realized her flashes of insight were coming when they felt like it, not on command. "Let's trust our instincts. It would seem whoever is behind this wants to mark both of us."

"Like a fox marks territory?"

"Yes." Marion, having spent a lifetime with fox-hunters, understood the game.

"A beautiful woman from India, and you and me?" Sister shook her head.

"We aren't dead yet."

CHAPTER 13

Tattenhall Station glowed blue in the twilight, the western sky still showing traces of scarlet and gold. Sister drove through and turned right, down the long lane leading to Faye Spencer's farm. She'd called Faye at work, asking if she might drop by.

The door opened the minute Sister's boots touched the front porch, the overhead light already shining.

"Come on in, stranger," Faye greeted her. "Tea? Hot chocolate? You name it. I even baked cookies yesterday. Still fresh."

"Hot chocolate."

Once the chocolate was poured, Faye and Sister sat in the living room. The old clapboard farmhouse had been built when the railroad first came through, for the foreman who oversaw Tattenhall Station's construction. The fire crackled. On the baby grand piano, its top down, a shawl artfully draped over the ebony, stood a photograph of Gregory Spencer in uniform.

"We've missed you in the hunt field."

Faye, pretty and in her early thirties, sighed. "Oh, Nighthawk threw a shoe, took a little chunk of hoof with it. We'll be back once my farrier gets to work on it."

"How's everything else?"

Faye ran her fingers through her glossy auburn hair, cut in a pageboy. "Coming out of it. Two years. Sometimes time flies, sometimes it crawls."

"Sounds about right. The first year of Ray's death I hurt, plain hurt. The second year I felt numb. Then in high spring of that year I started to revive. I suppose we grieve in our individual ways and you're young, whereas I was in my fifties. I don't know if that made it easier or not."

"I miss him. Don't get me wrong. I do, but now I can think of Greg without bursting into tears."

"He was a focused man." Sister smiled at the memory of him. "He loved the army. You know what they always say about war, it's the brave lieutenants and captains who die in the largest numbers among officers. Those who survive usually become senior officers if they stay in the service."

"I do know that."

"Greg would be proud to see how far you've come with the company."

"There are days when I think the name Warp Speed is so-o-o wrong." She drew this out humorously.

"You could change it to Three Speed." Sister laughed.

"Might be a good idea. Three Speed. Some days I think we're almost there; other days I feel sucked back by an ebb tide. It's exciting, though, Sister, to think we may be on the cusp of developing a twenty-first-century Rosetta stone. You write the phrase you want to speak into computer or cell phone and you receive a script of the translation. If you're online with someone from another country, their input is translated. We're so, so close. I believe the day will come when this can be done phonetically. Right now, though"—she held up her hand as if to stave off an onslaught—"we're concentrating on text."

"Sounds like a miracle."

"No, just hard work. Every language can be broken down into nouns, verbs, adjectives, and so on. Structure is relatively similar among the Indo-European languages. It's when we reach into Chinese and Japanese that we go back to the Bible and read about the Tower of Babel."

"Ideograms?"

"Oh"—Faye waved her hand, her wedding ring golden in the reflected firelight—"no way. Everything has to be put in our alphabet; that's just the first hurdle."

"What about Russian?"

"That's easier because the Cyrillic alphabet mostly parallels ours. And the structure does too. Russian will be next; we aren't working on it now. I love this. I really do. I'm glad I'm not the linguistic expert, though. I stick to the nuts and bolts."

"Bucknell University served you well."

"Did." She drank more hot chocolate. "Met Greg there. Funny, because we were both from Virginia. That's what connected us in the first place."

"Leave home to find home," Sister said.

"Greg had this calling," she recalled fondly. "He followed it and I followed him and then I found mine. He was so sweet. When he was posted to Iraq, he said, *Honey, you supported me. I'll support you.*"

"Think he would have stayed in the army?"

"No. His idealism tarnished in Iraq. He wanted to complete his tour of duty and his time in the service, and then he said he'd work for me. I don't know if that would have been a good idea, but I suppose we'd have found out."

"What would he have done? He wasn't in your field."

"Sell. Greg could talk a dog off a meat wagon."

Sister nodded. "Yes, he could." She changed the subject. "Only three weeks left in the season. Can't you borrow a horse while Nighthawk heals?"

"Clayton Harper stopped by and said I could borrow his young mare. Think I will."

"Have you seen Marty Howard lately?" Sister was glad Faye would be back hunting.

"No, but Crawford comes around the office. He likes to check on our progress. I keep meaning to call Marty for lunch."

"Me too."

"Well, I don't know what you're going to do about her." Faye knew the situation. "Say, High Vajay dropped by Saturday after the hunt with his friend, Kasmir, can't say his last name—"

Sister filled in. "Barbhaiya."

"Couldn't have been more polite. Anyway, he asked me some questions about Tattenhall Station and the community. He said he was in contact with Norfolk and Southern. You gave him the information."

"The grass doesn't grow under his feet."

"Seems like he'd be a good addition to the place."

"Does." Sister placed her cup on the woven coaster. "Well, I've got to get back. A new horse came in yesterday, settling in, but I'll check on him."

"Kilowatt?"

"News travels fast."

"Yes, it does," Faye agreed.

"It occurs to me that you're—I guess the phrase is *cutting edge*—on the cutting edge of technology. What do you think about the murder of the woman in research at Craig and Abrams?"

A shadow crossed the young woman's features. "I don't like it. I wonder if she knew something."

"Technical?"

"That or sabotage."

"Political?"

"Hmm, probably not. I was thinking, what if one company wanted to destroy or drive down the stock prices of another? Let's stick to price. If she had information about development, it's possible for someone in a competing company or one that wanted to gobble up, say, Company A, to delay the development project. It's not that difficult if you have information. Look in another arena. Toyota overtook General Motors as the number one carmaker in the world. Yet even with all their resources in every department, it took Toyota years to develop a full-sized truck to compete with the American half-tons. And then they had to delay its entry onto the car lots by almost six months. Now I'm not saying there was sabotage, but even without, launching a new product is hazardous."

"Back to what you first said. Could such information be worth millions?"

"Yes. If the shark company bought up Company A after stocks were depressed thanks to a delayed product release or whatever, it would save millions for the buyer, then ultimately make them billions. The lady in question, had she lived, could have wound up in a high position with stock options Midas would envy."

"Good Lord."

"Business can be ruthless."

"What if the situation were reversed?"

"What do you mean?"

"What if she refused to tell?"

"Actually, that's worse."

"Why?"

"Because, Sister, anyone with valuable information can usually be scared into giving it away. If she didn't, she was brave and it cost her her life."

Sister leaned back. "Seeing her"—she stopped and thought—"got to me. You're in a field somewhat similar to hers. My curiosity is getting the better of me."

"Curiosity killed the cat. I'd be very, very careful." Faye said this protectively.

"By the way, Ben told me someone shot out the night-light." Sister changed the subject again.

"That's not all. When I was at work, someone hooked up the garden hoses, ran water in them, shut off the water, didn't drain the hoses. So of course they froze. Little irritating shit. Excuse my French."

"Do you know why someone would want to bother you?"

"No idea."

"Odd."

CHAPTER 14

A h, Lakshmi." Kasmir stared deep into his brandy snifter and shook his head.

The two men sat before the fire in the study at Charing Cross, the walls, painted lobster bisque, reflecting the light.

Upstairs the children slept. Downstairs their father agonized.

"Saturday." High's jaw set hard, then he covered his eyes, simply mentioning the day his wife would return.

"At least she didn't mention divorce." Kasmir ever sought to find the silver lining.

"Not yet. What could I do?" He threw up his hands. "The sheriff had to question her. He had the decency to give me some hours to compose myself before he called her in Phoenix." He paused. "Her sister will suggest divorce." He paused again. "She's never liked me."

"I remember." Kasmir thought Mandy's sister was one of those people who looks for what's wrong instead of what's right. The world is full of people like that.

High took a long sip of his brandy. "I didn't kill Aashi. I didn't even know she was in Warrenton."

"Maybe she wasn't," Kasmir replied.

High sat up, leaning forward in the deep-seated wing chair. "Why would I kill her? I liked her. She was so full of gaiety, laughter, and energy. She made me feel young."

"We aren't that old, you know."

"Old enough." High put his snifter on the coffee table. "Old enough to start worrying about getting old."

"Young women are an antidote. But I thought you had ended the affair. You wrote me last year that you had." He half smiled. "I liked receiving the letter, but you made me laugh, saying you didn't want to have this conversation on your cell, too many people could listen in. True, but why would they be listening to us?"

"Between us we possess stores of information."

"Only about money." Kasmir smiled.

High fell back into his chair. "Exactly."

"Well, what are you going to do?"

High opened his hands, palms outward. "Cooperate with the authorities."

"Of course. I mean, what are you going to do about Mandy?"

"Isn't it more, what is she going to do about me?"

Kasmir pursed his lips. "She'll rage and cry when the children are out of the house. Maybe she'll throw things at you or force some penance upon

157

you. I've heard jewelry or a new car absolves many such sins."

High grunted.

They both stared into the fire; then Kasmir spoke again. "When did you fan the embers?"

"Never really died. I couldn't get her out of my mind. The funny thing is, I love my wife. You know that. I love our children. I love our life together, but I needed Aashi. Is it so hard to understand?"

Kasmir shrugged, "We're men. Men understand. Women don't. But let me pose the question: What would you do, were the situation reversed?"

"She'd never," High answered, too quickly.

Kasmir nodded in agreement, while noting the haste. "Yes, yes, but what if, my old friend?"

"Well"—High shifted in his seat—"well, I'd be furious. I wouldn't hit her; I might want to but I wouldn't. If the man were someone close, that would be a double betrayal. I'd want to kill him."

"Yes. That's usually the case."

High grunted. "At least I spared her that—the double betrayal, I mean."

"She knew Aashi from when she was your secretary."

"Aashi wasn't my secretary for long. She was bright. I helped her move up and out. Better for me too. Sometimes people can sniff those things out in an office. I don't think anyone did."

"Someone did."

"No, they didn't." High looked quizzically at Kasmir, comfortable in his cashmere robe.

"Who told the authorities you were having an affair with her?"

High sat bolt upright. "I never thought of that."

"You're too upset to think clearly," Kasmir said, to soothe him.

"Who could it be?"

"Someone who observed you closely, perhaps."

"I'm retired. If they told the police anything from our office days, it would be old news."

"But whoever told the police indicated the affair was ongoing. Correct?"

"Correct." High felt even worse now.

"Let us consider this logically, difficult as it is. Someone knew you and Aashi had either continued your affair or revived it; that detail will emerge in time, I suppose. Now, why would that be important?" He answered his own question. "You are a suspect. Men do kill their mistresses for all the old reasons. If there are new ones I know them not. You didn't kill her. So whoever informed the sheriff—as I recall, the counties here have sheriffs, not police—at any rate, this person either thinks you are guilty or wants others to think so."

High's right hand came to his forehead. "Kasmir, it can't be true."

"Why?" the portly man pressed. "Why would someone wish to cast you in such a dreadful light? Do you have enemies here? Is someone seeking revenge from Craig and Abrams?"

"I helped Craig and Abrams double their profits."

High, not an egotistical man, did know his worth. "Yes, there were those with whom I was not close, people I even disliked, but not to this degree. You remember. I told you who would drag their heels, no vision, or who would complain about my administrative habits."

"You did. Sometimes, Lakshmi, seemingly mild breasts harbor a deep reservoir of self-regard and hatred of others. It has been my experience that they reveal themselves when one is at one's lowest."

"Possibly but—"

"Is there anyone here, anyone you have crossed? Women like you. Perhaps some Virginia lady fell victim to your charms and her husband felt otherwise."

"No. I flatter the ladies, as you do. That's what one does. Sometimes Crawford Howard, Ramsey Merriman, Clayton Harper, and I would drive to D.C. I'd slip off for an hour, but I don't think they knew."

Kasmir sighed. "Then allow me to suggest a truly offensive possibility but one not out of the realm of my observations of life. What if Mandy killed Aashi?"

"Are you out of your mind, Kasmir? She is the most gentle of women."

"Not now. She may have taken the news with relative calm on the telephone, but once home I wouldn't expect the calm to continue."

"Murder? My wife murder another woman? No."

"Aashi wasn't just another woman. She was your

mistress and she was some twenty years younger than your wife, who was one of the world's great beauties, to be sure, but is now middle-aged. This preys on a woman's mind even as it preys on our own. Madhur"—he used her real full name—"must be facing the loss of this beauty, or the power of it."

"She's not that superficial."

"Lakshmi, a woman's face is her fortune. Myself, I believe your wife is more beautiful than ever. The years have burnished her beauty, motherhood has softened her, but a mistress, especially a young and gorgeous one, strikes at a woman's heart."

"I know," High said quietly, feeling wretched.

"Was there time for Mandy to kill Aashi?"

"I don't know. I didn't keep a leash on her at the ball. I suppose." He threw up his hands. "This is absurd. She would never do such a thing."

"Yes, yes, but what if she had cracked your passwords or your communication with Aashi? She could have sent her an e-mail telling her to meet you at the Hampton Inn. Simple."

"You're supposing my wife ransacked my computer, found my secret files, and then proceeded to bait Aashi?"

"Your wife can use a computer better than most of us."

"She wouldn't."

"She had powerful motivation. So now I come to my next question. If she did kill Aashi, will you protect Mandy and say you did it?" Kasmir wanted to know if High loved his wife as much as he said.

High shut his eyes and covered them with his right hand. "Yes."

CHAPTER 15

That same evening, Tuesday, February 26, light shone through another glass, this one filled with single cask brandy and firmly gripped in Clayton Harper's fist.

A small group of dedicated people had met at Tri-corne Farm, a modest but pretty place owned by the Franklins, for the purpose of considering fund-raisers for the Thoroughbred Retirement Fund.

Betty and Bobby Franklin, Peggy Augustus, Ilona and Ramsey Merriman, Cabel and Clayton Harper, Sister Jane, Tedi and Edward Bancroft, and Sam Lorillard comprised the group.

All were in agreement concerning the fund-raiser party, but Cabel shocked everyone by saying the theme should be Lady Godiva—lots of naked women on horses. Ilona nearly slapped her. Cabel apologized for her insensitive humor and flounced off. Bobby winced when he heard gravel and snow churn in the drive as she peeled out.

The meeting over, the gathering congenial, they broke into small knots to talk horses, hounds, people.

Sister picked up a cleaned-off vegetable tray and walked back to the kitchen to refresh it. She and Betty had the run of one another's houses, so it wasn't rude of her.

Clayton followed her into the kitchen, reaching for some small scrubbed carrots. "Betty fixed this herself. Some folks just buy stuff from the supermarket, ready made. But that frozen tomato cannonball she makes can't be duplicated. I've begged Cabel to make it and she does, but it's not the same and Betty won't reveal her secret."

"Does Cabel use crushed pineapple?"

"Yep."

"What about Worcestershire sauce?"

"Yep." He took a big gulp of his brandy. The glass had been almost full, so great was his tolerance for alcohol. "You wouldn't happen to know the recipe, would you?"

"She won't even tell me and I'm her best friend." Sister laughed. "Maybe the great question is Hellmann's or Duke's?"

Southern women were divided between these two mayonnaises, fiercely defending the virtues of each, although one is to make one's own mayonnaise. Who has the time, hence the debate.

"Matters even more than Coke or Pepsi." Clayton's laugh was deep and comforting, and for a moment the tiny broken veins in his puffy face seemed to recede. "You're a Duke's."

"What a memory."

"I remember a lot of things." He sipped once more. "I may drink like a fish but my mind's still good."

She turned to face him, setting the tray back on the counter. "Clayton, stop."

"Stop what?"

"Stop drinking."

He put the glass on the counter next to the vegetables and folded his arms across his chest. "Give me one good reason to take away one of the sustaining joys of my life."

"Your life itself. You'll kill yourself with that stuff."

"We all have to die sometime, and I'm having a good time while I'm doing it."

"I don't think you are."

He looked into her eyes, saying without apology, "I'm a coward."

"I don't remember you being a coward. I remember you working your tail off, building a good business, riding hard to hounds in the bargain. I remember you raising three great kids, all married and doing well."

"Cabel can take most of the credit for that. I think the mother usually can. I did my part, although I worked too late and too long, but it always comes back to the mother."

"I don't know. I've seen some sorry mothers. But that begs the question. Clayton, look at yourself."

He unfolded his arms and hugged her spontaneously. "You're one of the only people in my life who will tell me the truth."

She hugged him back. "I will and I am. I care about you, Clayton. Many of the people in the club care about you. You can stop."

"Then my nerve endings will wake up."

"That's the point."

"Jane, Cabel has many good qualities, but for the last ten years or so, they've been lost on me. Goddamn but she's a whistling bitch! I suppose part of it is, the more she nags the more I drink. Her revenge is to spend money. And for a smart woman she can be dumb. She's having some health problems, little things. Her hair is falling out. She wears a wig. Her legs hurt. No one knows but Ilona. Will she go to a doctor, no! She won't get a mammogram, blood work, just won't." He shrugged. "I just sleep with as many women as will have me. Drives her crazy. I told her she could sleep with whomever she wanted; I didn't care. She slapped me." He laughed.

"Leave."

"Yeah, I think about that when I wake up in the morning, before I pour a little Knockando in my coffee. But you know, it was her money that started my business. I owe her that."

"You've repaid her many times over. Divorce her. Split your assets and gird your loins for all her stories about what a shit you are."

"Well, if I sober up I'd better call all the women I've slept with, because she'll ferret them out and tell everyone."

"She already has."

Betty walked in, perceived the intense conversation, picked up the filled tray, and sailed out. Sister looked after her with affection.

"There are some she doesn't know about."

"Good on you." Sister laughed.

He laughed back. "You'd be surprised how a fat drunk can still get the girls."

"You're a lot more than that. Women like you. Always have." She put her hand on his forearm. "Clayton, Sam Lorillard fell far lower than you could imagine falling. *He* changed."

He gulped the rest of his drink as though he'd crawled across the Sahara. "Cabel declares she loves me, but it never felt like love. It felt like a vise, even before I married her."

"So you married her for the money and for the feeling of being central to someone's life?"

"Male ego. A woman tells you she can't live without you. *I love you* doesn't cut as much ice as *I can't live without you.*"

"I'll take your word for it."

That made Clayton laugh. "Clear-eyed as always. I wish I could be more like you."

"Look, Sam is out there. He'll help you. We'll all help you." A gust of anger swept over her. "Clayton, you have balls. Use them!"

He put the empty glass in the sink, washed it out slowly, and turned to her. "You know, Jane, I wouldn't take that from anyone but you."

"I know." She tactfully left the kitchen so he could compose himself. A few minutes later she saw Clayton and Sam talking in the living room.

Betty smiled at Sister, who smiled back.

CHAPTER 16

Thick icy fog shrouded the soft rolling hills of central Virginia. Early colonists called this a *pogonip,* a word borrowed from the Native Americans and no doubt somewhat altered in the process. A pogonip freezes on trees, stones, and rooftops and then melts on the earth, warmer than the air. Superstition has it that evil spirits frolic but Marion, driving very slowly, thought superstition just that.

Usually on Wednesday she trooped in a half hour before opening, it being her "late" morning. But last night she had had a dinner date with an old flame and had neglected to take her paperwork home. Why sit through dinner fretting over paperwork? Better to rise early and knock it out at the office.

She could barely see the store as she turned into the top drive and parked next to the building. But approaching the door she gasped, stopped, and her hand flew to her heart. A corpse sat astride a child's hobby horse. She forced herself to breathe deeply, then gingerly approached the naked white figure. The fog intensified her dread. Not until she was up close did she discover the corpse was a mannequin.

She slumped against her front door. What a sick joke. Furious, she reached over to push the wretched thing over and smash it to bits but then stopped herself. The sheriff would want to see this.

Flipping open her cell, she speed-dialed the

department, the first number she had programmed on her new phone. Since the murder she'd put the number on speed dial, hoping she wouldn't have to use it. She wanted someone over here fast because the mannequin needed to be removed. The townspeople wouldn't enjoy the joke any more than she did.

Thank heaven Trigger was in the store. She couldn't have faced a mannequin on him.

Next she dialed Sister.

"Good morning," came Sister's cheery voice. The hounds could be heard in the background for she was in the kennel.

"Sister, someone put a naked mannequin on a hobby horse in front of the store. Thank God there's a thick fog."

"You're kidding."

"How sick is that?"

"Sick. I assume you called the sheriff."

"Someone is on the way. I want to get this damn thing out of here. I can't believe it. My heart stopped. Stopped. I couldn't breathe. All I could think of was *Why?* and then I was terrified I'd know the victim."

"Is the store all right?"

"I don't know. I'll go in right now." Marion fished out her keys, opened the lock, stepped in, and hit the lights. "Well, it's a quick look, but I don't think anyone has been in here." She exhaled loudly. "I could kill. I could just kill!"

"We might have to," Sister replied, over the roar of

the girls flying into the feed room. "Let me go into the office. Can't hear myself think." She waved at Shaker as she left the large room.

"What do you mean we might have to kill?"

"Just popped out of my mouth." Sister sat on the corner edge of the desk. "Do you think kids did it?"

"I don't know." Marion's voice dropped a bit; she suddenly felt tired. "I guess I'm a little more on edge than I realized."

"We all are. Why don't you come on down here for a vacation?"

"Thanks. I can't. I'm buried under an avalanche of work. Everyone is."

"Take a rain check then."

"How's everything there?"

"Oh, fine, if you consider I have an outlaw pack to contend with, plus scenting conditions have gone to hell in a handbasket."

"Here too. Joyce Fendley breezed through yesterday saying the same thing. It's the temperature bounce; it's responsible for all the colds and flu. I think so, anyway."

They talked until the deputy came. Sister returned to the feed room and then walked over to the barn. She brought in each horse, putting him in his stall. Kilowatt looked good; he had wonderful ground manners.

She threw an alfalfa-and-orchard-grass mix out to the brood mares and the two retirees. Feeding, filling water buckets and water troughs, and checking over each horse took two hours and she was efficient. A dawdler would have stretched it into three.

She then hopped in the GMC truck—twenty thousand miles on the odometer—to drive to the dentist's office for her cleaning.

She shook off hay before walking into the pleasant sitting room. Looking up from *W* magazine was Ilona Merriman.

"Ilona."

"How are you? I see you just came from the barn."

"Thought I brushed off all the hay."

"Not quite. Here. Turn around." Ilona brushed off some bits of rich tiny alfalfa leaves. "You missed a drama last night at Walter's."

"What happened?"

"He had a poker party."

"That's right. I forgot about that. Which reminds me, he said he could organize a poker tournament for the Virginia chapter of the Thoroughbred Retirement Fund. Haven't had time to call him since our meeting at the Franklins'."

"I can tell you, Sorrel Buruss's sharp at cards. I didn't know that. Walter will have her help if he does the fund-raiser. Well, anyway, there were four small tables—play three games, then switch tables. He had it organized like musical chairs except no one was left standing."

"Who won?"

"Kasmir. Faye made out all right too. Well, Clayton was shaking like a leaf. He could barely hold a hand

and Cabel kept sniping at him. Walter unfortunately put them together for the first go-round. You won't believe this, but Clayton has stopped drinking. He's suffering too. I think he should go away to one of those clinics. Wouldn't it be easier? People who understand can help you."

Sister sat down. "Maybe Clayton *will* go to a clinic. I hope so. He needs help."

"Cabel won't help him. She ignored him. When he made a bad call—this was before Walter moved him—she said he thought better when he was drunk. That's vicious. I mean, I adore Cabel, you know we are best-best friends, but the man is suffering and he's trying. For the first time in his life, he's trying."

"She probably doesn't believe he'll make it. Maybe she's steeling herself for a relapse. I don't know."

"It's revenge. I swear. I shot her a look but to no avail. If she wants to be hateful to him, do it at home. She was bad enough the other night at the Thoroughbred Retirement meeting."

"Yes, she was."

"I swear, I don't know what got into her; she needled Faye every chance she got. She'd insinuate that High Vajay spent a lot of time visiting his neighbor. As the night wore on the insinuations became outright accusations. Faye took it with good grace until Cabel—and I swear *she'd* been drinking because I've never seen her like this, I mean it—Cabel said, flat out, that men think beautiful young widows are starved for sex, so she, Cabel, expected they'd worn a path to her door. And Faye looked straight at her and said, *Are you worried Clayton was one of them?*"

Sister's eyebrows shot upward. "Faye Spencer said that?"

"She'd had enough. Well, Cabel threw her cards in Faye's face, grabbed her purse and coat, and stomped out. We could hear the motor when she floored it; two times this week she's ripped up someone's driveway. Clayton didn't move a muscle. Faye picked up Cabel's cards and said *Lousy hand,* and showed us a pair of threes."

The hygienist appeared from the hallway. "Mrs. Merriman."

"Coming, dear." Ilona stood up. "You should start playing poker, Sister. You don't know what you're missing."

"Apparently not." Sister smiled but thought to herself that life was gamble enough, why squander her money on cards? It wasn't noon yet and already the day had been popping.

It was three thirty when Sister walked through her kitchen door, sun finally peeping through low clouds. She heard a clatter and the sound of a large pussycat running. Raleigh and Rooster, awake at the sound of the truck, rushed to greet her. One of the good things about Shaker's living on the other side of the kennels was he would let the dogs out when she ran errands. She petted them, bestowed kisses, and threw her gear on the farmer's table to go in search of what Golly had done. She knew the calico well enough to know the cat had pulverized something.

Nothing in the kitchen. Nothing in the dining room. The living room glistened pristine. Small wonder, she hardly ever used it. Had to be the large pantry or the den. She walked into the den first. Raleigh's beloved stuffed pink flamingo toy lay in tatters, the squeaker carefully dismantled by clever claws. One of Sister's needlepoint pillows, she'd done it herself, sported long dangling threads.

"Golly, damn you!" Sister walked out and yelled up the stairway at the cat, peeping down at her from the top of the stairs.

"Death to dogs!" was Golly's response.

Raleigh, on Sister's heels, mournfully carried the flamingo bits.

"Wicked. That cat is wicked," Rooster grumbled.

"I told you I'd get even." Golly remained motionless on the step, ready to run under a bed or spring over everyone's heads, a trick she'd perfected.

Instead, Sister returned to the kitchen, the dogs with her. She gave them large milkbones, picked up the paper, turned on the teapot, and sat down to read the day's fresh hell worldwide.

The phone rang.

"I hope Alexander Graham Bell is in the lowest circle of Hell."

Nonetheless, she stood up, slapped the paper down, and picked up the wall phone.

"Sister." It was a young voice, trembling.

173

"Felicity, are you all right?"

"Yes," came the wavering reply.

"Honey, what's the matter?"

"Well, I had a meeting with Mrs. Norton. She was great. But she said I needed to talk to Mom and Dad as soon as I could. So I called them on my cell. I mean I started talking to them and asked them to come visit me. Mom got all worried. I only once ever asked them to come to Custis Hall, and that was freshman year. Well, anyway, I told them. Everything."

"You did the right thing. I'm sure your mother thought the worst when you said you wanted her to come to Virginia." She paused. "How'd she take it?"

"She told me to get rid of it." Felicity was sobbing now.

"Felicity, why don't I drive over there and pick you up?"

"Val said I could use her Jeep. I'm going to get Howie. May we both come to you?"

"Of course." She hung up the phone as the teapot whistled.

Howard and Felicity arrived at four forty-five. She glanced up at the wall clock when she heard Val's Jeep and smiled for a moment, thinking how generous Val could be, even when angry at her friend.

The two knocked on the mudroom door.

"Come on in."

They did. Sister poured coffee, set out cookies and cake.

"Thank you for seeing us." Howie sat down gratefully, a young man with a burden on his shoulders.

"Would you like to talk here or in the living room?"

"Here."

Howard, eighteen years old with an open, All-American face, began. "I called my parents after Felicity called hers. Mom's pretty okay. Dad's furious. He said he won't give me any money for college."

"Think he'll stick to it?" Sister asked.

"Yeah. You don't know my dad."

Sister thought to herself she was glad she didn't. "You can go to Piedmont Community College at night, if you want to continue your education."

Felicity, a little tense, replied, "But Sister, he can't play football there and he's so good."

"Felicity." Howard's voice was soft, but there was power in this kid. "It's just a game. My chances of playing in the pros are pretty slim even if I have a great college career. What's more important, football or you? You."

Felicity sniffled. Sister rose, picked up a box of Kleenex from the counter, and set it near the young woman.

"Howard, have you been accepted at any colleges yet? I know April is usually when the notices go out, but given that you've been recruited, have any coaches promised you anything?"

"Well, they can't exactly promise but I'm pretty sure I'll be accepted at Wake Forest, and maybe at the University of South Carolina."

"Any Virginia schools?"

"I applied at Tech but I don't think I have a chance."

"What about William and Mary?"

"My grades aren't good enough. If Tech or William and Mary did take me, I'd have to be tutored over the summer and take the College Boards again. I didn't do very well."

"He's not good at tests," Felicity simply stated.

"How badly do you want to play football?"

Howard looked down at his big hands. "Not bad enough to leave Felicity." He looked up at her, his light brown eyes serious. "Maybe this is the best thing to happen to me."

"How so?" the older woman asked, warming to this young man.

"You get treated different, you know? Football spoils you. You work hard on your physical stuff but you can think you're better than other people. I don't want to end up like that, Mrs. Arnold. I'm not better just because I can throw a ball."

"Felicity, what do you want to do?"

The thin girl held her coffee cup in her hands. "I'm going to get a job, go to Piedmont at night, and have the baby." She looked at Howard. "If you go to Wake, I'll support you. You don't have to stay here with me and the baby."

"No way. I'm supporting you. And I'm going to marry you."

Felicity smiled but didn't reply.

"You'll turn eighteen soon enough, Felicity, and then if your parents don't give their approval, it doesn't matter," Sister said.

"I never thought my mother would be like this." Shock registered on her face. "They were always behind me. I can't believe my mother told me to have an abortion."

"Every woman has to face that issue alone."

"I graduate in June. I've already sent in my application to Piedmont. I know I don't really have to for night school, but I wanted to be sure. If I get a job I can work until I have the baby and then go back as soon as I'm able."

"Who will take care of the baby while you're working?"

"I don't know yet but I have some time to think about it."

"I found a job already," Howard said.

"You did?" Felicity grabbed Howard's hand.

"Working for Matt Robb's construction company. He said as soon as I graduate from Miller School to show up at the office. I like construction."

"Matt's good. You'll learn a lot," said Sister.

"And I'll be outside. I can't sit at a desk, Mrs. Arnold, I just can't."

"I understand. I can't either." She smiled in accord. "What can I do to help you two?"

"You've helped us already." Howard smiled at her.

"Mom and Dad are flying in for the weekend. I'm going to hunt Saturday, I don't care."

"Felicity, much as I love having you in the hunt field, please spend as much time as you can with your parents. Have they met Howard?"

"No. They will over the weekend. They aren't talking me out of my baby," Felicity declared defiantly. "And they aren't talking me out of marrying Howie."

"You finally said yes!" Howard leaned back in his chair and let out a stream of air; then he grabbed Felicity and kissed her, but not too long because of Sister.

"Congratulations, Howard. You've won yourself a fine young woman."

"I love her, Mrs. Arnold. I know people say we're kids. I mean, you should have heard my folks. But whatever comes, we'll deal with it."

"I believe you will." She thought a long time, placing her hand on Raleigh's head when he came up beside her. "Plenty of young couples get off to rockier starts than you two. I'm no expert on marriage even though I was married myself—you all never knew Ray, of course—and I've observed marriages that work and marriages that don't. What I can tell you is don't stop talking. If something bothers you, get it off your chest and get it over with. Never go to bed angry. Put up with the little irritations of character and life. Forget them. And most of all, keep your sense of humor."

"Thank you." Howard squeezed Felicity's hand. "Honey, I have to get back."

"Okay."

As they stood up, Felicity hugged Sister, and Howard spontaneously did the same. Then he shook her hand. "Thank you!"

"Howard, you and I are going to know each other a long time, and I look forward to it." She smiled broadly.

Felicity hugged Sister again. "I love you."

"I love you too, honey. Keep your chin up and remember that your parents want what's best for you even if you're on opposite sides of the fence. Real troubles don't seem to upset people as much as shattered expectations. Try to remember that."

As they left, hand in hand, Sister thought they had a lot going for them. She dialed Garvey Stokes.

"Sister!"

"You handsome thing, what are you doing?"

"Just came back in from the bullpit." This was the factory area where his workers poured aluminum and put together window frames and other objects, much of the work computerized.

"Garvey, it's been over a year since Angel Crump died."

Angel had been his right-hand "man," so to speak, ever since he started his business. She had passed away at work in her mid-eighties, and he had never hired a replacement or changed her office, which sat empty.

"Think of the old girl every day."

"Would you hire a new girl if I recommend her?

Someone who possesses Angel's tact and is every bit as smart? Of course, she doesn't know where all the bodies are buried. That Angel could work a deal because she knew so-and-so's great aunt got hooked on laudanum back at the turn of the century."

Garvey let out a belly laugh. "She did, she certainly did. Who are you sending me?"

"You know her: Felicity Porter."

"She's not going to college? What a waste."

"She'll be going to Piedmont at night."

"Why?"

"I can't tell you that, Garvey, but if you will consent to interview her, she will do well. She's steadfast. Once she learns the routine, she'll fit in, and I think she'll become fascinated by the business. I thought she'd become an investment banker, but you know, Aluminum Manufacturing may wind up being more exciting for her."

"I like the kid."

"Will you interview her? I'll drive her over next week. She doesn't have a car."

"Of course I will."

"I have a feeling about this, Garvey. Forgive me for the prophecy, but I believe wonderful things can grow from this."

She hung up the phone and returned to the table. Her tea was cold so she turned on the kettle. Raleigh looked at her with his sweet Doberman eyes, brimming with intelligence. Rooster, now next to him, also looked up to her.

"Beggars." She gave them each a cookie.

Into the room sashayed Golly, leaping to the table, where she paused for some conspicuous grooming. She sat on the newspaper, of course. Forgetting her needlepoint pillow, Sister absentmindedly stroked the cat. She thought of the two kids sitting at her table, each willing to sacrifice for the other. Sex might bring people together but it didn't keep them together. Those two seemed to have a great deal of what keeps people together.

She was surprised when the tears rolled down her cheeks.

CHAPTER 17

Heavy frost silvered the rolling pastures, fields, and the rooftops of the old stone buildings of Mousehold Heath, a new fixture fifteen miles southeast of the kennels.

As is always the case with a new fixture, it takes perhaps two years to figure out the fox population, most especially how they run.

Established in 1807, the simple farmhouse and outlying clapboard barns acquired its name owing to the unusually large mouse population. Over the centuries, generations of hardworking cats somewhat reduced the numbers of these little marauders, as did foxes, owls, and hawks, but Mousehold Heath still boasted regiments of mice.

Sister noticed Faye Spencer parked as far away

from Cabel Harper as possible, down by the old cattle barn. The two pointedly did not speak. Ilona, with quiet glee, was observing every nuance.

It must have killed Cabel that Clayton dropped his mare at Faye's farm.

Betty Franklin noticed too, simply shrugging as Sister said nothing. Human dramas bored Sister. Her focus was on foxhunting in particular and animals in general, although she did care about her Custis Hall girls. They were young, experiencing powerful adult emotions for the first time. They needed a friendly ear, perhaps a friendly nudge. Adults should be accustomed to such tempests, although Sister had come to the conclusion that adults were just wrinkled children with greater resources to inflict greater damage.

She swung her leg over Matador, the two still getting acquainted. The sixteen-hand flea-bitten gray, light gray with dark flecks in the coat, former steeplechase horse looked wonderful, and she accepted compliments as she rode along the trailers.

Ascertaining that the small Thursday crowd out on this cold crisp day was five minutes from ready, she checked her watch. Well enough, five minutes to the first cast.

Sister did not wait for people who showed up late or fiddled with tack. Scent, often a fragile thing, demanded her utmost attention. Why punish all those who did arrive on time by letting slip an opportunity to pick up a fox, scent possibly fading as the hands on the clock kept ticking?

Like every leader before her, regardless of the organization, the sum is greater than the parts and the group takes precedence over the individual. She'd bend over backward to help a hunt club member, even Cabel, but when it came to the actual hunt, you'd better mind your p's and q's.

Hounds rocked the party wagon, they were so eager to hunt. Wisely, Shaker and Sister had brought only seasoned animals. No reason to risk a young hound's becoming confused in new territory and perhaps skirting off.

"Let's decant 'em." She smiled at Shaker, already mounted.

Sybil opened the back door to the hound trailer.

"Hold up." Shaker quietly commanded the eleven couple of hounds, which stood patiently but with high expectation.

Sister scanned the small field, noting that Vajay appeared drawn, Kasmir elegant, and Cabel and Ilona stuck next to each other. Weekdays the field included more women than men. Those men owning their own businesses might take one morning off during the week but they usually couldn't take two.

Sybil swung her leg over Bombardier, her tried-and-true horse. Betty sat on Outlaw, those two like an old married couple.

Having discussed the morning's draw before arriving, Shaker stuck to the plan, which was to cast behind the cattle barn, across the pasture, and thence to the back pastures and cornfields.

Hounds eagerly dashed behind the cattle barn, feathered, but didn't open. A thin but fast-moving stream separated the barn field from the next pasture; the eastern hillside faced the barn. A million tiny rainbows glistened. The temperature rising on the eastern slopes would soon turn that glittering sight into thick dew. Shaker urged hounds forward, Cora being the strike hound today, Dragon left in the kennel.

A long row of rolled-up hay lined the southern side of the twenty-acre pasture, like giant biscuits of shredded wheat. Shaker asked hounds to investigate the round bales, for mice liked to make warm nests in the sweet-smelling hay.

"Hey," Dasher called as the whole pack worked, noses to the hay.

Cora joined him. *"H-m-m."* Her stern moved faster.

Trudy, now in her third year, leapt atop the hay, jumping from one bale to another. She could hear the mice inside. The humans couldn't but all the hounds both listened intently and inhaled deeply.

They covered the ground. The fox had been there; a deep hollowed-out spot in the hay bale marked one entrance. It was a red dog fox that they could clearly smell. This fox had decided to live with his food supply, but he wasn't there.

As it was the end of February, the hay fox might be coming home from courting. They cast themselves farther away. Scent picked up, then frittered away.

Hounds moved across the pasture, easily clearing the three-foot-two-inch coop at the end of the field.

Throughout the summer, staff and some members had worked to prepare the fixture.

A small covert on both sides of a deeper stream pointed down to a larger creek. Hounds burst in and burst out. This time yet another fox, a good-sized gray, shot in front of them.

Betty, on the left side, hollered, "Tally-ho!" when he burst out.

To everyone's surprise, he made a large circle and then dashed into that same covert.

Betty called, "Tally back!"

The fox was young and became unnerved by hounds when he bolted from his den. He wouldn't make that mistake again, and he was lucky to pop back in and save his brush.

Shaker dismounted, flipping his reins over Gunpowder's neck as the sweet older horse stood. Shaker slipped going into the covert but recovered. The thick brambles impeded progress, but he could make out hounds digging at the den. Fighting his way through the thorns, he reached the den, blew "Gone to Ground," and praised his charges. He returned, favoring his right leg a bit, and swung up on Gunpowder to head toward the woods across the pasture.

They fiddled and faddled in there but nothing—still too cold—so he emerged on the eastern side, hunting back below the cattle barns in the opposite direction. Ardent picked up a line and they ran for perhaps ten minutes, but it faded and that was pretty much the day, although they kept trying.

Still, when they returned to the trailers Sister felt positive. They'd only hunted Mousehold Heath three times. The owners, a young couple determined to make a profit off a combination of cattle, timber, and hay, came out from the house to join the impromptu tailgate.

"Won't you all come inside?" Lisa Jardine asked Sister.

Sister declined. "We'll track up your house."

"It can't be any worse than what Jim and I do. Come on. It's cold out here."

They carried the food into the big old country kitchen, a white porcelain table in its middle.

Jim joined them. "Twenty degrees this morning. How do you keep your feet warm in those boots?"

Shaker replied, "You don't."

After forty-five minutes of thawing, drinking hot coffee, and eating the ubiquitous ham biscuits, these made by Faye Spencer, the whole gang returned to the trailers.

Sister, hand on the crystal doorknob with a center of mercury, smiled at the well-built pair. Country life kept them strong and healthy. "Thank you. This was an unexpected treat."

"You know I rope cows. I can ride pretty good." Jim, at first thinking foxhunting a sport for toffs, was coming to understand it was quite the reverse.

She challenged him. "Well, Jim, let me put you to the test."

"Can I ride Western?"

"Jim Jardine, you can ride anyway you want. We'd be honored to have you join us, and you will see your beautiful farm in a new light."

"Can I wear my chaps? Haven't got any special gear, you know."

"You can." She thanked them again and walked back to the trailer.

Jim Jardine would get hooked. The only people who didn't succumb to the lure of foxhunting once they rode out were those who were terrified but couldn't admit it. Everyone else embraced the majesty of the chase. Even today, pushing off in the low twenties, her toes already throbbing, Sister thanked God for this bountiful earth and all its beauty. She never felt more alive than when foxhunting. Even making love, an activity that found favor with her, posted a dim second. Her reasoning was a great lover might last an hour. Wonderful and good. A great chase might last two hours and occasionally four. Do the math.

Strictly speaking, the square-built Jim shouldn't come out in chaps on a Western saddle. But landowners, special generous folk, could do whatever they wanted in Jefferson Hunt. As far as Sister was concerned, she was damned lucky to have him. Over time he'd realize the traditional hunting kit served a purpose, one tested over centuries. Then, too, if she were a man she wouldn't want to take a jump in a Western saddle. That horn could be lethal to one's reproductive career. Hell, Jim could ride naked if he wanted to! But then she regretted that thought, for it brought Lady Godiva to the fore.

No sooner had she reached the trailer than she heard Faye Spencer and Cabel Harper yelling at each other.

High and Kasmir ignored them. Betty and Sybil did too, but their responsibilities as staff precluded such intrusions. Ilona was vainly trying to pull away the puce-faced Cabel.

Shaker stepped up to Sister. "You might want to speak to the ladies."

"How long has this been going on?"

"Um, maybe two minutes, maybe five; the air is sulfurous."

"Yes, I can hear that."

"You slut! You piece of white trash!" Cabel screeched.

"And you're not?" Faye shot back, but at lower register.

"Cabel, come on now. You're making a spectacle of yourself." Ilona pulled at Cabel's elbow, only to be shaken off as Cabel spun around on her.

"Leave me alone! You don't think your precious Ramsey hasn't rammed his dick up her?"

This vulgarity shocked everyone more than the fight. Cabel had never been a vulgar woman.

Sister, towering over the women, said firmly, "That's enough."

"Who the hell are you to tell me what to do? We aren't hunting." Cabel now spun on Sister. "You lured my husband away."

"Years and years ago, Cabel, and I can now see I was wrong. You're overwrought." Sister wondered if perhaps Cabel wasn't ill; something was pulling her down. "This doesn't become you."

The fact that Sister didn't scream back at her, but remained calm, began to have an effect.

Ilona, glancing at Sister, voice low, pleaded, "Come on, honey. You're upset." Then she said, "I'm going to tell Sister."

"Don't."

"It's too late, Cabel. This isn't like you." She turned to Sister. "Clayton asked her for a divorce. I don't know why she wants to keep him, but that's love for you."

Cabel burst into tears. "I made him! I made him what he is today!"

Sister had to bite her tongue because she wanted to say, "Yes, you did." Instead she spoke sympathetically. "Cabel, that's painful news, I know. Certainly I have no advice except to say, if you can't patch it up, end it and go forward. You have a lot of living ahead of you."

"How can he do this to me?"

Sister couldn't say a word to that.

Ilona murmured, "He's going away for twenty-eight days; that might change things." She turned again to Sister. "He says he's truly going into rehab."

"I see." Sister, seeing that Cabel, though sobbing, had stopped attacking Faye, walked over to the younger woman, who had retreated to her trailer. "You all right?"

"Yes. She flew at me like a harpy. Scared me half to death."

"He's asked for a divorce."

"Well, it's not because of me." Faye bit her lip. "Oh, he came around sniffing. That's Clayton. But I certainly didn't go to bed with him."

"She thinks you did."

"She's lost it. She thinks every woman in this club has gone to bed with him."

Sister smiled slightly. "Ah, well, some of us did back in the Bronze Age. I know this is hard to believe, but he was so handsome. So handsome and so much fun. The years work on all of us, I reckon."

"Some more than others."

"Well, I thank you for not throwing a punch at her. It was bad enough."

"It was. I shouldn't have lost my temper and said what I said," Faye looked imploringly at the silver-haired woman, "but I'm sick and tired of it."

"I understand. Do your best to keep it in check."

As Sister rode back to the farm in the truck, Betty at her side, the two rehashed the day's hunt and then touched on the human explosion.

"We make ourselves miserable." Betty played with her gloves, which she'd folded over in her lap. "We do, we make our own Hell."

"Yes, we do."

"Speaking of Hell, how about Heaven? Today's saints?"

"Herefrith, Bishop of Lincoln, most likely killed by

190

the Danes in 873, and also Oswald. Now *he's* really interesting. He was the bishop of Worcester in the late tenth century and then became archbishop of York. He came from a Danish military family. By now the Danes controlled huge sections of England; the Saxons in the north were weak at the time. Oswald must have been quite something. He was much loved, and eyewitnesses commented on his splendid physique and his beautiful voice."

"Did he get murdered too?"

"Died on February twenty-eighth, reciting the Gradual Psalms. For an archbishop, that's the way to go."

"Ever think about your own death?"

"In my teens. I suppose the reality that I would die intruded on my consciousness, but the intrusion was intellectual. Now I know it emotionally so I accept. Not that I want to go. I'm quite happy to live."

"Sometimes I wonder," Betty mused, "then I banish it from my thoughts. Nothing I can do about it. We're all going to go."

"Think about Herefrith. So many of the saints died terrible deaths. Being cut down by the sword was relatively kind. And here it is, over a thousand years later and some of us remember their sacrifice. I don't know if I could die for an idea. I could die for a person. I could die for a hound. But an idea? No. I know I've said this before, but it bothers me. I can't understand a person dying for an idea."

"I don't know if I do either, but then you think

about World War Two. Did those men die for democracy?"

"I suspect most Americans died because they didn't want to let down their buddies. Maybe some thought about what would happen if the Axis powers overran the world, but mostly I bet they marched on, sticking to their comrades. You know, about sixty million people died in that war. We're way past that, we're in the billions now, and we still can't get along."

"Must have been easier when you could just dispatch an enemy with a sword."

"Nothing has changed, Betty. We still kill our enemies. I'll bet you if Cabel, in her rage, had had a weapon she would have brained Faye. Blind rage."

"Distorts the features," Betty dryly replied, and they both laughed.

CHAPTER 18

The noise of the vacuum cleaner irritated Sister. Years ago, when the market sank like a stone, she had cut way back on personal expenditure, even letting her once-a-week maid go. She gave the woman a thousand dollars severance pay. When the market rebounded years later, the former maid had become a real estate agent. Sister learned to repent of her economies.

Housework, apart from vacuuming, soothed her, particularly ironing. When her schedule picked up, the housework would slide; she'd fret and then remind herself that she'd never read a tombstone that said SPOTLESS HOUSEKEEPER.

All the downstairs rugs, now free of animal hair, had brightened. She'd attack the dirt upstairs tomorrow. She kept to the old school of washing on Monday, ironing on Tuesday, and so forth. Although this was Thursday, errand day, the dirt had finally gotten to her, hence her vacuuming fit. This evening she congratulated herself on performing two big chores on one day: errands and vacuuming.

Just as she was closing the broom closet door, her cell phone rang.

"Hello, Jane Arnold here."

"Sister, it's Cabel Harper. I'm so ashamed of myself. Please forgive my deplorable outburst today."

"You're under great pressure. Of course I forgive you."

"And forgive me for carrying a grudge all these years. I haven't done you any favors, or myself either." Cabel sounded miserable.

"That was all a long time ago, and I was no saint."

"You're not responsible for my marriage. If he wanted to run around. . . ." Her voice trailed off for a moment. "Who could resist him?"

"It was his sense of humor more than his looks."

"He's lost both." An edge sharpened her tone. "God knows how many times he's caught gonorrhea or syphilis. Thank God for antibiotics."

"You know that expression, *What goes around comes around*?" Sister couldn't resist the poke.

"Yes, of course."

"It's true, but not in such a simple manner." She grew serious. "Sometimes I think our lives are a secret book. We write in every page. There are plenty of pages no one reads but ourselves, usually to our own dismay. At any rate, I didn't mean to go on. I hope you can find some balance. On the bright side, there's your demeanor in the hunt field. Your turnout has always been correct. I like that you have never bowed to fashion."

Thinking herself quite fashionable, which she was, in a provincial Virginia way, Cabel asked, "What do you mean?"

"Back in the seventies, when hunt coats began to be cut shorter and rust breeches hit the stores, you continued to wear the longer-cut coats that are so flattering to the figure, and you never abandoned your mustard breeches."

Surprised, Cabel stammered, "Thank you." Then she perked up. "You know, you can't find the mustard anymore. Beige, tan, but not mustard. I have to go up to Middleburg Tack Exchange or the Old Habit and flip through the used sections. Sometimes I can find an old pair that fits."

"Isn't that something? Some of those breeches—I say this because I do the same thing," Sister confided, "were made in the 1920s. Quality."

"Same with derbies and caps. I look for the old Locke's."

"Me too." Sister laughed. "Thank you for calling, Cabel. I truly do hope things even out."

"To somewhat make up for being tacky, on Saturday I'll bring three heavy carpet mats for the puppy palace. The puppies won't be able to drag them. Ilona will help me load them, but maybe Shaker can unload them. They really are heavy."

"That's unnecessary, but I do thank you."

"Well, I don't do much for the hounds except pay my subscription. Time I gave them more attention. Time I did a lot of things." She paused. "I'll see you Saturday."

"I look forward to it." Sister clicked off the phone and wondered at what prompted people to change. Usually it was a crisis. If only we could better identify problems, nipping them in the bud, instead of expending huge stores of energy in denial. Or say we commit to a course of action that doesn't work. Do we change it? No. Our egos get the better of us as we doggedly pursue ruin.

As these ruminations occurred to her, Sister pulled on her old bomber jacket, red cashmere scarf, a few holes making it more individual, and lined waterproof work gloves. The cold still crept into her fingers, but the lining helped for the first forty-five minutes.

She stepped out into the clear, cold night. The dogs wanted to follow but she said no to their forlorn looks.

She went past the kennel, where a few of the boys out for their evening constitutional said hello. She walked on the farm road, heading toward the apple orchard. The ground, frozen, wasn't too slippery but the ruts demanded attention.

Once at the old orchard, she checked the feed bucket. Still three-quarters full. She checked Georgia's den. A neat pile of chicken feathers, now frozen, stuck on the ground about two feet from the entrance.

"Where did you get that chicken?" Sister called into the den.

Georgia, full, unmotivated to leave the warmth of her den, replied, *"I'll never tell."*

On hearing the young fox's light chirp, not a full yap, Sister smiled and returned to the stable, where she checked the tack and the small heavy bowl of tiny broken-up sweets she left on an aisle tack trunk for whatever undomesticated animal wanted them. Inky often would eat some, as would Georgia. Once she had walked into the barn in the early morning to find a cowbird gorging on the goodies.

A bloodcurdling shriek stopped her cold. Little wings beat overhead as Bitsy rose to her nest in the rafters. A barn owl also lived up there. They got along just fine but they kept different schedules.

"Dammit, Bitsy, you about gave me a heart attack."

The screech owl dropped down from her nest to sit atop a stall beam, across and four feet above Sister, who looked up at her.

Bitsy opened her wings and then folded them. *"News, news, news. I just heard from the tufted titmouse who heard it from the red-shouldered hawk that the jolly Indian man moved into Faye Spencer's bungalow, the one she rents as a hunt box for visitors. How's that for news?"*

Sister heard the little gurglings and beak clicks. She knew those were happy sounds from an owl but the content eluded her.

She rattled the candies in the bowl. "Good night, Bitsy."

"Good night." Bitsy blinked and wished humans were smarter. Being in possession of information thrilled the little owl, so she flew out to tell Lafayette, Keepsake, Rickyroo, Aztec, and Matador. Their interest was not as high as she had hoped, so she flew back to her nest. Well, when the barn owl returned from foraging, at least she'd listen.

Sister checked the electric heater in the water troughs. Running heavy-duty cords was a pain but trenching, dropping a line—that got expensive. Plus the electric company had to come out, and the telephone company, all to mark their buried lines with different colors of spray paint. Someday she'd get to it, but for now, winter meant running heavy orange extension cords to the paddocks for the horses. Horses prefer warm water to icy cold, and if the ice on top is too thick they may try to break it with a hoof.

All was well. She walked back to the house marveling at the clear February sky, the startling blue-white stars.

After she hung her coat on the peg in the mudroom,

she heard Betty's old Dodge truck rumble down the drive. Once in the house, Betty told her what Bitsy had just mentioned.

"That's good news," Sister replied to Betty's tale.

"Because he's staying?"

"Yes."

"I expect the Vajays, like all of us, have a point at which even the most pleasant of houseguests wears out his welcome."

"High and Kasmir are old friends, so I'm sure Kasmir knew the exact right time to find a rental. And I think he's serious about buying Tattenhall Station."

"He'd be a godsend."

Sister then described Cabel's call, ending with *that eases the tension.*

"Who knows how she'll treat Faye this Saturday?"

"Let's hope Cabel calls upon her social discipline. All those years of cotillion."

Betty laughed at this because she, like Cabel and Sister, had passed through the years of rigor known as cotillion. Southern girls and boys learn their manners even if they hate the process: All those old biddies hovering over your every word and move. Ultimately the discipline learned was worth every discomfort.

"I didn't mind walking with a book on my head and learning how to say no without saying *no.*" Sister sighed. "Northerners just can't get that. They think being direct is such a virtue and they think we're devious because we go about it by another route."

"Sign of no imagination." Betty laughed as she

rummaged in her small duffel for her nightgown.

"Well, that said, I agree being direct saves time, but it destroys all the joy of social intercourse, which really is dancing with words. Where was I? My cotillion. The ice-water teas. About killed me."

"Me too. Hated them!" Betty agreed, for what could be more boring than over and over again pouring ice water from a lovely teapot into an equally loved china cup, perched on its saucer. She changed the subject. "Do you think Cabel is having a nervous breakdown?"

"Well, she wouldn't be the first."

"And here I thought we'd get through a season without one." Betty's fuzzy slippers entranced Golly.

"Who knows what else will happen? Cabel's probably the least of it." She stared at Betty's slippers. "Those are a libido killer."

Betty laughed. "What's it to you?"

"Well, you've got me there." Sister snuggled under the covers. "Betty, you really don't need to babysit me like this."

"I do." Betty hopped on the bed so hard that Golly, now on a pillow, grumbled.

"Gray and you have obviously organized a pajama party for each night. You're the first person to sleep in my bed, though. I stick the others in the guest room."

"Liar." Betty smiled.

"I am not."

"Lorraine Rasmussen didn't stay in the house last night. 'Fess up."

"All right." Sister slipped deeper under the covers. "She stayed with Shaker, but I'm fine and Shaker is just on the other side of the kennels."

"Someone needs to be in the house at night."

"I have Raleigh and Rooster."

"What if someone poisons or shoots them?"

"When?" Golly perked up.

The two dogs lifted their ears.

"Betty, what a horrible thought."

"Murder is horrible and there's a sicko out there. You're not on the good side of whoever that is, so get used to company, sweetie."

"You aren't going to do this every night. Who else is?"

"Sorrel, Tedi, and Sybil for starters. Ilona volunteered, as did Cabel, but I demurred. If we run short you might be stuck with them."

"Christ, Betty, I think I'd rather face Lady Godiva's killer."

Betty sighed at Sister's remark, then replied, "I suspect we already have."

A long silence followed. "I—well, I feel some kind of dread I can't name." Sister changed the subject. "You and Gray are in cahoots obviously."

"Obviously." Betty turned off her light.

Sister affixed a tiny book light with a flexible stem on her copy of Captain E. Pennell-Elmhirst's *The Best of Fun* published in 1903. "This won't keep you awake. I have to read before I go to sleep."

Betty turned on her side, studying the light. "Nifty."

" 'Tis."

Betty rolled on her back. "Funny, how you can know someone so well but still not know things."

"Are you referring to my reading light?"

"No, I'm referring to your lack of nightgown."

"Betty, when you and I go on road trips to other hunts, on those occasions when Bobby doesn't come along, we bunk up. Right?"

"Right."

"And half the club, the female half, troops through our rooms."

"Right," Betty agreed.

"Do you really think I'm going to sit there naked?"

"No."

"But I'm in my own bed with my best friend hovering over me. So?"

"All right. I just want to know how you stay so tight."

"Work."

"Well, I lost all that weight but I've got some flabby parts."

"If it really bothers you, go to a personal trainer. I think you look wonderful."

"You're too kind, but then you haven't seen me without my nightie."

"Do I have to?" Sister slammed her book down in mock irritation.

Both women laughed.

"I'm trying to sleep!" Golly raised her voice.

"Intruder!" Raleigh leapt to his feet and ran out of the bedroom, thundering down the stairs.

Rooster followed.

Both dogs howled, the hounds starting up too.

Sister shot out of bed, threw on her robe, and opened the window. Cold air rushed into the bedroom. She saw a pair of red taillights recede down the driveway just as the lights went on in Shaker's upstairs window.

"Dammit." Sister slammed shut the window.

Betty started down the hall.

"Wait," Sister commanded while she grabbed her .38 from the nightstand drawer.

The two women hurried down the stairs and opened the back door, carefully—keeping the dogs in, to their dismay—to behold a plastic shopping bag at the mudroom door.

Betty poked it with her foot, felt a square edge, and picked it up. She opened the bag and plucked out a DVD. *"Lady Godiva."*

Sister took the movie from Betty's hand. "Made in the fifties."

"If I find who left this, I'll wring his neck." Betty, furious, heard the phone in the kitchen.

Sister trotted back and picked it up. "Someone left a movie. About Lady Godiva." She inhaled. "Fragrance. I can't place their perfume but I've smelled it before."

Shaker's strong voice replied, "You don't know what's on that video." He'd heard the car leave.

"You're right."

"You're okay?" he inquired.

"I am." She was glad to hear his voice. "I'll see you in the morning."

Next she called Ben Sidell.

Accompanied by the dogs also smelling the fragrance on the plastic bag, the two women repaired nervously upstairs.

"Anything?" Rooster asked after checking the bag.

"No. I couldn't identify anyone. Too much plastic odor."

"Too cold too." Rooster's ears drooped a bit.

"We're going to have to sleep with one eye open."

"Yep."

"Now I'm wide awake," Betty complained. She had a big day tomorrow at the printing press she and Bobby owned.

"Shall we?" Sister, flat TV discreetly by the wall in the bedroom, popped in the movie. "If we're going to be scared on a cold night we might as well watch the goddamned thing. You know there's a scent on it." She handed the plastic bag to Betty. "Recognize it?"

"No."

"I can't place it," Sister said, then got back into bed.

The two watched a tepid film about Lady Godiva, then fell asleep.

The next morning Sister made waffles for Betty, fortifying her friend for a long day ahead.

CHAPTER 19

February 29, Leap Year Day, roared through on the teeth of a low-pressure system. Trees bent over, hounds stayed in the kennels, horses stood with their rear ends to the wind. Even loquacious Bitsy hunkered down in her nest.

Sister, fearing the power would be cut off, hurriedly vacuumed the upstairs. That done, Golly reentered social exchange by removing herself from the closet.

"You're scared of the vacuum cleaner," Rooster teased her.

"Yeah, you burrow in all of Mom's cashmere sweaters. Cat hair everywhere." Raleigh picked up the game.

"Cashmere is goat hair. What's a little cat hair after that?" Golly sniffed.

"Chicken," Rooster taunted.

"Bubble butt." Golly thumped down the carpeted twisty back stairs to the kitchen. Many old houses have a narrow stairwell from the kitchen to the second story as well as the wide stairwell off the center hall.

Rooster, hot on her tail, snapped, *"I don't have a bubble butt."*

"Fatty, fatty, two-by-four." Golly started the nasty childhood chant.

Raleigh had barreled to the main stairway and taken

the steps three at a time and was already in the kitchen when the two squabblers emerged.

Even with the carpet on the back stairs, Sister could hear the two animals thumping down toward her. They burst through the open door, complaining vociferously.

"Pipe down, I can't hear myself think," she admonished them.

Raleigh sat there like an adoring angel, which really offended Golly, who walked up to the Doberman, sat right in front of him, and batted his long nose with one lightning strike.

"Ouch."

"Brownnoser." She jumped on the counter and pushed around Sister's tiny cell phone sitting in its recharging cradle.

Sister grabbed the phone and cradle before they clattered to the floor. She looked at the small blue square that read CHARGE COMPLETE, unplugged the charger, put it in a cabinet drawer, folded the phone over, and stuck it in her back jeans pocket. While wearing a cell phone holder on her belt might have proven more efficient, nothing could induce her to do it, just like nothing could induce her to wear a sissy strap under her chin on her helmet. Some things were just too weenie.

She opened the cupboard containing treats, tossing a big pig's ear to each dog and a large green chewy at Golly. The pigs' ears remained fresh in large sealed bags. The pungent aroma would fill the kitchen were the bags not sealed.

"I'll bet you-all don't know why we have leap year."

Head turned sideways as she gnawed on her greenie, Golly replied, *"Do I need to know? I've lived all these years in contented ignorance."*

"The calendar year is different from the equinoctial year so time can move backward." Seeing that she had only one interested party, Raleigh, Sister addressed this to him. "A calendar year is 365 days. An equinoctial year—that's the time it takes the earth to make a complete revolution of the sun from equinox to equinox—is actually 365.242199 days so periodic events would slowly move backward. To keep things on time, we had to add a day every four years. We've had calendars for thousands of years; humans struggled with this but I think Pope Gregory the Great set things to rights. He switched us off the Julian calendar, which made some provision for this but not enough." She threw up her hands. "I used to know all this. Anyway, St. Oswald—that's an English saint from the tenth century—used to have his festival on February twenty-ninth, but in 1930 the Catholic Church moved his feast day to February twenty-eighth. Poor fellow wasn't getting enough of the party. Of course, now many of the saints have been dispatched, but I still pay attention."

"See, I didn't need to know any of that."

"Dunce." Raleigh dropped his pig's ear, which rattled on the heart pine.

"It doesn't make any difference. What do I care if

festivals move backward? What's St. Oswald to cats?
If he grew catnip—well, then I'd pay attention."

"*She knows a lot."* Rooster enjoyed the rich flavor
of the pig's ear.

"*Human stuff, most of which is irrelevant. Nature*
can kill them all if she wants to, and then what of
Leap Year?" Golly puffed out her magnificent chest.

"*Crab,"* came Raleigh's tart reply.

Golly might have attacked the Doberman again, but
the lure of the greenie overcame the desire for violent
revenge. The long-haired calico was a great believer
in violence artfully applied.

The cell rang. Sister forgot she'd left it on so she
retrieved it from her pocket. "Hello, Jane Arnold
here."

Marion's lilting voice said, "Can't you just say
Hello? Who else would use your cell phone?"

"I've been thinking." Sister launched right in, since
Marion was accustomed to her going straight to the
point and vice versa. "Well, let me back up and say
that there's a wireless carrier, Leap Wireless International—good name for Leap Year, right? Anyway this
company, in which I've bought shares, sells service to
low-income, young, and ethnic people. They operate
under the name Cricket. This particular market is
deemed too small for the giant carriers."

"Sounds pretty smart," Marion replied.

"It is. Forty dollars a month. No credit check. You
sign up and you've got service."

"What's the catch?" Marion was suspicious.

"Roaming charges are high. The system is designed for people who don't travel much, so if they don't use roaming they'll save money. Cricket requires customers to pay each month in advance. Obviously, in that income bracket they need some protection. But isn't it a terrific idea?"

"It is. How long before they are absorbed by a huge amoeba?"

"Not long, I expect. Since our Lady Godiva had information concerning this kind of technology, I've been investigating in my own small way."

"How often does your cell phone die on you?" Marion queried.

"At least once a day. I attribute that to dead zones, especially here by the mountains."

"Sister, I'm a few miles more east of the mountains than you are. Happens to me too."

"Guess you like your new cell phone." Sister teased her.

"Better looking than the one I threw in the fire, but I hit those dead spots too. Sometimes I'll be in the store and nothing. I'll be in the middle of a conversation yakking away, and suddenly I realize no one's on the other end. Maddening."

" 'Tis."

"What if a huge company with extraordinary research facilities goes about buggering—forgive the word—other wireless providers? Meanwhile, it establishes a reputation for reliability. What are most of us going to do eventually? Switch to the reliable company." Marion paused. "Our beautiful victim could have been a part of a number of illegal activities. If she was, I hope someone figures it out."

"Me too."

"I had another thought. This one's really dark. I know the money involved in gaining hegemony in the wireless market might lead some people to murder. But this would be a *direct* route to murder. What if our government, fearing an overheated economy and inflation, actually slows business by two percent—just two percent; that would have an enormous effect. The old phone companies and the wireless companies would cooperate in exchange for favorable treatment down the road via tax breaks, protection for outsourcing, or other plums. The deal would be that the phone companies disrupt calls, not an outright break in service but a disconnect like you and I experience with our cell phones. We attribute it to bad signals, dead air space, but what if it is deliberate? It's possible."

"Marion, in a million years, I wouldn't have thought of that."

"I trust government less than you do."

"Maybe." Sister thought a moment. "Maybe, but it comes down to the fact that you're brilliant and I'm merely intelligent."

"Bull."

"Oh, take the compliment and shut up." Sister laughed at her.

"Okay. I'm brilliant, but you know in Hollywood

when they want to fire you they first tell you you're brilliant."

"A much-used word then." Sister laughed some more. "No word on who played the prank with the mannequin?"

"No, but if I ever find out, I'm stripping him or her and parading them around town on a horse—or maybe I'll tie them to the hood of my car, a nice big ornament." Marion took a deep breath. "Can't decide if it was a prank or a warning."

Sister then told her about the old movie being left in the mudroom, which upset Marion too.

"Excuse me. . . . I do too." Marion cupped her hand over the mouthpiece, then removed it. "Sorry. My appointment has appeared five minutes early."

"Go do biz."

"You too."

"You've given me a lot to think about."

"You know, the Chinese have this expression: *I throw out a brick in the hope that someone else will throw out jade.*"

"Got it." Sister liked the concept. After switching off her cell phone she put it on the kitchen table. "Could it be possible?" A long pause followed. "Kids, this is a case of what you don't know can hurt you. I haven't a clue about the technology involved in a scheme like that, but a few people in this world do. I wonder if Aashi was one of them."

CHAPTER 20

One of the people who had a grasp of wireless technology was High Vajay, riding out today. He needed a blast of energy, given his marital troubles.

It was Saturday, March 1, and the field was quite large. Less than three weeks remained in the season. The day had proved so mild, in the low fifties, the trailers jammed Foxglove Farm.

The horrendous cow Clytemnestra, together with her equally worthless son, Orestes, had been placed in a five-board fenced paddock with extra grain, a brand-new salt block, and mounds of hay. Five boards wouldn't stop Clytemnestra any more than three if she chose to bust a move, but it made Cindy Chandler, the pretty blonde owner, feel better.

Caneel, one of her hunters, watched everyone from an adjoining paddock.

Kasmir and High rode with Faye. The Merrimans were out, as was Cabel, which showed pluck on her part. She'd apologized individually to everyone who had witnessed her meltdown at Mousehold Heath. All the Custis Hall regulars came save Felicity, whose parents had descended upon her.

Sister made a mental note to speak with Charlotte Norton about Felicity. The worst thing the Porters could do would be to yank Felicity out of school. She sincerely hoped that wouldn't be the case. Not only would it interrupt what should be one of the happiest times of a young person's life, it would set her against her parents.

Val, noting Cabel's difficulty mounting Mickey (for she'd forgotten her mounting block), gave Cabel a leg up. "Mrs. Harper, I've always wanted to ask you why you spell your name as you do. I thought Cabel had two *l*'s."

"Does," came the quick reply. "I kicked the *l* out of it." She laughed, as did Val.

The warmth worried Sister in terms of scent, but the low cloud cover might help a bit. She had read every book there was about scent; there weren't many. She'd pored over other people's old published hunt diaries and read the work of hunting correspondents for the British papers over the last two centuries. They didn't know any more about scent than she did.

What she did know is that two lovely foxes lived at Foxglove. One, Grace, kept close to the stable because Cindy put out jelly beans, corn, and other tidbits that Grace devoured.

Another fox, larger, lived under the old schoolhouse used from 1870 to the 1940s.

She counted seventy-two people, a nice number. The Custis Hall girls rode at the rear of first flight.

Shaker cast hounds away from the stable toward two ponds with a pretty little waterwheel. It was a dwarf compared to the giant waterwheel at Mill Ruins, Walter Lungrun's place. Cindy was forever improving her ponds. Originally, a long pipe poured water from the upper pond to the lower, and the water was then recycled back up by means of a pump in an enclosed pump-house. She had recently installed this small waterwheel, finding the soft lap of water on the paddles soothing.

Hounds found no scent around the ponds, which surprised Sister, for usually there was a hint near the cool dampness. Hounds moved up the meadows past the woods to their left where the old springhouse stood, still useful. They feathered by the schoolhouse. Iggy, the schoolhouse fox whom hounds called Professor, was nowhere to be found.

Shaker jumped the coop over the road and then the coop on the other side of the dirt road, hounds casting in the rougher meadow there. They'd been out twenty-five minutes at a walk. Cooler air touched Sister's cheeks; a little wind current fluttered across the meadow.

Dragon, out today because Cora was footsore, sniffed, feathered, moved faster, then opened. Within the blink of an eye the entire pack was flying. Dreamboat, Diddy, Darby, Doughboy, Dana, and Delight did wonderfully, as did the third-year hounds, Trudy, Trident, Tinsel, and Trinity. Two young entry came out today, Parker and Pickens. Both Sister and Shaker thought Saturday a bit much for first year, but these two had matured faster than their littermates and currently ran smack in the middle of the pack.

Hounds ran straight as an arrow until reaching Soldier Road, the local east-west route that climbed laboriously over the Blue Ridge Mountains. Interstate

64 farther north took most of that traffic, for which everyone was grateful.

Soldier Road had narrow ditches on either side for runoff. Sister and Keepsake, happy to be out today, cleared one clambering up the low embankment to the macadam road. Watching her hounds, she noticed the macadam did not throw them off. Scent had to be red hot. The oil odor of macadam, especially when warming, conceals scent. She cleared the second runoff ditch, plunging into unkempt fields. They blasted through those fields, skirted the base of Hangman's Ridge, veered east into the wildflower field, awaiting spring's clarion call, and up and over the hog's-back jump into After All Farm.

Dragon, in the lead, was stretched to his fullest. Right behind came Diddy, then Trinity. To her surprise, once she cleared the hog's back, Sister saw Pickens fourth as the hounds ran in the woods, the denuded trees offering some views.

On and on they screamed until arriving at Pattypan Forge, impressive in a forlorn fashion.

Aunt Netty lived at Pattypan Forge, Uncle Yancy leaving out of frustration once she arrived. But hounds hadn't been on Aunt Netty snug in her den, furious about this commotion outside her tidy abode.

Hounds cast around the forge, large heavy stones set in place in 1792. This time Diddy picked up the signature odor and off they ran again.

Straight through the trees, into the pinewoods, scent thick in the air, needles cushioning hoofbeats, then out and into the hardwoods again, and down into Broad Creek. The crossing had become tricky. People dotted the last few miles, four coming a cropper at the crossing alone. The temperature was cool enough to feel uncomfortable if one is soaking wet.

Onward. Keepsake, nostrils wide, ears forward, loving every second just as much as the silver-haired woman on his back, scarcely touching the reins.

The scorching pace now told on those whose horses weren't fit. Some people themselves had gotten out of shape over the holidays and hadn't recovered form. Bathing-suit weather usually took care of that.

On and on those hounds ran, Shaker behind them. Betty, on Magellan, a huge grin on her face, whipped in on the left. Betty disappeared in the woods. Sister caught sight of her once more, bursting into the open; same with Sybil, riding Postman today, covering the right.

Her whippers-in stuck to their places as well, using good judgment. The staff work today proved as good as the hound work.

On they ran. Sister glanced behind her, the field strung out like pearls that had popped their string. Tedi and Edward were close behind, once again demonstrating the wisdom of riding fit Thorough-breds. Gray was nowhere to be seen. In that quick glance she caught a glimpse of only a dozen people.

Good God, she thought to herself, *what's happened to them?* That thought lasted only a split second because the Custis Hall girls rode tail and they were

equal to most crises; also the pace, flaming, inciner-
ated the thought.

Hounds leapt into the graveyard at the old Lorillard
place, where they threw up. Scent disappeared as if a
magician had put the fox back in the hat instead of the
rabbit. They whined a moment and cast themselves
away from the large pin oak in the middle of the
graveyard, guarding Jemima Lorillard's grave among
others.

Nothing.

Shaker removed his cap, wiping his brow.

Sister did likewise.

Tedi and Edward remained behind her but close.
Walter, on Rocketman, caught up. She counted heads:
twenty-three people. No sign of the hilltoppers.

"Where is everybody?"

"Lost the hilltoppers at the crossing," Walter
replied. "Bobby is bringing them the long way
around."

"Jesus," was all she said, because the long way
around meant he circumvented one mile north for an
easier crossing. "Hilltoppers are supposed to be able
to ride. They should also be able to jump at least a log
in the road."

"Well, he had some green people today; better safe
than sorry," Walter replied, and he was right.

"The run of the season." Edward lifted his top hat
to salute the hounds.

"By God, it was!" Walter agreed and did likewise
with his hunting cap.

Coming up behind was Kasmir and he, too, lifted his topper. High and Faye had succumbed to the pace but Kasmir, although a touch portly, was as fit as his mount.

"Couldn't help it," Sister bragged. "Those young ones were fabulous." She wanted to shout to the heavens, *Thank you, Jesus!* but instead sat quietly while horses, hounds, and humans recovered their wind. One by one, riders straggled in, the number now thirty-two, still a far cry from seventy-two.

"We ran an eleven-mile point." Walter flipped his Reverso wristwatch, the perfect watch for hunting despite its expense. "One hour and fourteen minutes with a brief check at Pattypan Forge."

"It truly was the run of the season." Tedi needed a pickup from her flask, which contained an excellent port. "Sister?"

"Forgive me, folks." Sister, parched, took a draft, even though staff is not to drink alcohol during a hunt, one of those rules usually observed in the breach.

Everyone who had a flask reached for it.

Shaker rode up and Walter handed him his flask. "I know, I know." Walter smiled. "But you must be dry as a bone."

Shaker shook his head no. He kept sweet tea in his flask. He'd learned the hard way that he couldn't drink, regardless of occasion.

Sister also kept iced tea, unsweetened, in her flask, but Tedi's exquisite port lured her.

"Boss." Shaker sighed with deep joy.

"Huntsman." She smiled at him. "I say we head back."

So they did, and not halfway into the woods, just at the edge of where the old Lorillard property adjoined After All Farm, they hit again. The music filled the air, echoed off hills, gave horses another burst of energy.

This fox happened to be Uncle Yancy. Why he was this far east was anyone's guess, but he took them straight to Pattypan Forge again, where he ducked into his harridan's den. This time hounds dug at the entrance with conviction, because they could hear squabbling inside.

"You lazy, good-for-nothing, what makes you think you can come into my den?"

"Hounds were hot on my tail, my sweet; then again, I haven't seen you for far too long." He blinked with a sweet expression.

"I ought to throw your sorry tail right out of here." Aunt Netty swished her own tatty brush.

"Now, my sweet, don't be hasty," he cooed.

Trinity whispered to Dasher, *"Will she throw him out?"*

"Nah, they fight all the time."

After blowing "Gone to Ground," Shaker hopped back up on Kilowatt—he was already in love with this game, athletic horse—and they walked slowly back to After All Farm.

Along the way they passed some of those who had turned back early.

They rode up on the Custis Hall girls in the wildflower field, helping guests who had parted company with their mounts. Sister thanked Val, Tootie, and Pamela for catching the horses.

The walk back took forty-five minutes. Sister wouldn't take any jumps. Most accidents occur skylarking on the return when many horses are blown.

Keepsake, Kilowatt, Magellan, and Postman could have popped over. So could Tedi and Edward's horses, but it wasn't worth it. It's a foolish field master who risks life and limb going home. When hounds are running, that's a different story.

Finally the stable at Foxglove Farm came into view, the weathervane's arrow point indicating a slight wind from the northwest.

However, what caught Sister's eye and everyone else's was the squad car at the stable.

"I hope no one's seriously hurt," Sister whispered to Walter.

No one was hurt, but Faye Spencer, naked, tied to Cindy Chandler's mare, Caneel, sat in the paddock. Caneel had been drugged. Faye had been shot through the heart.

CHAPTER 21

Lady Godiva," Sister whispered, trotting to the paddock.

Ilona Merriman, sobbing, screaming, was forcibly removed from the scene by Ramsey. Cabel Harper and High Vajay stood in mute horror.

Nonni threw a shoe, so Ben Sidell, who had turned back early, took charge. He estimated Faye had been in the paddock for perhaps a half hour. She remained quite warm. The ropes tying her to Caneel had not yet rubbed her wrists and ankles raw. One by one, he had noted the names of the fifteen people who had reached Foxglove Farm first.

Sister rode up to him. "What can I do?"

"Herd everyone away from here. The people who were here need to stay briefly. They're in the stable."

"Fine."

Diddy had shot off to the crime scene. She wanted to know what the fuss was. She stood on her hind legs, sniffing Faye's foot and left leg. Shaker called her away, and she raced back to squeeze through the door held partway open. She then told the pack what she'd smelled.

"Blood?" asked Ardent.

"No, perfume. Ladies wear perfume," Dragon said.

"Not supposed to," Tinsel added. *"The only person wearing scent should be the fox."*

"Would you recognize that perfume again?" Diana asked.

"Sure."

"Could be Faye's perfume," Trinity logically added.

"Could," Diddy agreed. *"But if I catch wind of it again, I'll tell you."*

"Shaker, you, Betty, and Sybil ask everyone out here to please leave. The people who came back early are in the stable. Ben requests that we get everyone else out to cut down on the confusion," Sister commanded.

"Right." He could see the ghastly figure in the near distance, Caneel with her head down, half asleep.

"Be sure to get the Custis Hall girls out. They don't need to see this. They should be back any minute."

Sister dismounted, loosened Keepsake's girth, threw a rug over him, removed his bridle, and put his halter on in four minutes flat, then ran to the Custis Hall van looking for Charlotte Norton. The headmistress and the riding coach, Bunny Taliaferro, weren't back.

She passed Sybil on her return to the paddock.

"Sister, are you all right?" the second whipper-in asked.

"I don't know," Sister replied. "Seeing this once was bad enough. Twice is horrifying. But I swear to you, Sybil, this bastard is on my turf now and I will get him."

"Be careful."

"You too." Sister touched Sybil's shoulder and raced back to the paddock.

Two sirens ruined the quiet of the day, now 12:20 P.M.

Ben turned to her. "Like Warrenton?"

"Yes. The obvious difference being Caneel is a real horse and Faye is tied, but same modus operandi, naked and shot through the heart."

He walked around Caneel, in step with Sister. "No

sign of a struggle. No bruises. No sign of torture obviously."

"Caneel is untouched."

He blinked, realizing once again how sharp this old woman was. She knew he'd concentrate on the human; she focused on the horse. Every second might yield a clue that would be lost within minutes or disturbed in removing the corpse.

"Whoever did this knows horses." Ben returned to his starting point.

"Yes." She named a tranquilizer. "I expect Caneel's shot full of Banamine. She'll be fine when it wears off."

"Will you go in the stable, write down everyone's name, the time they returned, anything they noticed?"

"Boss," Shaker called over the fence, "some of the people can't go because they're vanning with people in the barn."

"Tell them to wait," Ben answered. "Shouldn't be too long."

Sister walked into the barn. Cindy was there, ashen-faced. "I need a tablet and a pencil," Sister told her.

Wordlessly, Cindy opened the door to the small office, reappearing with a spiral notebook and a small green golf pencil.

Ilona, slumped on a tack trunk, couldn't stop crying, gulping in huge gasps of air.

"High Vajay," Sister asked, "when did you return?"

"Noon."

"When did you notice Faye?"

"Perhaps five minutes after that. I opened the gate to the paddock and ran over. She was already dead."

"Ramsey?"

"I was behind Vajay. I ran into the paddock too. Ilona came right after me."

Sister looked at Ilona, thinking she'd speak to her last. Perhaps by then a deputy would be here who would be better at this than she was.

Ronnie Haslip, Henry Xavier, Cindy Chandler, Cabel Harper, and Lorraine Rasmussen were each questioned.

Ty Banks, Ben's young deputy, walked into the stable. He conferred quietly with Sister as the emergency vehicle pulled to the paddock.

Ilona, startled, ran to the open stable doors. She started screaming again.

Ramsey hurried to her. "Honey, please. There's nothing you can do."

"Who would do this?" Ilona wailed.

Ramsey put his arm around his distraught wife, guiding her back to the tack trunk, where she collapsed with a thump.

Sister whispered to Ty, "I don't think Ilona's ever seen a corpse. She's usually sensible."

Sister's generation had seen death more often than had younger generations whose families died mostly in hospital beds. Perhaps it was not a good thing that people today were so removed from the normal life cycle.

As Ty took over, Sister walked out with Cindy.

"Maybe I should stay in the barn. I came back early," Cindy said, forlorn.

The two women walked back in. Cindy asked Ty what he wanted her to do. He told her he'd get to her, but since this was her farm she might be needed outside.

The two women walked back out.

"Have you talked to Ben?"

"No. I came in around eleven and put my horse up. By eleven twenty I was in the house getting things ready for the breakfast."

"Did you hear any cars?"

"No. But I wasn't listening. Same with people returning. The windows were closed and I didn't pay attention. I didn't know anything was wrong until I heard Ilona scream."

"Do you recall looking at the paddock when you rode up?"

"Yes, Caneel whinnied to Booper. She performed a pirouette and that was that."

Booper was Caneel's stablemate, the horse Cindy rode today.

"No sign of Faye, alive, I mean?"

"No. There were some horses tied at trailers, but I didn't pay attention. I figured it was the usual case of broken tack, thrown shoes, you know."

"Can you remember how many horses?"

"Oh, dear." Cindy frowned. "Three? Four?"

Sister grabbed Cindy's hand. "Come with me."

They stepped quickly to Faye's trailer, a well kept two-horse. Clayton's mare, the loaner, was untacked, wiped down, a fresh cooler draped and cinched over the pleasant animal.

"Well, she had time to put up the horse," Cindy noted.

"Or someone else did." Sister stepped up into the small tack room. She touched nothing. "Everything looks in order. I'm going to stay here so no one comes in this room. Will you run to Ben and tell him he needs to dust this tack and the halter? If there are prints other than Faye's we might get to first base."

Cindy dashed for the paddock, not wishing to see the dead woman but knowing Sister's plan was vital. She hastily told Ben and turned on her heel. Before she bolted through the gate, Ben called out, "Cindy, do you want me to leave Caneel in the paddock?"

The answer was yes.

Sister remained in the tack room for another twenty minutes. As she did, she observed the fifteen people filing out of the stable, all disturbed.

Once the fingerprint team arrived, Sister returned to Ben, now at the gate, as Faye's body, in a plastic bag, was rolled out on a gurney.

"Had she been cleaned up?"

Ben nodded. "Yes, but this time the killer didn't have much time. My guess is she was hosed down at the outside pump." He pointed to the frost-free water pump, hose attached. A puddle, slowly being absorbed, was on the ground. "I looked around for rags. None. When we lifted her off, we noticed she had been sprayed; she was still wet."

"Faye was beautiful even in death. Two beautiful victims," Sister stated.

"Faye knew electronics, right?"

"She was on the cutting edge."

Shaker joined them. "Charlotte came in just before the girls. She and Bunny got them out of here before they could see the body."

"Good. You can't protect young people from the world, but with something like this you must try." She lowered her voice to a whisper. "Could they be in danger? The kids?"

"I don't know," Ben honestly replied, "but right now I would caution every woman to be careful. If you leave the hunt field, leave in twos. If you go out at night, go in twos." He spoke directly to Shaker. "Watch out for Sister. The punch bowl in her stable office is hardly a good omen."

"I will."

"Sister, carry your thirty-eight. You have a permit for a concealed weapon. Do not leave your house without that gun. I mean it."

She appreciated their concern, making light of it. "I'm not young and beautiful. I'm safe." Then she changed the subject. "Wonder if the wound was made by the same gun?"

"We'll find out. I'm willing to bet she wasn't sexually molested."

"Same killer?" Sister's silver eyebrows lifted, then dropped.

"I'm not supposed to speculate, but I think it is. The

public display of the corpse?" He paused a long time. "Let's just say something like that infuriates and motivates those of us in law enforcement. The killer is thumbing his nose at us."

"All of us," Shaker added. "Ben, I'd like to get the hounds back. They hunted hard."

"Sure."

Ty Banks walked in, folding back his cell phone. "Called her office. Two people working on Saturday. Figured you'd want to question them, so I asked them to stay at work until we get there."

"Good."

Betty, patiently waiting for Sister, waved when she saw them looking in her direction.

"May I be excused?" Sister asked Ben. "I need to get the horses back."

"You may."

"I just noticed the daffodil in your buttonhole. For St. David's Day, the patron saint of Wales?"

He nodded. "Mother's proud of her Welsh blood."

"A strong people. You'll need that strength on this case."

CHAPTER 22

Everyone invested heavily in Faye's company." Gray, nightcap in hand, sat in the club chair in the den, cashmere throw over his aching legs.

Gray hadn't ridden that hard in a long time.

Sister, opposite him on the couch, Golly in her lap,

sipped hot green tea laced with fresh lemon. "Even I put a little money in."

"First I've heard of it."

"You know, I haven't thought much about it. It was a small amount." She was quiet for a moment. "Sometimes I forget to tell you things and other times I elect not to because I don't want to be a pest always asking for advice." She changed the subject. "It's been a day none of us will forget."

"In a way I'm glad I came back late, but I wish I could have helped you." Gray had dismounted, walking his horse back the last two miles since both were weary. "Who else put money in Warp Speed?"

"Crawford, High, Clayton, Ramsey; even Edward chipped in a bit. I don't know about Kasmir. What would any of those men have to gain by Faye Spencer's death?" Sister answered her own question. "I suppose it depends on whether they wanted the company to succeed or fail. Craig and Abrams might be working on a similar product. It's possible High Vajay would want her to fail. Investing a substantial sum would provide a cover, plus he'd be able to report on her progress. God knows, he has the money. On the other hand, he might want Faye to succeed so Craig and Abrams could buy Warp Speed and use their research without incurring the cost of duplicate effort. Someone like Crawford might want to take over the company, although killing Faye is a stupid way to do it. Crawford's not stupid, not in that way."

"No." Gray half closed his eyes as the warmth of

the scotch worked its way down to his stomach. "Honey, I don't know if Lady Godiva's special, but this has something to do with injustice. It's revengeful. Displaying a woman like that, even dead, is humiliation. Everyone who sees her will remember her naked."

"In the case of Aashi and Faye, they were gorgeous naked."

"But it's still humiliation." Gray stuck to his point.

"Yes. Yes, it is, and the murderer wants us all to witness the humiliation. If the killer wanted to scare us, he'd disfigure the corpse. Here it's the reverse. The women are cleaned up."

"Odd. Compelling."

"When I spoke to Marion today she used the same word, *compelling*." Sister noticed a blue flame leap up among the yellow gold ones. She sighed deeply. "God, what an awful day. And it was the best damn run of the season. Once I got home I went into the kennels and thanked every hound that was out. Took my mind off Faye. I liked Faye."

"Timetable. Cindy Chandler was the first person back, that we can identify. Others had to be back; you said Cindy remembered horses tied to trailers." Gray took another much-needed sip of scotch.

"Imagine how Cindy feels." Sister shook her head. "She's in her kitchen while Faye Spencer is being shot behind her stable or at least washed up there. She said she never heard a shot."

"If a person drove up, killed Faye, and drove out,

someone would have seen the vehicle. Whoever killed Faye was either waiting here or rode back with the first group of people. And the gun could have had a silencer."

"How else would the killer know Faye turned back early, right?"

"Exactly." Gray smiled.

"Let's pick someone we know would never do this: Lorraine Rasmussen. Lorraine asks Faye to ride back with her. Any excuse will do. Faye agrees. Lorraine is in collusion with the killer, already here."

"Could be. Whether that's the case or not, there was some kind of plan and a desire to cut it close. I doubt there was as big a thrill to killing the woman in Warrenton as there was to this. The killer wanted everyone here."

"Is this a true serial killer, you think?"

Gray rubbed his aching thighs. "Yes, I think it is. Because of the media we associate serial killers with sex. Either it's a man who kills prostitutes because he's determined they're evil, a man who preys on young men, or a man who kills women, regular women, who may resemble one another. But it seems to me that killing could be an incredible high, a tremendous exercise of power. Sex doesn't have to be part of it."

"That's what bothers me. It is in the sense that the women are beautiful and they're naked. Something's missing."

"I half want to find it and I half don't."

"Oh, I want to find it." Sister's cheeks blazed. "My hunt club member is shot, my field sees this grotesque parody of Lady Godiva. I want to find it—and him."

"Sweetheart, I admire your sentiments, but there are times when you are too bold."

"Like the time I decked Crawford?"

This made Gray laugh. "That was justice served."

"Maybe this is too."

CHAPTER 23

Sunday, the traditional day of worship, brings families together. Sunday, March 2, brought some together and rent others asunder.

High Vajay found himself the main suspect in the death of both Lady Godivas. Uncomfortable as this was, Mandy's wrath proved more unsettling.

As they were Hindu, not Christian, they did not attend church service. Mandy asked Sybil Fawkes if she would take the boys for the day since she and High had issues to discuss. They'd kept a lid on it until they could have a day together. Neither one wanted to get into an argument when the boys were in bed and awaken and frighten them. Sybil's two sons and the Vajays' two sons had become friends, and Sybil readily agreed.

So at nine in the morning, across a highly polished kitchen table, husband and wife had already been going at it hammer and tong for forty minutes. Mostly it was High being hammered. When you're the anvil, have the sense to keep still. He did.

"So?" Mandy's eyebrows were raised, her face perfect even in anger.

"What more can I say? I was wrong. I was foolish. I risked everything for momentary pleasure."

Even at home, Mandy was dressed exquisitely, this morning in a cream-colored silk shirt, camel-colored pleated skirt, and low-heel Gucci boots. Mandy was five feet eight inches in her bare feet. She listened impassively, her anger spent.

High kept going. "I didn't call her to come to Warrenton. I swear to you, I did not."

"Then why was she there? You renewed the affair."

He leaned forward on his elbows, misery etching every feature on his handsome face. "I did. I went back up to Washington. You remember, Tim Pasternak called me up."

Tim Pasternak ran the small office in Washington, D.C., more as a presence than a power. Craig and Abrams occasionally needed the cooperation of the government. The U.S. headquarters was in New York City.

"I remember. Three months ago."

"It was one night, Mandy, that's all."

"It was one night that fired up the affair. You didn't stop at one night. Don't play me for a fool, Lakshmi, or I will take you for everything you've got. We're in America now, remember?"

A flash of pride almost made him say, *Take it all. I*

can make it all over again. Instead, he wisely pushed down his ego and demurred. "The affair was more over the phone and the computer. I only saw her one other time, and we didn't go to bed."

"You expect me to believe that?"

"It's true. If you don't believe it there's nothing I can do." He was resigned now.

She got up from the table, folded her arms across her chest, and paced the large kitchen. "How about the children? Did you not think of the children?"

"Madhur, men don't think of things like that when lust blinds them. To our shame. To my shame. For me the affair was like a good round of golf. Fun and relaxing, not central to life. Men do this. It doesn't mean that much. But it means much to women and there's no denying that we know that. We hope not to get caught. And when we do, we realize how bloody goddamned selfish we've been. I will do anything to win you back. Anything."

She walked to the window and looked east as light flooded the immaculate brick buildings, painted white, that constituted the stable, the cow barns, the huge garden shed with greenhouse, all restored to perfection during their ownership. "All right then, Lakshmi, you have your chance. I have never meddled in your business; that isn't my sphere. But I know when you're building something, you're tense, excited. What are you doing?"

He looked up at her, his dark brown eyes troubled, but he answered. "Trying to drive up Craig and

Abrams stock. If I'm successful, our investment will spiral to the heavens."

"And exactly what are you trying to do, apart from sleeping with a young woman now murdered?"

He raised his shoulders then dropped them. "I want to destroy or buy out the competition."

"Cell phones?"

"Well, the technology that connects your phone to your TV, to your landline, to your car, to your iPod, the technology to drive everything from one tiny unit, is not an inch from us. There's a little work to be done but the real next step is marketing."

"And Faye Spencer? God, did you sleep with her too?"

"No. Ramsey Merriman was doing that. I know Clayton tried but I don't think he succeeded." He went on quickly. "I liked Faye enormously, but I was in enough trouble and she's not my type. Wasn't my type." He closed his eyes. "What a shocking sight. Thank God you were on the plane coming back from Arizona."

She returned to sit down. "Is what you are doing legal?"

"Yes. Well, a gray zone."

"Which is?"

"One thing Craig and Abrams is doing, covertly, obviously, is to disrupt other companies' service. Then offer better contracts and service. It costs Craig and Abrams three hundred and fifty dollars for each new client; that's one of the reasons we need the year-long contract. But there's a small company now that provides service to the poor without a contract. And there are other companies undermining what we've established in the wireless industry, trying to make what the Americans call an end run around Craig and Abrams. The sheer size of the company is both our strength and our weakness." He paused. "That's capitalism."

"Do you destroy their towers?"

He half smiled. "Nothing that dramatic."

"What do you do?"

"We can interrupt the wave, literally. Craig and Abrams is light-years ahead in some areas but woefully behind in others. Our research and development department is the best in the world; our marketing is abysmal. That's one of the reasons I keep getting called back because I have the ability to talk both to the strange gnomes in research and to the marketing men, all of whom dress like bad models from *GQ*. If I see one more French-blue shirt with a tie the same color I think I'll rip it off the man's pencil neck."

That made her laugh. "Not everyone possesses your incredible sense of style. You know, that was the second thing I noticed about you: Everything you wore fit perfectly. You stood out without being flashy. I don't like flashy men."

"What was the first thing you noticed?" He couldn't help it, his vanity was being massaged.

"Your eyes. What was the first thing you noticed about me?"

"Everything. Hiroshima. Boom!" He threw up his hands.

"Then why other women?"

"One other woman. Mandy, I love you. You are my wife, the mother of my sons. But how do the Americans put it, *A stiff dick has no conscience?*" He shook his head. "Who could be as beautiful as you? And you are a good woman. But sometimes a man is weak or away from home and lonely." He shrugged.

"And you don't think women get lonely?"

A three-car alarm look crossed his face, "Yes. No. What do you mean?"

"Only that women, too, need solace. We're better at hiding it. Have I cheated on you? No. Rest your pride, for that's what it is. I have my circle of friends. I think my relationship with my friends is different from yours, but no matter. Back to Craig and Abrams. If what you are doing works, Craig and Abrams will emerge as"—she thought a moment—"the Toyota of wireless, of personal technology."

"Military hegemony too. Those applications are not known to the public. We will be number one in the world, an Indian company. What's that other American expression? *When the tide's in, all the boats rise.* So it will be for our country."

"Strange. I have love and pride for my people and for India in general, but I feel more American. Sometimes that bothers me. Am I faithless? Am I so easily won over by their freedoms, many of which are scurrilous or illusory? Or is it their attitude? What my father always says was called *can do* in his day. But they are like that, you know. Americans think they can do anything so they do. They aren't chained to fathoms of history as we are. When I'm here I forget about Hindus hating Muslims. I don't care. I don't care that I think Mumbai residents combine the worst of Los Angeles and New York. I look out at the Blue Ridge Mountains, much smaller than the mountains of my childhood, and I feel peace. And strange to say, my husband, I feel power."

"You have always had power, Mandy."

"Beauty is power, but beauty fades."

"Not yours."

"Ha. Mine most of all. When you are called one of the world's most beautiful women, everyone searches your face for that first wrinkle. Well, I have more than one wrinkle now and some gray to season my hair as well. No, this power is different. This is from within. Beauty is without."

They sat in silence for a long time.

"I love you," High said, voice overflowing with emotion. He rose from his seat, walked over to his wife, knelt before her, and wrapped his arms around her knees. "Forgive me. Please forgive me."

"I do, but I must know: Did you kill Aashi and Faye Spencer?"

He looked into her eyes. "Never. Never would I kill a woman."

"Do you know who did? It looks bad for you, Lakshmi; you discovered Faye and you are on the list for killing Aashi."

"I don't know who did it. I wish I did because I fear him."

"Why?"

"Because he's not finished. I feel it."

"I see." She stood up, pulling him up with her, and hugged him, then kissed him passionately on the lips. "I love you too. That's why it hurts. But I must protect myself and my children. If you want me in your life as your partner, you must go to McGuire and Woods"—she named a prestigious Virginia law firm—"and assign half of your assets to me *now*. For one thing, should you predecease me, that will cut down the inheritance tax, and for another, if you do this again, I walk away a rich woman and a free woman."

He didn't flinch. "It will be done."

"And Charing Cross Farm. I can never leave here. I have found my heart's home."

"That too."

"If, for some reason, you awaken tomorrow morning and wish to run heel"—she used the fox-hunting term whereby hounds become confused and run backward on a fox's line—"I will reveal what you are doing."

At that moment, although he had been married to her for all these years, he truly appreciated the depths of her intelligence, exploding within him like a depth charge. He needed her on his side as much as he loved her. "I will not run heel. I will do as you ask. But I too have a request."

"What?"

"Please don't ever tell our sons what a fool their father is."

"I will not, but who is to say as they grow older they won't find out? The first Lady Godiva's life can't remain a secret forever."

"My second request. Let us not speak of her between us."

"Lakshmi, I can't promise that. With Faye's dreadful murder, the first murder is fresh all over again and the sheriff's department knows of your involvement. We can't pretend it never happened."

"I know that, but don't throw it in my face."

"I won't, but I must ask you particularly, since you think the killer will strike again, do you know who else Aashi was sleeping with?"

"No. Why would she tell me?"

"I assume she knew people with whom you do business."

"She knew Faye and Warp Speed's work. She knew Ramsey, Clayton, Crawford, and Edward, all because of their investments in Warp Speed but also sometimes, as you know, we'd drive up to Washington together."

"Faye. Anyone other than Ramsey?"

"I don't know. I only know about Ramsey because once Ilona, when we were hunting, made a cutting remark about Faye. I'd be hard put to prove it, but it fits if you know both their patterns."

"Yes, it does. I liked Faye. I liked her tremendously. She never wasted my time with twaddle. When I would call upon Faye or vice versa, we sank our teeth into interesting subjects. Did you know she was passionate about poetry? Unusual for a science type, I think."

"No, but I didn't know Faye as you did."

"How is Kasmir?"

"Shocked. He's taking care of her dog and her horse. I told him tomorrow I'd call around to find a farm manager. I don't even know if Faye had a will or relatives. She rarely spoke of them."

"She had a brother in Naples, Florida. Just a brother with whom she had a good rapport. Her parents were killed in a car crash on the Florida Turnpike in the late 1990s," Mandy replied.

"Ah, poor fellow. What terrible news."

As the Vajays found their way back to each other, the Porters were becoming further estranged.

Felicity's mother tried every manipulation of which she was capable: grief, guilt, anger, tears, more guilt. Nothing worked.

Her father accepted his daughter's decision with scant enthusiasm. Perhaps his vanity was tweaked. He hadn't planned to become a grandfather until his late fifties and here he was just forty-seven, plus he thought Howard Lindquist was a dumb jock.

When her parents finally vacated Custis Hall, Felicity crossed the quad from the administration building back to Old One, the oldest dorm on the campus. She'd call Howard but she needed to collect her thoughts. She had thought her parents really loved her. She was grappling with the dismal reality that they loved her only when she was what they wanted her to be.

Halfway across the quad, bundled up against the cold and the March winds, appearing right on time, trotted Val and Tootie.

When they reached her, Val slipped her arm through Felicity's right arm and Tootie took the left. No one said anything. Felicity's tears came not because of her parents but because she realized her friends loved her. Val disagreed with her but she loved her. You can't pick your family but you *can* pick your friends.

They gathered in Val's room, the corner room traditionally given to the president of the senior class.

Val put a kettle on her hot plate. It was illegal to have a hot plate, but most of the girls jimmied up some way to make coffee, tea, and hot chocolate just like they snuck in liquor, pot, and the occasional gram of cocaine, all of which would horrify their parents, who pretty much did the same thing way back when.

"Mrs. Norton was very nice to give us the little conference room. Spared you all from hearing Mom wail down the hall."

"Bad?" Val pulled out three mugs, proudly displaying how clean they were. "SOS pads."

"That's the first time you've scrubbed them since you were a freshman." Tootie couldn't believe it.

241

"They were clean. Stain's not the same as dirt," Val replied, then turned to Felicity. "Coffee?"

"Yes."

"Are you tired?" Tootie noticed the dark rings under Felicity's eyes.

"I never knew how much this stuff—well, it makes you more tired than physical stuff. Mostly I want to sleep for a week. At least I'm rid of them and they aren't going to pull me out of school. Won't pay for night school, though. Won't pay for an apartment or anything like that." She stopped, chin jutting out. "I don't want their money. Whoever gives you money owns you."

"Won't be easy, Felicity. You're used to having a lot," Val said, not in a dismissive manner.

"I don't even know what I have—I mean, how would I know until I have to do without? I don't know how to run a house. I'm pretty good with money, but I don't even own furniture." She sat on the worn but comfortable reading chair.

"Sister will help." Tootie listened for the water to boil; she was thirsty. "If she asks hunt club members they'll find stuff. Your place won't make *House and Garden* but, hey, you'll have a bed to sleep in."

"I don't want to bother her. She's put herself out for me with Garvey Stokes. I can't ask for more."

"Felicity, Sister would be upset if you didn't ask. She knows about these things." Val agreed with Tootie.

"I'll think about it."

Val and Tootie looked at each other, silently agreeing that they'd talk to Sister.

"There are lots of places to rent," Val said cheerfully.

"Once I'm working full time we can afford something cheap. Howie should make some money at Robb Construction. Remember, we need a car too."

"Forgot about that." Val had.

"Val, I know how you feel about me, about Howie. I know you're furious I'm not going to Princeton, should I get in."

"We'll get in," Val boomed out.

"You will." Felicity's eyes misted again. "Thank you for standing by me even though you don't agree with what I'm doing."

The water boiled. Val poured hot water onto powdered cocoa, then coffee, and finally another cocoa for herself. "If I can't change your mind, I might as well help," she finally responded.

"I mean it. I hope someday I can pay you back."

"That's what friends are for." Val smiled, handing her a cup, a spoon, and powdered milk.

"All for one and one for all." Tootie smiled.

Felicity, who had had quite enough of talking about her future, changed the subject. "I heard about the hunt. Faye Spencer. Tell me."

And so the grisly tale was repeated, with Felicity wretched that she'd missed the hunt just so her parents could try to grind her down.

What is it about horror that excites the mind?

Just as Val and Tootie were doing, other Jefferson Hunt members all over the county were recounting the story to their friends.

CHAPTER 24

How much do you have in the kitty?" Sister asked, as she drove Felicity to Aluminum Manufacturing.

"Seven hundred and one dollars and ninety-five cents." Felicity enjoyed the high view the truck gave her. "Most of it from Val."

"Cusses a lot, does she?"

"Not around you." Felicity's wry humor hadn't abandoned her despite her predicament.

"Better not." Sister slowed, turning left into the parking lot behind the brick office building.

Felicity saw the manufacturing building behind the brick building, which was obscured by rows of pines along the road. "Huge."

"Garvey calls this the bullpit. Window frames are made here, caps for broom handles, you won't believe the stuff they make. It's fascinating, really."

"Once our second grade visited a dairy." Felicity observed a stream of white smoke curling upward from the big chimney at the rear of the building. "I mean, I knew milk came from cows and all that but I didn't know how much happened before we drank it: machines to milk cows, what goes on at the processing plant. That's when I became interested in how things actually get done. And profit." She smiled shyly.

"Profit's the hard part. There's no way anyone can pierce the future. All decisions are based on insufficient evidence. But I do know, should you end up in business, a good rule of thumb is, whatever something costs today, it will cost more tomorrow."

Felicity flipped down the passenger sunshade, a mirror on the reverse side. She checked her face. "Do I look okay?"

"Fresh as a daisy."

"Should I tell him I'm pregnant? It's kind of like lying if I don't." The strain was showing on her young face.

Sister cut the motor. "Yes, but wait until the interview is mostly over. Garvey's a good man, a fair man, and if your interview has gone well—and I'm sure it will—he'll work it out with you."

"I like Mr. Stokes. He doesn't do stupid things in the hunt field."

"I like him too. Ready?"

"Yes, ma'am."

They walked over the macadam, little bits pilling up over the years. Macadam doesn't have a long life span. The bits crunched underfoot.

Reaching the glass door, Sister stepped forward to open it for Felicity.

The office building was rectangular, brick with lots of windows. Built in the 1930s, the entire structure, front and back, was no-nonsense. Sister appreciated function so she didn't find the place ugly at all.

The small lobby contained samples of their products as well as colored framed photos of special projects over the years. A curved reception desk, a deep navy Turkish rug, and six Barcelona chairs offered testimony that Garvey possessed some aesthetic sensibility and was willing to pay for it. True Barcelona chairs are anything but cheap and the desk had been handmade specially by Aluminum Manufacturing, the aluminum top smooth, highly polished, and gleaming.

Bessie Tutweiler, a woman in her mid-fifties, was helping as a temporary bookkeeper and receptionist.

She pulled off her tortoiseshell glasses, hanging on a silver chain, and they dropped to rest on her ample, cashmere-covered bosom. "Sister, haven't seen you since Moses parted the Red Sea." She beamed.

"Bessie, that was a long time ago. I don't even remember what Ramses wore."

They both laughed.

"And how are you since that distant day?" Bessie inquired.

"Fine. Yourself?"

"Can't complain."

"This is Felicity Porter." Sister introduced her to the older woman instead of vice versa. Sister's manners were impeccable. "Bessie, she's a wonderful young lady and she has an interview with Garvey." She turned to Felicity. "This is Mrs. Thornton Tutweiler."

Bessie stood, extending her hand, which Felicity shook.

Bessie looked sharply at Felicity, liking the package, for the still slender girl was modestly dressed in becoming colors. "Honey, you sit down and he'll be out in a minute." She glanced at the small switchboard, a few dots of light showing, and flicked a button that turned on an orange light on Garvey's phone, alerting him that his appointment was in the lobby.

Sister sank into a Barcelona chair. She smiled at Felicity, who returned her smile, trying not to let nerves get the better of her.

Within a few minutes Garvey walked down the hall, entered the reception area, came rapidly to Sister, and bent over, kissing her on the cheek. "Master, you look wonderful."

"Thank you." She wasn't immune to compliments.

"Best run of the season Saturday!" He took both of her hands in his. "Just the best. I try to forget the rest of it." He reached over to Felicity, offering her his hand. "Come in, young entry," he said, winking.

Hearing a foxhunting term relaxed Felicity a little.

When Garvey's door closed, Bessie said, "She looks like a sensible kid."

"A brilliant one. She has a real mind for business. And she is pretty sensible, no drugs or drinking, you know." Sister left it at that, for Bessie would learn in good time about the rest.

"Faye Spencer." Bessie sucked in her breath. "How awful for you. I just can't believe it!"

"None of us can."

"What could that lovely widow have done to deserve such a death? A nicer person you'd never find."

Bessie put her glasses back on to check a new light on the switchboard, then removed them to look at Sister. Angel had researched and updated the office equipment, but she had died before being able to update their interior communication. Garvey kept meaning to get around to it, but that's easier said than done. At least Bessie knew how to work the switchboard.

"Faye was a delight to all who knew her. And she worked hard, Bessie. After her husband was killed she picked herself up and kept going. Faye never asked for sympathy or favors. I hope I find out who did this. I'll skin him alive."

"I'll help you." Bessie pursed her lips. "We live in a strange and violent world, Sister. No respect for life. It's all money, money, money."

"Do you think Faye might have been killed over money?" Sister couldn't lean forward in a Barcelona chair without sitting on the edge but she raised her voice a tad.

Bessie threw up her hands. "Who knows? I guess if her business takes off—well, she'd have been worth millions, wouldn't she?"

"Yes, I think so," Sister replied.

"I think there's a fiend out there. I don't really think this is about money." Bessie settled in to explain her theory. "Ever watch the true crime programs on TV?"

Sister shook her head. "Well, from what I can gather from them, most criminals, if they aren't stupid and can't control their impulses, which is most of the criminal population, if they're intelligent, they believe that what they are doing makes sense. It's right. They truly believe they are right, their acts aren't immoral. You know, like the men who kill prostitutes because they believe they're filth. Wouldn't it make more sense to kill the men who buy their bodies? I mean, we do live in a world of supply and demand. Seems to me the retribution is one-sided, but then those killers are always men, aren't they?"

"Serial killers are, with one or two famous exceptions." Sister knew Bessie, while not a flaming genius, possessed a sturdy intelligence, better in the long run.

"They truly believe their actions bring justice because the system is slow and unjust." Bessie repeated the main thrust of her thoughts.

"Never thought of that. I thought killing provided an adrenaline rush, a thrill, power."

"Probably does. I hope Ben Sidell gets this guy. Makes me look over my shoulder to think he's out there—I mean, out there on our streets."

"I'm looking over my shoulder too." Sister changed the subject. "How's Thornton?"

"Oh, happy as a clam. Orthopedic surgeons never run out of patients. If it's not a football player, it's a skier, and if it's not a skier, it's a kid who fell off his bike. He loves it." She laughed. "Show Thorn a broken bone and he's in heaven. Isn't it funny, he was just as enthusiastic when I met him in med school. Blind date and here we are." She laughed again. "Just love him, just love him to death."

"Ever notice when someone finds the right one it's easy"—Sister paused—"or as easy as a relationship can be."

"Yes, I have noticed."

"Bessie, it certainly is good of you to fill in here while Garvey is shorthanded."

"I worked before the kids were born, which you know, and now that they're married—well, how can I put it? I was drifting along. When Garvey called last month I thought, *Why not? A few months will be fun and the pin money never hurts,* and you know I quite like it. I like the hustle and bustle." Bessie's vocabulary sounded older than she was, no doubt a result of all that time spent playing bridge with her mother-in-law.

"He's lucky to have you."

Bessie rose, came over to sit next to Sister, and lowered her voice. "You're sweet to say that. I spoke to Thornton last night, testing the waters. He said he thought it would be fine if I went back to work, so today I'll talk to Garvey about it. Even if he hires that pretty Porter girl, he needs one more person on office staff full time. Someone has to work the dinosaur." She indicated the switchboard. "You wouldn't believe how much work there is to do here. Mountains." She emphasized mountains.

"Better get your climbing gear because I know you'll have a job."

"Think so?" Bessie sounded breathless.

"Of course."

They heard Garvey's door open so Bessie returned to the desk.

Felicity and Garvey were walking in step, both smiling.

"Bessie, Felicity will start tomorrow, working Monday, Thursday, and Friday after lunch, part-time, until school's out. Then we've got ourselves a full-time girl, I mean woman." He did try not to call women *girls,* but it confused him that an eighty-year-old woman would call another eighty-year-old woman *girl.*

"Wonderful." Bessie meant it.

"Angel's office," Garvey mentioned.

"A good omen." Bessie smiled again. "Congratulations, Felicity. You'll like it here. You can't believe how much activity there is, so much to learn."

"I can't wait, Mrs. Tutweiler."

Out in the parking lot, Felicity threw her arms around Sister. "Thank you, thank you!"

"Honey, I just opened the door. You had to walk through it. I knew you'd impress Garvey." She waited a moment. "The baby?"

"Oh, he was so sweet. He said I should work until I became too uncomfortable and then come back when I was ready; he'd hold my job. I'll be back in a week. I need to work." She stopped, then looked Sister straight in the eye. "I don't want anyone's money. I'm glad our parents won't help us. Howie and I will do it on our own. No one can throw anything up in our faces then."

"You're right about that, Sugar. Come on, let's get in the truck. It's colder than a witch's bosom."

Once rolling back down the road they chattered away.

Felicity quieted a moment. She was usually quiet, but the relief of getting a job had pulled the stopper out of the bottle. "Sister, what am I going to do about Parson?" Suddenly tears welled in her eyes.

"I've been thinking about that."

This was a surprise. "You have?"

"He's a good horse. He's got a little age on him, but he's well made, smart, kind, and will take care of his rider."

"He's a good jumper."

"Lorraine Rasmussen is coming along with her riding. She'll be ready for first flight next season. I'll have a word with her. You keep Parson, and when the season's over, bring him here. I think we can work something out, and I bet you could ride him some-times, although with a new baby I don't know where you're going to find the time."

"You did."

"Sweetie, you didn't know my husband, but let's just say I married well. We could afford help. And even with help, there were days when I was over-whelmed when RayRay was a baby. I do better with children when they can walk and talk but RayRay didn't know that so I sure learned."

"He must have been a good guy, your son."

"He was. I think of him every day, every hour, and I long to hear his voice." She smiled. "Your child opens your heart, or maybe I should say opens a part of your heart you didn't even know existed until that door opens."

"I'm kind of excited. Kind of scared."

"Well, Felicity, join womanhood." Sister laughed. "Every one of us feels that way and then out pops the baby and you're on the roller coaster."

"I can never repay you." Tears welled up in Felicity's eyes.

Sister's engagement ring and wedding ring glamed with that odd burnish of platinum as a ray of sun caught her hand on the steering wheel. "You can."

"How?"

"Love the land. Teach your child to love the land and the creatures upon it and in the sea and in the air. Teach your child respect for life. Even trees are alive and"—she paused dramatically—"put that little thing's bottom on a horse as soon as he or she can actually see. Hold them up there and I'll take the lead line. You make a foxhunter for me."

Felicity grinned. "It's a deal."

"Now, what about Howie? I take it he can't ride yet, so use your womanly wiles. The family that rides together learns to ride out troubles together too."

"Howie can't ride a lick."

"He'll do it for you. He'll do it for the baby."

"I'll work on him."

"Felicity, men are easy," Sister said, a glint of deviltry in her eyes.

Passing through the huge wrought-iron gates, Sister again admired the grounds of Custis Hall. She parked behind Old Main, the administration building, as she had business with Charlotte Norton.

The two walked to the back staircase of the oldest building on campus, once serving multiple functions but now confined to housing administrators.

Sister kissed Felicity on her cheek. "You're on your way."

Solemn, a little nervous, Felicity said, "Will you be godmother to our baby?"

Without a second's hesitation Sister replied, "I would consider it a great honor."

Felicity felt tears well up in her eyes again. She struggled to know herself because she wasn't given to emotions and now they skimmed on her surface. "Thank you."

Sister kissed her again. "Go on, young 'un."

Inside the reception room to Charlotte's office, Teresa Bourbon, Charlotte's able and discreet assistant, waved Sister in.

The silver tea service, expensive then, a fortune now, given to the president by the class of 1952 back in 1952, sat on the coffee table, steam spiraling out of the teapot spout.

"Egg salad and tuna salad sandwiches for starters."

Charlotte stepped out behind her desk. "And your favorite afternoon tea, real orange pekoe."

"I need it." Sister sank onto the sofa as Charlotte poured a bracing cup and handed it to her.

Then she poured one for herself and sat next to Sister. She picked up the tray of sandwiches. "Nourishment."

"I really am famished."

They ate their sandwiches, drank their tea, and talked forthrightly, for over the years the two women had taken each other's measure.

"Got the job."

"I'm glad," Charlotte replied. "Much as I'd like to see her at Princeton, I know she's strong-willed and I hope this will work."

"Wonder if they'll all get into Princeton?"

Charlotte leaned back. "They have the qualifications but I doubt if admissions is going to take three girls from the same school."

"There is that." Sister reached for another delicious sandwich. "You know, Charlotte, I have a feeling about Felicity. Like I get a feeling about hound puppies. That girl is going to be a success, a big success. She has drive. Fate appears to be handing her a bad card, but I think it will be the making of her."

"I hope so." Charlotte didn't sound 100 percent convinced. "Her parents flamed me like a blowtorch."

"Immature people need a target for their anger."

"Felicity is more mature in many ways than her parents." Charlotte poured another cup of tea for Sister and herself. "You'd be surprised how many times I see that here."

"Bet I wouldn't."

Charlotte spoke next of the unavoidable subject. "I've hired extra security. There's always fat in every budget, so I squeezed some out. Chances are, whoever this perverse killer is, he isn't interested in Custis Hall, but I can't be too careful, and both victims were young and good-looking. Who's to say?"

"I certainly hope the girls are safe. You did the right thing. The only common thread I can find—well, two—for the victims is that both were quite beautiful and both had knowledge of wireless technology."

"Yes, I thought of that too. Naturally, I don't want to alarm the girls but I did have the career counselors give each girl a questionnaire concerning last year's summer jobs. It's not obvious—there are lots of questions because it's designed to support finding a job this summer for those who want to do that as well as supporting life experience information for college applications—but there are a few questions about working for cell phone companies and computer chip companies. Just in case." Charlotte smiled a tight smile. "As it turns out, Val worked last summer for Alltel back home."

"You're way ahead of everyone else," Sister replied. "Let's hope Val's knowledge is limited, just in case."

Charlotte held a plate of chocolate cookies and

shortbread ones. "One good thing that's come out of this is that interest has spiked in the early Middle Ages." She paused. "It was taught to me as a low point in European history—well, not as low as the so-called Dark Ages but low—and I don't think it was at all. The advances in agriculture were significant."

"And the clothing design was gorgeous," Sister added.

"Twelfth century. The lines," Charlotte enthused, for she believed clothing revealed a great deal about a culture's dreams as well as its reality.

"Long fluid lines." Sister agreed with her. "I think the true Dark Ages for European culture was the twentieth century. A sea of blood."

"Exactly." Charlotte paused. "You know, the sum of suffering was so great we can't apprehend it. But we can understand two dead Lady Godivas. Understand and fear."

"Do you think the killer wants us to be afraid?"

"I don't know. I am."

"I wonder if he's laughing at us."

"Is it possible he wishes us to be both fearful and amused?"

CHAPTER 25

On Thursday, March 6, Sister and a large contingent who managed to get off work or had already retired drove up to Casanova territory, east of Warrenton. Ashland Bassets were meeting at Eastern View, owned by the Fendleys.

Hunting on foot separated those with wind and those without, which became apparent twenty minutes into the hunt.

Joyce and Bill Fendley ran along, as did Marion, who took off early from Horse Country because Ashland hounds cast at two in the afternoon.

Sister had to laugh because Cabel Harper showed up in brush pants, very intelligent decision, and a true tweed jacket to repel thorns, topped off with a hunter-green Robin Hood hat, a pheasant feather stuck in for allure. Ilona confined herself to a baseball hat, while Betty Franklin, remembering those nasty thorns, also wore brush pants but she tied a wool scarf around her neck, tucking it into her jacket. The last time she hunted with the bassets she had cut her throat, and blood had poured over her shirt and jacket.

Charlotte Norton allowed the Custis Hall girls to hunt so long as they wrote a paper about it for class. Val drove them in her lime-colored Jeep. By the time the kids reached Eastern View, all but Val agreed a Wrangler wasn't meant for long trips. Their fillings rattled in their teeth.

Al Toews, Master of Bassets, held the horn this March 6 and his joint master, Mary Reed, whipped in to him. Al and Mary had been in the custom of taking turns hunting the hounds but Al declared he would give it up to Mary after season's end because his wind was shot. No one believed him since he could outrun anyone, but this declaration was made with solemnness. Al's wife, Kathleen King, also whipped in to him today. The two were psychic when they hunted together. Aggie de la Garza, Miriam Anver, Frank Edrington, Sherrod Johnson, Mary Dobrovir, and Nancy Palmer whipped in as well.

Camilla Moon and Diana Dutton acted as first flight field master and second accordingly, although they didn't exactly specify it that way, but the field seemed naturally to break into two groups as time ran on and so did the bunnies.

At a check, Tootie whispered to Sister, "Why so many whippers-in?"

"Bassets are harder-headed than foxhounds. Need more control," Sister whispered back.

Camilla, a true canine student, turned as the Jefferson Hunt people were behind her, the Ashland members gracefully allowing the guests pride of place. "Second-best noses in dogdom."

Tootie already knew that bloodhounds possessed the best so she rightly figured that foxhounds must come in third.

Naturally, harrier people, coonhound folks, and beagle devotees could argue the point. Even Plott hound lovers who run bear would argue, but foxhunters, like all hound people, prove marvelously resistant to others' opinions.

Al bounded into a hateful covert of brambles, a thin swift-running blade of water, deep-sided, cutting it in two, a perfect abode for the cottontail.

Before first cast, the tall lanky Vietnam veteran had asked Sister if she would care to hunt hounds with him. Flattered as she was by the prospect of being that close to these aggressive hunters, this would be her only time to be one of the field as opposed to leading. Joyce Fendley enjoyed being in the field for the same reasons. She had no decisions to make. Camilla and Diana had to make them.

Hounds began to feather, then tails whipped like propellers. One lone deep note from Tosca alerted the others, followed by a crescendo of sound, beautiful spine-tingling music for the only pack voices as beautiful as these belonged to Penn-Marydels.

The rabbit, still in the covert, headed along the stream, then shot out over the pasture and ran a tight circle, hounds in hot pursuit and humans pursuing as hotly as their legs would carry them.

This rabbit could run, and the chase lasted fifteen exhausting minutes up and down the pasture—which had a steep roll to it—and then the rabbit disappeared, just popped down a hole. No amount of furious digging could dislodge Peter Cottontail, who lived to run another day.

Rabbit scent is fragile, but the afternoon proved a good one and hounds worked another narrow covert. Mary Reed hollered, "Tally-ho!" Al quickly pushed the bassets up to the line, and off they ran again.

Sister noted at the next check that most of the Jefferson Hunt people hung in with first flight, but huffing and puffing were evident. She was breathing hard too, and all those broken bones of decades past began to speak to her.

After another short burst, light fading and temperature falling, the group walked back to the old silo to enjoy a tailgate.

Betty asked Cabel if she'd heard anything from Clayton.

Gratefully drinking mulled wine, the warmth most welcome, Cabel airily replied, "He can't call out. It's lockup."

"All for the best, I'm sure."

"I'm lost," Cabel suddenly blurted out. "He plucked my last nerve. Let's call a spade a spade; my husband is a philandering drunk but we've lived together for twenty-two years and I miss him. If nothing else, he did take out the garbage, drunk or sober. I can't believe how much I miss him. . . .

"How do those Custis Hall girls get out of school? When I went there you were only let out of class if your mother died." Cabel nodded toward Val, Tootie, and Pamela, abruptly changing the subject.

"Where's Felicity?" Ilona asked. "Val, Tootie, and Felicity are the Three Musketeers."

"Aluminum Manufacturing," Betty answered. "She's working three afternoons a week."

"I thought the Porters had money," Ilona said.

"They do." Betty wasn't about to tell them Felicity was pregnant, as well as the rest of it. "But she wants real-life experience, as she puts it."

"Good for her." Cabel nodded. "What else do they have to do at that age except drink, drug, and have sex?"

"Cabel, we didn't." Ilona recalled her own Custis Hall days.

"Speak for yourself," Cabel wryly responded.

Betty held up her hands, palms outward. "I was a bleeding saint."

"Spare me." Cabel rolled her eyes, then stared at the girls again. "They *are* beautiful girls. Well, Pamela's a pudge, though she's losing some of it. But Val and Tootie are two of the prettiest girls I've ever seen."

"The men notice, and they notice which other men are looking. Bobby tells me everything," Betty noted. "He said if anyone lays a hand on one of those kids— did I get it right, lay? Well, if anyone does, he and Walter will dismember them. But I don't think the men in our club are like that."

"They all are," Cabel stated flatly. "I'm amazed that Clayton didn't make a pass at one of them. Too loaded."

"Never stopped him before," Ilona said uncharitably.

"Ramsey's better?" Cabel fired back.

"Ladies, good to talk to you." Betty backed away.

"Oh, Betty, don't be so goddamned proper. You've seen us fight before. We're joined at the hip. We're bound to fuss sometimes. If you want to know who I think has really been dipping his stick throughout the county, let's discuss High Vajay. I'll bet you dollars to doughnuts he was sleeping with Faye Spencer. All he had to do was fall out of his own bed to fall into hers." Cabel warmed to her subject.

"Wouldn't want to be in his boots right now." Betty avoided the sex suspicions. "He's the main suspect for the Lady Godiva murders."

"Boots? How about pants? I'm surprised he isn't singing soprano. Mandy must have an iron will and a forgiving patience," Ilona marveled.

"There are worse things than a husband who cheats." Betty opened her mouth before thinking.

"Such as?" Cabel and Ilona said in unison, both incredulous.

"Wanton cruelty. Loss of honor."

"You don't think sex outside of marriage isn't cruel?" The pheasant feather bobbed on Cabel's hat.

"I think it hurts, but I don't think the intent is cruel." Betty held up her hand to stay the protests. "Would I be devastated if Bobby ran off the reservation?" She used the old phrase. "I would, but I would be far more upset if he was cold, critical, and cruel to animals and people. Or if he proves a coward when Gabriel blows his trumpet. A man with no honor isn't worth having and neither is a woman. As to sleeping around—well, sex is irrational and in a different category from other human endeavors."

"You have a point." Ilona was thoughtful. "But consider the intimate betrayal. I don't know if I will ever completely trust Ramsey. I love him but I don't trust him. That's not good. And have you ever considered that your straying husband might bring home a gift that keeps giving, like AIDS?"

"I know it's terrible. It must eat you from the inside

out." Betty was compassionate. "But look at Sister. Neither she nor Ray was monogamous, and they had a good strong marriage. Gay men are like that too, or so it seems to me, and their relationships last longer than most heterosexual ones, a fact the sex Nazis can't concede. I don't want Bobby fooling around, don't misunderstand me, but I truly believe there are worse sins. We make a small god of monogamy."

"I hope you never find out." Cabel headed back to the food.

"I'm sorry. I've upset her," Betty said to Ilona.

"She's having a hard time. She'll get over it." Ilona smiled. "We all do and if we don't, we're pretty stupid, aren't we? You can't spend your life massaging old wounds."

"Plenty do," Betty said. "Virginians mistake personal injustice for history."

"Isn't that the truth! There are a lot of embittered injustice collectors out there." Ilona started for the food, then turned back to Betty. "I was on my way to becoming one of those people. Finally couldn't stand myself, and I said, 'Ilona, you've got to do something or you'll turn into a snitz.'"

Snitz is a dried apple.

"Glad you got hold of yourself," Betty complimented her.

"Me too."

Betty then joined Al and Mary, the whippers-in, the Custis Hall girls, and Sister. She slipped her arm around Sister's waist.

Neither woman thought a thing about that. They loved each other deeply and were not afraid of touching. Touch is healing. Men are denied this except with their wives and their children; they don't get the same loving reinforcement from their own gender.

"Master." Tootie addressed Al, who was a natural teacher. "Why did you draw the first covert up one side and then down the other? Shaker doesn't do that."

"Because Shaker is hunting a predator. I'm hunting prey. A rabbit will survive more often than not if it is still, if it sticks in its warren. The bassets have to bolt them. When you hunt foxes, you usually pick up their line when they themselves are hunting or returning to their den from a night's hunt. So I have to make good the ground in a very different way."

Mary chimed in. "And fox scent is heavier than rabbit scent."

Sister and Betty were as enthralled with this information as were the young folks. True hunters find no bottom to their enthusiasm, much to the despair of those around them.

Al thought things through in systems, in checklists. He broke down complicated problems into discrete parts, which is natural for a combat pilot. A man has a much better chance of living through a war if he does this, and the equipment Al flew was the most sophisticated for its time. You'd better have a checklist or else. He applied this relentless logic to hunting the bassets, but like all good huntsmen he could be flexible.

Tired but full from all the food, the Jefferson Hunt gang bid their Ashland friends good-bye as they piled into trucks, SUVs, old station wagons still providing service, and Val's Jeep.

Tootie hesitated for a moment before stepping over the lip into the sturdy vehicle that really could go anywhere.

"Will you stop being a prima donna!"

"Val, you're not sitting in the back," Tootie said.

Pamela replied, "Neither am I. Come on, Tootie, I rode back there on the way up."

"All right, all right."

Sister walked by. "Be grateful you don't have old bones."

"They'll be old by the time I get to school." Tootie laughed and climbed in, the door swinging shut behind her.

Sister and Betty drove past Marion, who was starting her car.

Stopping, Betty lowered her window. "Come on down. We're hunting Mill Ruins Saturday. You've never seen Peter Wheeler's old place. The mill still works."

"I don't know if I can take off work, but it's a wonderful invitation."

As Sister and Betty rolled down Route 29 they reviewed the hunt, the tailgate, their lengthy discussion with Marion as to the status of the Warrenton murder, and the murder at Foxglove. Then they replayed Al's wonderful talk on hunting with bassets.

"It's funny, all the years I've whipped in and I never thought about hunting a hunter. All I know is fox. Well, deer occasionally, but hunting with hounds, all I know is fox," Betty said.

"Since a prey animal is in some respects weaker than a predator, camouflage and stillness are essential." Sister loved talking about these subjects. "But you know, a cow is prey and a horse is prey, but of course they're large. They don't have to remain still and they have hooves to kick the daylights out of a predator."

"Or me." Betty laughed. "Remember the time that doe charged Archie?" She named a now-departed beloved hound. "When was that? I remember, 1997. Outlaw was green then, his first season, and after the doe charged Archie she charged us. Scared the hell out of both of us. Outlaw came up with all four feet off the ground."

"Bet your heart flew up too." Sister smiled. "Every now and then something happens out there and the rush is incredible. Sometimes it's good and sometimes it's bad, but at least you know you're alive. Hard to believe the season's almost over. Always gives me the blues. Then I snap out of it. When the puppies start coming and the garden blooms, I pick up again."

"You've got a green thumb."

"Thanks." Sister sat upright, making Betty look

ahead, wondering if something ran across the road. "Betty, what if our killer is a prey animal?"

"What?"

"What if our killer feels weak? Here we've been assuming this is some kind of sex thing, which it may be, or that it's tied into wireless competition. But what Al said about a prey animal sitting tight, then having to be bolted? Maybe that's our killer, sitting tight, only coming out to kill when the coast is clear. Aashi and Faye were seen as predators."

Betty thought hard. "Weak things *can* kill, can fight back. After all, the doe did."

"One has to provoke them, right? The first defense is to hide. I guess the second is to flee, but if we can bolt the killer, we'll know him."

"High Vajay doesn't strike me as weak," Betty said. "Too smart."

"You don't think High's the killer?"

"I don't know, but I doubt it. He has too much to lose by committing that kind of felony."

"Unless he had more to lose with the two women living."

"True." Sister noted a streak of turquoise over the crest of the Blue Ridge Mountains.

"I thought weak people poisoned their victims. Guess that's one of those stereotypes. You know, kill by stealth." Betty wondered how to flush out the murderer.

"Still a useful way to send someone off planet earth. All the labs in the world can't point to who put the poison in the cup. They can only identify the poison. But, see, this is what bothers me. If someone used poison, wouldn't you assume they don't want to be caught?"

"Sure." Betty reached up for the Jesus strap as they took a curve. Reaching for the strap was force of habit.

"Part of me thinks our killer, like most murderers, wants to get away with it, and part of me thinks not. The Godiva part is too public."

"People do get away with public murders. What about all those political murders in places like Ireland, Serbia, Iran, and Iraq? I'm not even counting Africa. I guess it's a matter of scale. The more people you kill the better your chances of escaping justice."

"Pinochet proved that." Sister pointed to the flaming sunset over the Blue Ridge Mountains. "But, on the other hand, we judge everything by the comfort of America. Look at Spain, a hideous civil war. Did that war lay the groundwork for Spain's resurgence today? Same with Chile. Did all those murders of Allende's people lay the groundwork for that country's economic revival? We don't like to think about things that way. I mean, we don't like to think that sometimes forests have to be burned for fresh growth."

"Yeah, it's repulsive."

"I guess it is. The Chileans slit the bellies of those they killed, then dropped them from airplanes into the ocean so they'd sink without a trace. I consider that gross."

"Isn't that always the problem with a human corpse? How do you destroy the evidence?"

"Right. But here we have a killer who wants everyone to *admire* the evidence. I just don't get it. What I do get is, he's *here.*"

"And was at the Casanova Hunt Ball."

"Right. I've gone over the list. It's half our club."

"Ben Sidell has it?"

"Of course, he's questioned everyone methodically as to when they left the ball and what they saw. As far as I can tell, everyone has been cooperative."

"Too bad Crawford wasn't there, we could pin it on him." Betty laughed.

"He's like a bad penny, he'll show up when we least want to see him." Sister sighed. "Maybe I'll have a brainstorm."

"I rather hope not," Betty said firmly. "The last time you thought you could pin a murder on someone he nearly killed you. This person puts the silver bowl in your stable office, drops off a movie, parades a corpse at Cindy Chandler's. You stay out of it."

"How can I stay out of it? I'm in the middle and I don't even know why."

"Well, that makes two of us. Where you go, I go." Betty smiled.

CHAPTER 26

True to form, Crawford did show up on Saturday morning. He called first.

Both Crawford and Sister sat on the Board of Governors for Custis Hall. The administration had been searching for a new theater director as well as a head of alumnae relations. Crawford strongly opposed one of the candidates, personally visiting every board member. Sister was first on his list because he wanted to get it over with.

After hearing his objections, Sister replied, "Thank you for doing the homework. I support your nonsupport of Milford Weems."

Crawford folded his hands together. "Good. I won't take up more of your time."

"Before you go, I have a question for you. Do you intend to rent the Demetrios place?"

"I'd like someone who can farm. The house needs some fixing too."

"Allow me to suggest a young couple, very young but clean-living and hardworking, Felicity Porter and Howard Lindquist. They'll be married this summer, so I guess I should think of them as the Lindquists. He'll be working with Matt Robb's construction company, so he has the skills to repair the buildings."

"Felicity's not going to college?" He was incredulous, worried.

"Night school. Piedmont Community College."

"What a waste. That girl belongs at an Ivy League school."

"Most people feel that way, and you're in a position to help them. Obviously, they haven't a cent, although she is working part-time for Garvey Stokes and that will be full-time when she graduates. He'll be making some money but they don't even have a car yet." She held out her hands as a supplicant. "If they repair the house and paint the interior, would you consider a significant reduction in rent? They're good kids and"—she smiled—"they're in love."

He perceived the situation. "I'll talk to young Lindquist." He half smiled too. "Thank you for your suggestion. If I don't get someone in that place it will slide into ruin."

"They'll be good neighbors."

"Well, I don't know Howard but I think Felicity is mature for her years, very sensitive."

This time he stood up; Raleigh and Rooster stood too. Golly, lounging on the back of the den sofa, couldn't be bothered to see a guest out, even an unwelcome one.

Sister walked Crawford into the wide center hall, built to allow a breeze to cool the house in Virginia's sweltering summers, and to the front door, with its overhead fan and glass panels on either side.

"Awful thing about Faye Spencer," Crawford said.

"Yes, it was."

"Vajay is the man most under suspicion, but Ramsey Merriman had a lot to lose."

Sister perked up. "Have you told Ben?"

"Yes. I don't like saying stuff like that, but under the circumstances Ramsey should pay the consequences for his affairs." He shook his head. "Bragged about it. Said he seduced that Indian girl on one of his trips with High to Washington. Said High never suspected or perhaps never cared, I don't know. Then he said he tried to talk the woman into sex with him and Clayton. They'd pay her thousands. She refused and cut him off. What a fool. Anyway, he called and cussed me out and so did Ilona. I did the right thing."

"Yes, you did."

As she watched him drive away in his metallic dark-red Mercedes, she felt more confused than ever but she had accomplished two important things: She found a home for the kids because she knew Crawford would respond to them, and she put loyal people around one who was not loyal.

Always keep your enemy in front of you.

CHAPTER 27

Had Sister known her enemy had been in front of her all the time, the day might have been different. Some things are so unthinkable one doesn't see them, even though they're as close as the nose on your face. Not only do individuals suffer from these blind spots, entire nations do as well.

The lulling lap and spray of the water off the three-story waterwheel at Mill Ruins was beautiful, spellbinding. Century after century, people in the western world took this sound for granted. Only in the twentieth century did it finally subside, along with the clack of wagon wheels and shod hooves on cobblestone streets, vendors shouting their wares as they toddled down country roads, the constant swish of large overhead fans in the South, the ringing of church bells to signify the hour. A few places preserved these sounds so tourists could imagine themselves in another time.

Time without end people kill one another. If sounds and sights change, this dolorous fact does not.

It was Saturday, March 8, and twenty couple of hounds waited on the party wagon. The mercury at quarter to nine read 48 degrees, the barometer falling, good sign.

March, a breakheart month, raises the average person's hopes for spring. Daffodils, early ones, display their yellow heads, and crocuses cover lawns or dot woods tucked back where old foundations remain from prior centuries. Buds swell a tiny bit on the trees, the red glow apparent to those who study nature.

Then a snowstorm or a freezing rain will pound down as Old Man Winter once more reminds all creatures that he is not ready to relinquish his grasp.

Foxhunters liked that, of course. Better to keep that scent on the ground, for the warmth would lift it up over hound noses. But even the most dedicated foxhunter eventually longed for spring, the cascade of white apple blossoms, pale pink cherry blossoms, and deep magenta crab apple blossoms, the fragrance filling entire counties. Redbud bloomed along with peaches and pears, tulips held sway for a while, and the world rejoiced in new life.

Even Sister, who inevitably passed through a period of mourning after the season ended, discovered rejuvenation in her garden at last.

Today the field swelled with the regulars and visitors too. Tedi and Edward brought guests from Marlborough Hunt in Maryland. The Merrimans and Cabel, parked side by side, burst with good spirits. The Custis Hall girls turned out in full force along with Charlotte Norton and Bunny Taliaferro. Charlotte joked that if she was a golf widow in the summer her husband could be a foxhunt widower in winter.

Gray was repenting his promise to ride with his brother on a steeplechaser fresh off the circuit. Even before he mounted up, Gray noticed the nervousness of the rangy bay.

"You're crazy to ride these horses right off the circuit, Sam."

"It's the only way I'm going to know how he'll go in company. I know how he goes alone and he's a good horse, Gray. Just a little up."

As the brothers bickered, Lorraine Rasmussen chatted with Felicity on Parson. Sister had mentioned to Lorraine that Parson was a suitable and kind horse but that Felicity couldn't afford him once out of school.

Henry Xavier ignored Ronnie Haslip's taunts that his diet wasn't working. It was, but slowly.

Donnie Sweigart surprised everyone by showing up on a horse lent him by Ronnie Haslip. Donnie borrowed clothes from Shaker, since they were the same size; he even found a pair of boots that would fit. He looked quite nice.

He'd fallen for Sybil Fawkes and knew the only way he was going to be in her vicinity was if he learned to foxhunt. He could ride some and Bobby Franklin, bearing that in mind, knew he'd have to keep an eye on him. If nothing else, Donnie had guts.

Sybil noticed. She walked over on Bombardier. "Donnie, did you discover the hardest part of foxhunting is tying your stock tie?"

He smiled shyly. "Did. Pricked my fingers too."

"I wish I could hold out hope that it gets easier but I'm forever fiddling with it, folding the ends over the wide center knot, pressing the stockpin through." She glanced over to see where Shaker was in his preparation, for she had a job to do. "I'm delighted to see you out here."

"If nothing else, I'll provide amusement."

"There will be plenty of that. Always is." She reached down and touched his shoulder with her gloved hand. "Takes courage to foxhunt, and we all know you have that. Hope I'll see you after the hunt."

"Sure thing." Donnie was floating on air.

Back at Ronnie's trailer, a crop snaked out from the

open tack room as Ronnie neatly stung Xavier's bottom. "Could show a movie on that butt."

"You spend too much time looking at men's asses," Xavier growled.

Ronnie feigned a falsetto. "What a big hairy-chested man you are."

Xavier never could keep a straight face around his boyhood friend. "Hey, at least one of us is."

"Remember when RayRay sprouted his first chest hair right between his pecs, and we threw him on the ground and yanked it out?" Ronnie laughed.

Xavier smiled as he swung up on Picasso, built to carry weight. "I think of RayRay every day."

Over at the Harper trailer parked next to the Merriman trailer, Cabel and Ilona watched Vajay and Mandy chatting with Kasmir.

"He's cool as a cuke." Ilona noted Vajay's demeanor. "You'd never know he was under suspicion of murder."

"If I were Mandy, I'd—" Cabel stopped herself. "Look."

Ben Sidell, on his trusty Nonni, had ridden up to the three and passed a few pleasantries. Since nothing seemed untoward, the girlfriends sighed in disappointment.

Sister pulled out her grandfather's pocket watch. It was seven minutes to the first cast. "Seven minutes. I'll go on over and say a few words, along with Walter. That will hurry up the laggards."

Betty waited on the ground, holding Outlaw's reins.

Her job would be to open the doors to the party wagon and then swing up on her horse. She and Sybil took turns performing this duty.

Sister on Lafayette rode over to Walter on his wonderful Clemson.

"Good morning, Master." He tipped his derby.

"Good morning, Master." She touched her crop to her cap.

"What saint's day?"

"A mess." She smiled at the tall blond man whom she had grown to love. "Senan, an Irish abbot who died in 544; Felix of Dunwich, bishop of East Anglia, who died in 647. His task was to Christianize the East Angles, a work still in progress." She paused, then added, "John of God, who founded the Hospitalers and lived from 1495 to 1550. There's one more, but I forget."

"I don't know how you remember what you do."

"I have a funny head for dates and numbers. Hey, it's International Women's Day."

"I celebrate women every day," he joked.

"Well, come on, let's do the shake-and-howdy. I want to cast these hounds."

Walter said nothing because she was always eager to get on terms with her fox. So they rode over, called the crowd together, guests were introduced, the field master was pointed out—Sister herself—Bobby was noted as hilltoppers' master, and without further ado Sister turned to Shaker and called out, "Hounds, please."

Betty flipped up the long latch, pulled open the aluminum door, and out bounded twenty couple of excited foxhounds.

"I'm ready!" Trinity announced to the world.

Cora disciplined her. *"Will you kindly shut up."*

Trinity hung her head for a moment.

Asa simply said, *"Youth."*

Diddy, Darby, Dreamboat, Dana, Delight, and Doughboy stood on their hind legs but they didn't babble. Pookah and Pansy came out today, the excitement doubled in the first-year entry.

Calming, Shaker lowered his voice. "Steady now, relax."

Showboat, Shaker's horse, ears pricked forward, exhaled out of his nostrils as two downy woodpeckers flew out of the mill.

What in the devil are woodpeckers doing in there? Sister thought to herself.

Only they knew, but a stream of invective flew between the birds as they battled about something.

Shaker led the pack past the mill, the spray becoming a heavy mist, moistening faces, intensifying scent. A huge door allowed entry into the first floor, a small door with a small outdoor landing was at the second story, and a third wooden door opened over the very top of the waterwheel. If the wheel needed repairs, it was stopped and the workmen could use whichever door was closest.

Foxes had lived at the mill since it was built, but that didn't mean they'd give you a run. There was no way to bolt them from the lair, but often the pack could get one fox returning home for a bracing go.

At the rear of the first flight, the Custis Hall girls rode through the mist and fog rising from the mill-race.

"Fog creeps me out," Val whispered.

"Because you got lost in it," Felicity mentioned.

"So did everybody else," Val whispered, a bit louder.

"Not everyone else, just us," Tootie corrected her, as they rode over the bridge spanning the millrace.

They emerged from the fog and took a simple coop into the first large pasture off the farm road. Hounds, on hearing, "Lieu in," the old Norman words in use for over a thousand years, fanned over the pasture, the dew thick and cool.

No fox scent rose up from the earth. They reached the back fence line, took the jump there, and moved into the woods.

For thirty minutes hounds worked, the field walking along: nothing. Then they came into an area called Shootrough, one hundred acres, that used to be really rough but which Walter had cleaned up and planted with millet, winter wheat, switchgrass, and South American maize at the edges. The ground nesters flocked in, as did the foxes.

Dana found the line first. *"Red dog fox."*

Other hounds ran over, putting their noses down. Cora opened on the line, and in a flash the entire pack was flying through the wheat and millet, the long stems swishing, the slight westerly breeze bending and raising the thin stalks as well.

A stout timber jump led into true rough ground, covered in brambles, pigweed, and poke. A little path cut through that got them down to the creek, below where Sister thought the fox would jump in to foil scent. But he didn't. He turned back, running right on the farm road by the north side of Shootrough. The entire field viewed him as they emerged on the road. Having a good head start on the hounds, he hadn't yet considered evasive action.

As Lafayette thundered down the road, clods of red clay flying up behind him, Sister noticed ice crystals on the north side of the road just catching the sunlight as the sun rose high enough to reach them from the east.

The fox plunged into the woods on the right, a small patch off the farm road at the end of Shootrough, the larger woods being to the left. He ran over moss and through hollowed-out logs and then came back onto the road, where he ran right between Cabel and Ilona, who stopped and stayed put as did everyone else, once Cabel shouted, "Hold hard!"

Within minutes the pack ran through the horses.

Diddy stopped for one second, then ran on. When she came alongside Tinsel, she said, *"I caught the scent again."*

"We all caught it," Tinsel replied, nose to ground, wondering what had happened to Diddy's wits.

"No, the perfume on Faye Spencer's leg."

"Nothing we can do about it now," Tinsel rightly answered.

This time the big red dog fox did use the creek, running through it and climbing out a hundred yards upstream.

Hounds lost scent where he jumped in, but Cora took some hounds on one side and Asa kept the others on the takeoff side as they worked in both directions until finally Tinsel, again demonstrating her fine nose, hollered *"Here."*

That fast they were all on again, threading through the woods as fast as they could, till they finally lost him at an outcropping of huge squared boulders, very strange-looking.

Gingerly, Trudy dropped down on the other side to see if there was a den—but nothing.

Once again the fox proved to all he had magic. *Poof!* He was gone, his scent with him.

CHAPTER 28

Shaker reined in, cast hounds in a wide net, but that yielded not a jot.

He noticed that the bit of wind died and a stillness muffled sound in the woods. He could hear horses breathing about half a football field from him but no birds flew, no deer appeared.

Not only are there dead spots where wireless phones can't receive transmission, there are dead spots and dead times, period.

Sometimes this presages the edge of a low pressure system. Other times it's just a calm moment or calm spot, just as there are spots where little wind devils forever spiral upward.

Shaker turned, casting back toward Shootrough. Given conditions, he thought it better to head toward food sources like the ground nester paradise. Usually he didn't draw the same covert twice, but this time he thought he'd draw toward the north, then move out of Shootrough where, once through the woods and skirting a ravine, an array of fenced pastures beckoned, little coverts stuck here and there, all rich in game.

Back in the wheat and millet, a bobwhite flew up, then another. Asa moved to the edge of the large area where the switchgrass formed a border. He lifted his head, flared his nostrils, then lowered his head. Patiently, he worked this old line as it grew warmer. A gray fox came for breakfast, feathers everywhere as though the vixen played with them, which she well may have done. Finally, he had enough fresh scent to open in his deep basso profundo, a sound to send shivers up one's spine.

Hound ran a half circle around the edge of Shootrough, staying in the switchgrass; then, to the field's delight, the gray vixen burst out, making a straight blast across the fields, tall grass bent down from winter's snows.

Betty, to the left of the beautiful fox, jumped a deep ditch, new, thanks to runoff. Clods of red clay flew up behind Outlaw's hooves.

Sybil, on the right, moved into the edge of the woods because the gray swerved, heading for the woods; then she turned again, making a straight shot toward Mill Ruins, two miles away as the crow flies.

Close to their fox, hounds grew more excited, as did the field.

The vixen knew her territory, moving over a large patch of running cedar that baffled scent just long enough for her to put more distance between herself and hounds. She ran another quarter mile, then launched straight up, grabbing on to the rough bark of a mighty walnut tree. By the time hounds reached her, she was grooming herself on a thick limb, tail held in front paw.

"Come down here! Come down here!" Doughboy leapt up and down.

"Cheater! Cheater!" Pookah was beside herself.

The gray looked down and smiled. *"When pigs can fly."*

Shaker rode up, Showboat lifting his gorgeous head to behold the fox.

Sister brought the field up close so they could see the vision. Bobby had room to come up too, as no saplings grew around the spread of the walnut's branches.

Shaker laughed. "Is there a call for Climbed a Tree?"

Sister laughed too. "Well, give Gone to Ground a few doubling notes."

He did, and the young horse that Sam rode just blew up.

"Brother, I'd better head back," Sam said quietly. He knew the animal had had enough.

"I'll go back with you." Gray wanted to keep hunting but Sam should have company. "I'll tell Sister we're heading back."

Gray rode up and spoke quietly to Sister, who nodded, and the two men turned to pick their way toward the farm road on a well-worn deer trail.

Deeper in the woods than they realized, they kept pushing toward the southwest. Sooner or later they would find the farm road. The steeplechaser calmed down with the leisurely walk and the fact that Gray's stalwart foxhunter stayed low-key.

The deep ravine to the right helped them get their bearings. Neither Sam nor Gray had the best sense of direction, unlike Sister and Shaker, two human homing pigeons.

Gray sighed. "Whew. Know where we are now."

"Yeah, I was getting a little worried too."

"Sister would have put out drinks and a cooler with food. She'd feed us like the foxes, figuring we'd smell out the food," Gray teased.

"Wouldn't put it past her. Remember the time Ronnie Haslip sank in the bog? The horse struggled but Ronnie couldn't move for the mud sucking him in. As everyone tied their stirrup leathers together to throw him a line, she calls out, 'Don't worry, Ronnie, if you go under we'll throw a wreath on the spot.' Took his mind off his predicament."

"Funny, isn't it, how the mind controls the body?"

Sam snorted. "In my case it's usually the reverse." He looked toward the ravine. "Damn, sure are a lot of crows over there."

"Probably a deer carcass left over from deer season."

"Hate that. Hate it when they wander off and die." Sam grimaced.

"Well, a good hunter will track his deer when wounded, but sometimes they can get away. Come on."

They rode to the lip and looked down to see St. Just and his flock merrily feasting on a corpse. St. Just had an eyeball in his yellow beak. The cold weather had preserved the body, and the slight thaw allowed the crows to really dig in to this unexpected treat.

"Jesus Christ!" Sam exclaimed.

Gray discerned the dead was male but the crows so covered the body he couldn't tell much else. "We've got to get Ben Sidell."

"Try this first. Yell. I'd like to spare this horse if I can. You've got a voice that carries."

"Worth a try," Gray agreed, cupping his lips with his hands. "Yo! Yo! Yo!"

Country folk know three shouts is a signal of distress. When it comes to yelling there's no formula, but Gray continued using three repeats.

Sound carried well today and the field three-quarters of a mile away heard him.

Shaker had already cast hounds back toward the mill so they were coming in that direction but on higher ground.

Sister paused a moment. "Edward, take the field."

"Yes, Master." Edward Bancroft touched his top hat with his crop.

Sister cantered up to Shaker. "That's Gray. Either he's seen a fox or there's something else."

Often times, if at a distance with no hounds near, someone will tally-ho. As it is, one shouldn't tally-ho if hounds' noses are down. Then, too, how does a field member, who lacks the view up front that the field master has, know if the fox viewed is the hunted fox?

The protocol of foxhunting is grounded in common sense.

"I can hunt that way." Shaker took his boots out of the stirrup irons to wiggle his cold toes.

"I rarely ask you to do this, but given today's conditions, which are pretty darned good, please lift the hounds and cast them forward when we reach Gray. We might get a popping run out of it. If not, I'll bear the blame."

"Yes, Master." He didn't like it but Shaker as a hunt servant did what his master told him to do.

Then, too, Sister and Shaker had worked together, cheek by jowl, for nearly twenty years; usually she was right. He tormented her mercilessly when she wasn't but all in good fun.

Within four minutes at a relaxed trot they reached the Lorillard brothers.

The second Sister and Shaker saw their faces they knew a fox had not been viewed.

Seeing the crows fly up, Cabel Harper couldn't

resist walking toward the edge of the ravine to look down.

Shaker held up hounds.

Ilona hissed at her. "Cabel!"

A moment before Cabel reached the precipice, St. Just, possessed of a wicked sense of humor, flew right over her head and everyone else's with that juicy eyeball.

Cabel screamed bloody murder, looked over the edge, turned her horse and rammed High Vajay so hard she unseated him, and then almost trampled the hounds.

Diddy said loudly, *That's the lady with the perfume.*

Cabel flew through the woods toward the farm road.

Ilona, ignoring Ramsey, rode up to Sister, astonished at both Cabel and what she had seen deep in the ravine.

"Master, please allow me to go after Cabel. I think she's quite lost her mind."

"Go," Sister simply said.

Ben Sidell, already making his way down on foot, confirmed what Sister and Shaker had suspected, as crows lifted up when Ben drew closer. The crows' lunch was Clayton Harper.

In the distance, receding, people could hear Cabel screaming.

Ben climbed back up; his cell wouldn't work in the ravine. He called the department and flipped the phone back, leaving it on.

Kasmir helped Vajay back up. The horse was fine but Vajay had fallen flat on his back, knocking the wind out of him.

Mandy held the horse's reins, feeling an unspecified sense of dread. She shrugged it off, deciding that Cabel's screams were unnerving. Then again, St. Just's display of the eyeball certainly ruined the appetite.

"Sister, take everyone back, will you?" Ben turned to Walter. "When my team comes, will you bring us back here? You know the terrain better than I do."

"Of course." Walter nodded.

As the field rode back, everyone talked. Gray stuck with Sam, since in company with hounds, humans, and other horses Sam's steeplechaser grew restive. Fortunately few saw Clayton since Sister prudently kept them back, but everyone saw the offending king of the crows.

CHAPTER 29

Back at the trailers, Ilona caught up with Cabel. "What have you done?"

"Help me. Help me get out of here."

"Cabel, what have you done?" Ilona dismounted quickly, tying her horse to the side of the trailer, slipping the halter over the bridle first. "You told me he was in rehab."

"He figured it out. What else could I do?" Although rattled by Gray and Sam's discovery of her husband's body, she evidenced no regret. "He even figured out that I put the silver bowl in Sister's barn, because I left early for hunting that morning. What could I do?"

"For one thing," Ilona coolly responded, "you could have dumped him anywhere but a fixture."

"Didn't have time. We were driving out this way. Walter was at the hospital, so once Clayton cornered me I had to work fast."

"Did you shoot him?"

"Hell, yes, I shot him. Do you think I could strangle him? He was so fat I'd never get my hands around his neck." She snorted. "What a fool he was. Typical male. Thought he had nothing to fear from a woman. When I pulled my twenty-two out of my purse and shot him between the eyes—well, Ilona, that was one of the happiest moments of my life."

"Where were you?"

"Here. He'd been hectoring me, you know, citing the time I left the Casanova Ball, how I loathed Faye Spencer. I asked him if he'd slept with her and he said that was none of my business. He tried to pin it on Ramsey, who did call on her, but this is one instance where your dear husband bearded for mine. Or for all I know they bearded for each other. They fooled everyone. What shits." She smiled wryly. "One down, one to go, but I'll deal with Ramsey later. I need to get out."

"I'll deal with Ramsey. How did you ever drag Clayton down that ravine?"

"Easy as pie. I shot him in the bed of the truck.

First, I told him to drive down the Mill Ruins farm road because I wanted to help feed foxes at Shootrough, and when we neared the widest part of the ravine—where I remembered it anyway—I told him to stop. Then I climbed into the truck bed and lifted a twenty-five-pound bag of dog food but I pretended I couldn't quite do it so he clambered up and I shot him. It never occurred to him that it might be odd to carry your purse into the bed of a truck."

Despite herself, this made Ilona laugh. "No blood?"

"Hardly. I hit him square between the eyes. So he now has the third eye of prophecy. The silly bastard. I should have killed him first, you know, before dispatching that Indian slut to Shiva or whatever those people worship. Then again, waiting made it sweeter, plus he had to pretend he didn't know anything about her." She threw a cooler over her horse. "The hard part was getting back in the woods without scraping up the truck. Got as close as I could and then I kept rolling him until I rolled him right over the edge. The snows came as a godsend, I will admit. Covered my tracks. And you know what else? It also never occurred to him to ask me why I was feeding foxes. That's not my job. Nothing but air between those ears—which, of course, I found out for certain when I shot him. The bullet just sailed right through."

Ilona's head snapped up. "Cabel, I can hear the horses." She put her hands on her friend's forearm. "Give yourself up. You can't get away. There's not even time to unhitch your trailer."

Cabel realized Ilona was right. "Guess they'd catch me anyway." Her eyes blazed. "But I'm not going down without a fight. If I have to die, I'll die on my feet."

"Cabel, please, there were extenuating circumstances. A good lawyer can spare you the death penalty."

"Well, you're an accessory. I killed for you as well as for me; Ramsey slept with Aashi. You didn't have the guts." She sighed. "You always were a softie."

"I know." Ilona admitted what to Cabel was a flaw. "Yes, I am an accessory. I helped you with both women. But I'll face the music. We can't go on. We can't."

"Are you sorry?" Cabel did love her best friend.

"Yes and no." Ilona, tears in her eyes, confessed. "I'm sorry we're going to get caught but I'm not sorry Aashi and Faye received the deaths they deserved. I'm not sorry I helped you. After all, I owed you one." She smiled sadly. "Revenge is much sweeter than people want to believe."

"It is, isn't it?" Cabel laughed. "That's the point of Christianity, to remove revenge from our hands. Mine are covered with blood and I'd do it again."

They heard Shaker's strong voice. "Good hounds, good hounds."

Cabel grabbed Ilona, kissed her on the cheek, and sprinted to the old mill, opening the heavy door and closing it behind her.

Ilona stood there, face wet with tears. She turned to

take the halter and then the bridle off her horse, slipping the halter back on. She also loosened the girth for Cabel's horse, removing the bridle.

When Sister rode up she noticed Ilona's tears. "Where's Cabel?"

"I don't know. I couldn't catch up with her but I found Mickey tied to the trailer. She's so distraught there's no telling where she is. I'm afraid she might—"

Sister, thinking Ilona meant suicide, looked down from Lafayette's back and said, very low, "We'll check the millrace."

"Oh, God." Ilona burst into sobs.

Sister hurried to her trailer and handed her horse's reins to Tootie, who was already on the ground. "Tootie, I need your help. Take care of Lafayette." She walked over to Shaker, Betty, and Sybil, still mounted. "I'll get the door." She opened the party wagon door and the hounds walked in, glad for a fresh drink of water from the big buckets. Sister counted heads as they walked in. "All on."

Huntsmen and two whippers-in dismounted.

Betty patted Outlaw's neck. "A day not to be forgotten, for both good and ill."

"And it's not over yet." Sister rapidly repeated what she had assumed was Ilona's fear.

Shaker exhaled. "I'll walk the millrace."

Sister hurried back to her trailer with Betty. "Tootie, when you finish with Lafayette, help Shaker, will you? Staff has an extra chore." Then, hoping she appeared calm, she walked to the Custis Hall van.

"Val, will you tell Walter, he's in his stable, staff is walking the millrace. I'll explain to him later." She checked her pocket watch. "Be another twenty minutes before Ben's people reach us. Pamela, make sure everyone gets into the house for the breakfast. Lorraine's in charge today, but she'll need you and Felicity. People are at loose ends, obviously. If they're all together, maybe Lorraine—" She turned as Charlotte Norton rode up. "Charlotte, I've given the girls assignments. If I may, I'll give you one also. Pamela and Felicity will herd everyone into the house. Will you help calm folks? Keep them out of the way of Ben's people." She paused. "Just in case something else pops up." Realizing what she'd just said and thinking Cabel was in the millrace, she shut her eyes for a second.

"Of course." Charlotte agreed readily. "I'll wait for you or Ben to give me the all clear."

"Please excuse me. Staff has a chore to do, and I don't know when or if we'll get to the breakfast."

Gray and Sam were at Sam's trailer, one of Crawford's.

"Gray," Sister called out, "will you help Lorraine? Walter needs to get Ben's people back to the ravine."

Gray nodded. "Yes."

Sister watched Val run to Walter's stable and then walk back toward to the millrace. The water moved along, which meant if Cabel jumped in near the mill itself, her body would already be hung up in the paddles, slowing the wheel or slipping under. Since the huge wheel turned easily, if Cabel was in the race, her body hadn't yet drifted down. In her heavy frock coat, she'd be at the bottom. This gruesome thought pushed Sister onward. Drowning must be a painful death; one's lungs burst. She thought as she walked along the race in its swift course toward the mill that perhaps there were few easy, painless deaths. Best not to dwell upon it.

The millrace itself originated in a deep hard-running stream a mile from the mill. The hands that cut the race back in the late 1790s had turned to dust, but their excellent work bore testimony to their skill, as did the stonework lining the cut waterway. The expense of duplicating such a feat today, if one could even find the artisans, would spiral into a couple of million dollars, to say nothing of interference from local and state agencies.

Shaker soon joined her, as did Sybil and Betty, who moved much farther up toward the stream.

Tootie, finished with Lafayette, headed toward the house just as Val emerged from the barn. The two met on the wide bridge over the millrace, the mist from the spray enveloping them.

Tootie looked up through open patches. "Sky's changing again, pushing this down."

"Feels like snow." Val grinned. "I love it when it snows. The whole world is new."

"Guess we'd better get to the breakfast. Everyone's supposed to gather in the house, and I think they have."

"Mrs. Merriman hasn't." Val tilted her head in the direction of Ilona's trailer. The woman sat on her mounting block, head in hands, sobbing, as Ramsey attempted to comfort her. They had some sort of exchange, and Ramsey reluctantly left her for the house after kissing her on the cheek.

"Better not go there." Tootie wondered how anyone could find comfort, given that your best friend was coming apart at the seams.

The young women didn't know why Sister, Shaker, Betty, and Sybil walked the millrace, but they certainly noticed the staff members peering intently into the running water, the mist coming farther down now and skimming the water.

"Tootie, I have a terrible feeling about this."

It dawned on Tootie that the day's dreadful events might not yet be over. "Should we help?"

"If Sister wanted us, she'd ask." Val looked up at the large wheel turning.

The small wooden door near the middle of the wheel suddenly opened, the hinge squeaking. Cabel Harper leaned out, looked around, and closed the door.

Val ran across the bridge, Tootie in her wake. She opened the large door at the base of the mill and entered.

Tootie's instincts told her not to go in but Val was already through the door, so she cupped her hands to be heard over the turning wheel. "Master, Master!"

Sister looked in her direction as Tootie pointed to

the mill and then disappeared through the door. "Shaker, Betty, Sybil, come on!"

The four were running along the slippery millrace when they heard a shot. This spurred them on. Shaker was first through the door.

"Don't move!" Cabel called. She was standing next to one of the enormous slow-moving gears, each tooth catching the tooth of its mated gear.

Tootie, still as a mouse, was half obscured by a heavy shaft. Cabel could see her but couldn't get a clear second shot. She held the .22 to Val's temple, the barrel opening slightly warm from the fired bullet.

When the girls saw her, Cabel had rushed down the wide wooden stairs and grabbed Val as she came through the door. When Tootie lunged, Cabel had fired, but Tootie rolled and the bullet missed.

"Let her go, Cabel." Shaker kept calm, making no attempt to protect himself, but he didn't move. Neither did Sister, Betty, or Sybil.

"What do you take me for, a complete idiot? Val's my passport." Cabel grinned. "Now, if you all have the silly idea of rushing me, I have five shots left, one for each of you, and I'm not a half bad shot. Even if one or two of you don't get hit, I have plenty of time to reload."

"Then I'll get away," Val vowed, bold as she was on a horse.

"Oh, my pet, I'll shoot you first. Look at it this way: It's my Christian duty; I'm sparing you a life of pain, at the mercy of evil men."

Sister stepped forward, pushing past Shaker. "Cabel, swap me for Val. I'm old. Let her go."

"Spare me your nobility. I'm not letting any of you go. I know what you really are, Jane Arnold. You slept with my husband."

"For God's sake, Cabel, that was twenty years ago!" Sister exclaimed.

Sister hoped to create a diversion, as Tootie crouched and then crept toward Cabel, who grasped the collar of Val's coat and hauled her backward, toward the steps and up them.

Cabel ascended to the first landing, giving her better sight lines. "Val, if you don't struggle, I might let you go."

"Yes, Mrs. Harper." Val sounded ever so polite as her mind feverishly sought an escape.

Shrewdly, Betty moved next to Sister. "Cabel, what's happened? This isn't like you."

"Oh, it is. I am walking into my house justified." Cabel used the old southern expression.

Sister answered with another one. "What you're doing, Cabel Harper, is coming home by Weeping Cross."

"Oh, do shut up, you old bitch!" Cabel laughed uproariously. "I'll give you credit, though. You've shown good sport and you can ride. Yes, you can. 'Course, I'm not half bad myself." She laughed again.

"Cabel, please let her go. I'll put my hands behind my head and come up the stairs. Please don't harm that girl." Sister wanted to scream but kept her voice as modulated as if she were playing bridge.

"No. We're all going to heaven together, although if Val is a very, very good girl, I might spare her so she can tell everyone else what happened. There should always be one person left to tell the tale after a massacre." She looked upward at the next level. "I can see the coverage on TV now: *Massacre at Mill Ruins. Cabel Harper, upstanding member of the community, lost her shit and killed five people.* Guess they wouldn't say *lost her shit* would they?"

"And why are you saying it? You never used to be crude." Sister baited her.

A flash of anger illuminated Cabel's pretty features. "What does being a lady get you? You do as you're told. You marry well. You work hard. You participate in volunteer organizations. You vote. What does it get you? Nothing. It's a façade, a lure, so people like you or me don't look too closely at how things really work. At who really controls the world. We're cogs in the wheel just like these cogs in here. Eventually you get ground down."

"Was that Clayton? Is that why you ran off screaming?" Shaker stuck next to Sister because if Cabel fired he was going to jump in front. He had no more desire to be hurt than the next guy, but he never lacked courage and he would defend someone he loved. His feeling was "Why live if there's no one you'd die for?"

Sybil picked up the line. "You shot him, didn't you?"

When Sybil rode in to hold hounds she'd looked down into the ridge and thought she'd recognized Clayton's maroon windbreaker, although under the circumstances it was difficult to be certain.

One squad car and an ambulance drove across the bridge, no sirens.

"Damn," Sister whispered.

Tootie kept creeping until now she was under a gear parallel to the floor as she edged closer to the stairs.

"Shot that son of a bitch dead to rights. I should have done it years ago."

"Judgment is up to God." Sister's anger was coming to the fore no matter how hard she tried to keep it in check.

"Bullshit. God is another helpful illusion. If people believe that crap, you don't need as many cops to keep them in line, do you?" Cabel smiled. "Sheep. We're all sheep, but I woke up. I was wronged, but I fixed it."

"You killed Aashi and Faye?" Betty, too, was looking for a place to dive and then crawl toward the stairs.

"Did. It was a bitch, hauling those carcasses up on the horses, but I had help."

"Why did you clean them up?" Sister was curious.

"I didn't want anything to distract from their beauty or from the retribution, even though people didn't know why they were killed. Beauty lured Clayton. He was so weak. Well, you lured him too. You should know."

"He was weak." Sister agreed with Cabel, which pleased her.

"High Vajay is innocent?" Sybil asked, to keep Cabel talking.

"No. He didn't kill anyone, but he's a faithless pig like every other man."

"I resent that." Shaker hoped to draw her ire.

Tootie suddenly crawled as fast as she could, rolling under the stairs. Cabel fired, but too late.

"Now you only have four bullets," Tootie taunted.

"Tootie, stay where you are." Val's voice was strong.

"I'll kill you first." Cabel crouched down to fire under the stairs.

Val twisted free; at six foot one she was taller and stronger than Cabel. She grabbed Cabel from behind, struggling to grasp her right wrist. Cabel kicked backward, catching Val on the shin, but not hard enough to dislodge her.

Tootie bolted from under the stairs, vaulting them two at a time.

Sister, Shaker, Betty, and Sybil followed.

Cabel turned as Val held her as though twirling on the dance floor. Desperation increased the middle-aged woman's strength, and as a foxhunter she'd kept in good shape. She pushed her right hand forward with all her might, slamming the butt of the gun into Val's forehead and opening a wide gash. Val lost her grip, blood gushing into her left eye. Tootie was still six steps away as Cabel whirled to fire.

"No!" Sister screamed as Cabel took aim, but Tootie kept coming.

Eyes focused on Cabel's index finger, Tootie saw the squeeze and flung herself down as Val, wiping blood from her eye, bumped Cabel.

The bullet grazed Tootie's boot at the calf.

The bottom door opened. Ilona, hearing the shots, raced in.

Cabel looked down, then back at the two girls. She hesitated a second.

Ilona, tears running as fast as the millrace, shouted, "Cabel, no. Please, no!"

"Let's go together." Cabel, tears now in her eyes, aimed and shot Ilona through the heart. As Tootie rose to jump her, Cabel swung wide. Tootie ducked, as did Val.

Sister, Shaker, Betty, and Sybil closed in behind the two girls.

Cabel kicked Tootie hard with her boot and pushed her into Val, who was struggling to keep the gushing wound from bleeding into both her eyes.

Then she turned, running upward, the thump of her boots on the wooden stairs echoing through the vast interior. Sister passed the girls and charged after her.

"Boss," Shaker bellowed, "leave her to heaven. Let's get out of here." He reached over, took Val's hand, and led her down to the next level as Betty covered his back, glancing backward and upward in case Cabel would fire again. She had three bullets left.

Sister, fighting her rage and her desire to fight,

302

turned and came down in one leap, the sound as she landed booming through the mill, and grabbed Tootie, who was limping from the vicious kick and bullet graze. "Can you put weight on it?"

Tootie could, but she moved too slowly. Sister swiftly bent over, put one arm through Tootie's legs, lifted her up with the other, and swung her on her back in a fireman's carry.

Sybil, turning around, stopped, let Sister pass, then descended behind her like Betty, looking upward and back.

Had Cabel wanted to, she could have halted her ascent and nailed at least one of them, but she waited until she reached the top, right over the waterwheel, where another small half door was closed.

She called down to them as they reached the lower landing, ten feet above the ground floor. Her gaze was fixed on Ilona, knees bent under her like a resting horse, upper body bent back.

"I spared you girls. You love one another. Friendship is the purest love in the world. Trust me, kids, sex is a poison that infects everything. As for you, Jane Arnold"—she took careful aim—"drop Tootie."

Sister turned around, bent low so Tootie could slide off. "Go ahead. I'll take my chances."

"You've got brass ovaries." Cabel looked down the barrel, lining up Sister. "I'll give you that."

"Tootie, get down. Go with the others," Sister commanded.

"No."

"For Christ's sake, Tootie. Go! You're young. If it's my time, it's my time."

"No."

"Tootie, get out of the way," Cabel ordered.

Val, stock tie ripped off, pressed it to her head as she turned around to climb back up.

Shaker spun around, snatching the bottom of her coat. "No you don't."

"Tootie," Val pleaded.

Cabel couldn't get a clear shot. "Goddammit, if only we could have a proper duel." She pointed the gun upward. "You'll live a bit longer, you old bitch." Laughing, she opened the door, crouched, put one leg out, and then turned. Sister and Val had finally reached the floor. "Remember, friendship is the purest love. I'm going to be with Ilona."

CHAPTER 30

Walter had hopped into one squad car to lead them to the body. Ben jumped in too. Gray and Charlotte acted as hosts for the breakfast but he kept checking the back window. Lorraine, apprised of the situation, kept the food coming. Ramsey Merriman, ordered by Ilona to go to breakfast, also kept looking for her. Gray couldn't stand it anymore—Charlotte Norton did a better job than he did anyway—so he threw on his coat and walked outside, reaching the bridge just in time to see Cabel Harper crouching in the half door. The wide flat blades of the waterwheel rolled past her. She smiled and leaned forward, holding the edge of the door with her left hand. Simultaneously she stepped forward with her left boot and pushed off with her right. For one precarious moment she was poised on the wide blade of the waterwheel like a small car on a Ferris wheel. She put the gun to her temple and fired.

Her body hit the next blade, and the next, and then soared outward, her cap coming off and her wig with it, plunging into the water below, mists swirling above the surface.

As the small bedraggled party came out of the big mill door they couldn't see the bubbles rising and popping from the millrace. Gray blinked, then rushed to them.

"Gray, Gray!" Sister called to him as he approached. "Call Walter."

Gray saw the blood all over Val's face and her bloodstained shirt, saw Tootie limping, blood on the side of her leg. He reached into his inside pocket and dialed Walter. Then he threw his arms around Sister, holding her tight.

"Honey, honey. I need to breathe. I'll tell you everything later. Let's get these girls into Walter's bathroom."

"There's a bathroom in the barn," Tootie reminded Sister. "We won't have to deal with people there."

"Good thinking."

Betty came up and quietly slipped her hand into Sister's while Gray held the other one. They walked over the bridge. Val supported Tootie with her free hand, her other hand pressing her stock tie against her forehead.

Sybil moved up to help with Tootie so Val could keep the compression on her head. She fished in her pocket for a handkerchief, handing it to Val.

"Mrs. Fawkes, I can't use this. It's embroidered," Val said, ever sensitive to value.

"It's hardly as important as your wound." Sybil shoved the handkerchief at her and took her bloody stock tie.

Shaker had stopped to peer down at the bottom of the millrace. The mists swirled, as clear patches opened up, then closed again. He caught up with the others. "She's up against the end of the race."

Sister grimaced. "Let the sheriff's department fish her out."

"Who's going to tell Ramsey?" Gray had told them exactly what he saw as they reached the barn.

"Oh, let it wait a bit. Let it wait." Betty felt so exhausted she could hardly lift one foot in front of the other.

"I'll tell him." Shaker looked down at the center aisle of the barn paved with rubber bricks. "Can't have him running all over looking for his wife."

"Shaker, wait until Ben gets back. Ramsey might lift the body. Ben should see Ilona before she's disturbed," Gray said sensibly.

Walter arrived within minutes, driven by Ben in his deputy's squad car. Shaker flagged him down. Ben cut the motor and the two men flew out of the car. As Walter examined the girls, Shaker led Ben to Ilona's body, also pointing out where Cabel lay, slightly moving under the water as though alive, her body hitting the end of the race and moving away for a foot, then pushed by a paddle to hit the end of the race once more. The opening and closing mist made the sight even more eerie.

"Val, I need to stitch this up. It's going to hurt. I have procaine, which I'll rub on, but it's still going to hurt."

"Just do it, Master." Val also felt exhausted as she sat in the chair in the tack room.

"Sybil, my bag's in the front seat of the truck. Would you mind fetching it?" He turned to Tootie, boot still on. "Luckily the bullet tore your boot more than it tore you. It's the kick that is raising up the knot on your shin." He felt her skin under her breeches.

Sybil hurried off as Sister stood in front of Tootie, back to her, and pulled off the damaged boot. Tootie bit her lip as it came off.

"Put ice on that," Walter ordered. "Might take a week to get your boot back on, but it's not bad." He walked over to the refrigerator, took out an ice tray, dumped half of it in a clean work towel, and handed it to the diminutive Tootie. " 'Course, you'll have to repair the boot." He smiled.

Sybil returned with Walter's bag. He washed Val's wound, quickly smearing it with procaine and giving it a few minutes to work while he threaded a needle.

Val held a clean rubdown towel on the gash, red seeping through the rough white cloth.

"Did you know that a horse's skin is thinner than a human's?" Sister decided conversation might help.

"I did."

"You are so-o-o smart." Tootie was feeling better.

Val eyed the threaded needle. "How many stitches, do you think?"

"Five at the most. I make a nice tight stitch. There will be a scar but it won't be bad. All right, take that bandage away. Let me clean this one more time." Sister handed him a prepared antibacterial wipe that was in his bag. "Now, if this hurts we need to give the procaine more time." He carefully wiped the wound, still bleeding but less so. He checked the ragged edges. "Going to be swelling from the blow. You might not get a black eye though, since she hit you high on the forehead."

"I can feel what you're doing but it doesn't hurt much."

"All right then. If you can hold still, this will take three minutes. I'm fast!" He smiled reassuringly at her.

The small group had watched countless horses stitched up, even doing it themselves sometimes, so watching Val didn't faze them.

Sister held her hand. Tootie held the towel filled with ice against her shin.

Tears rolled down Val's cheeks. "Sorry."

"I know you're not crying." Walter smiled as he

pierced her skin for the third stitch. "Body's natural reaction. Girl, you took one helluva hit. If she'd smashed your brow, she could have damaged your eye."

"Luck." Val tried to smile.

Tootie thought to distract her friend. "Do you believe what Cabel said about sex poisoning a relationship?"

"Why, do you want to sleep with me?" Val returned to form.

"You are so conceited." Tootie exhaled through her nostrils.

As Walter started the fourth stitch, Sister, knowing the longer one sat the more difficult it became, answered Tootie. "No, sex doesn't poison a relationship. People poison relationships. Sex is the excuse."

"Well said." Gray nodded.

"We'll never really know what those two did," Betty said. "I mean, we know Cabel killed Aashi and Faye, but Ilona helped somehow. Cabel had a hold on Ilona ever since college. Can you imagine helping your best friend kill someone? Actually, don't answer that." Betty wanted to let her head drop on her bosom; she needed to talk to keep awake.

Sybil piped up. "Their sex lives certainly seemed poisonous. How do people get twisted like that?"

"I don't know," Sister replied, as she dabbed Val's tears with her own handkerchief. "Almost done."

"I wonder why Cabel spared us when we went

down the stairs?" Tootie tried to make sense of it, tried to keep her emotions at bay.

"God's grace." Sister smiled as Walter finished the last stitch, snipping the thread.

"Wait one minute." He smeared on a little more procaine, giving Val two tiny tubes. "Val, this is going to sting and throb. Use this for a day or two and then just endure it." He covered his work carefully with a gauze pad, taping the ends with white adhesive tape. "Change this at least once a day, because the wound will still seep. Rub a lot of this antibacterial cream on too, because you don't want the bandage sticking when you pull it off. Okay? Going to hurt when you wash your hair. If you can bend over a sink to wash it, that's better than getting in the shower."

"I'll wash her hair," Tootie volunteered.

"Thank you, Dr. Lungrun." Val stood up and just as quickly sat down.

Walter grabbed her when she wobbled a little. "Honey, you've suffered a shock. You just sit there. Need a drink or anything?"

A little dazed, Val shook her head. "No."

"Gray, will you take Tootie and Val back to Custis Hall in the Land Cruiser?" Sister asked him. "I'll drive the horses back with Betty." She turned to Sybil. "Tell Shaker we've gone on." Then she spoke to her joint master. "Walter, please take charge here. I need to get these horses back and I'm a little shaky myself. I'm not up to the crowd."

"I'll tell Charlotte the girls have gone on," Walter agreed.

The little group left the barn. Just as they reached the trailers, they saw Shaker emerge from the mill with Ben. Sybil walked toward the men.

Betty said, "I want to get out of here before Ramsey sees her."

"Yes," Sister replied.

The girls moved slowly with Gray to his big Land Cruiser.

Val, voice wavering, took Tootie's hand. "Thank you. I love you, Tootie."

"I love you too."

Once in the trailer, Sister hit the window button, calling out to Ben, "I'll give you the details later, Ben. Trust me?"

"Yes." He waved, face solemn, as behind him two deputies, already wet from mist, knelt over the mill-race to figure out how to haul up Cabel's body without going in themselves.

The motor cranked on the truck. Sister never tired of that sense of power.

Once out on the road, Betty covered her eyes a moment. "We were pretty close to a ticket out of life."

"I know."

"Cabel always hated you. Never stopped. Never could let the past go." Betty inhaled deeply. "Lot of people like that in the world. All it brings is misery and death." She paused. "I never saw it coming, did you?"

"No. Funny how the mind ignores evidence. I underestimated jealousy and hate, and I underestimated Cabel. Good actress, though. I kept looking for a male killer, not a female. I was blind, really."

"She just"—Betty paused, then used the southern explanation for tremendous misdeeds—"snapped."

"Took Ilona with her." Sister noticed the flock of crows overhead, St. Just in the lead. "I don't understand a lot of things in this world. I don't even try anymore. I accept that I can't understand and that, if there are answers, I won't find them. I don't know if that's maturity or resignation."

"Both." Betty leaned forward to watch the large flock of crows fly overhead. "Not much for crows but someone has to be nature's garbageman." She turned back to Sister. "You could have been killed."

"You too."

"Were you as calm as you seemed?"

A long pause followed. "Yes." Then she smiled. "When the Good Lord jerks your chain, you're going. He doesn't want me yet. Then again, what if I'm headed downtown, not uptown?"

Betty laughed. "Won't know until we get there."

After a few moments, Sister spoke, "Hindsight makes us all smart. It's obvious now but I didn't see it there. You know, Cabel's hair loss, erratic behavior, loss of self-control: She was in the last stages of syphilis. You lose your mind."

Betty rubbed her temples. "It's making a big comeback."

"She hadn't been to the doctor in about twenty years. He had. But he passed it on to her." She paused. "They both paid for it."

"Sometimes I think history should be written from the standpoint of syphilis, malaria, black plague, tuberculosis, AIDS."

"You're right." Sister sighed heavily.

"It will take years for this to really hit those girls," Betty added.

"Us too. But you know, it's the duty of the old to protect the young. The only person in that mill who should have hidden herself and wouldn't have been shamed for it was Sybil. Her sons aren't grown. For the rest of us—well, we did what we had to do."

"Not everyone thinks like that."

"We're not everyone." Sister suddenly felt a burst of emotion. "Not by a long shot. I don't give a damn what's popular, and I don't give a damn about fashions, including moral fashions. The old must protect the young."

"I know." Betty felt Sister's energy lifting her own. "But we're country people. We live close to nature."

"Makes no matter." As Sister saw her Roughneck Farm sign, a flood of gratitude welled up in her. "City people are as obligated as we are to take care of the young."

"They don't obey the laws of nature. They no longer know them." Betty worried about urbanization and the destruction of the environment by people who often thought they were protecting it.

"Well, you know what, sugar pie? Nature will one day reach into those steel towers and shake them loose. Hers is the ultimate power."

As they coasted to the stable, Inky and Georgia shot out from the barn, where they had been enjoying left-over sweet feed and a bowl of sour balls.

Sister and Betty led one set of horses off the trailer and then a second. They cleaned them, tossed fresh blankets over them, put each in a stall with fresh warm water and delicious flakes of hay, and added a couple of handfuls of sweet feed to their food buckets.

The routine of chores helped each woman calm down.

A cat door, cut into the stable office and well used by Golly, had also been used by Inky and Georgia. They left behind their signature scent, a fox calling card.

Chores done, Sister and Betty walked into the heated office for a moment to warm their hands, and both noticed the bowl of sour balls, wrappers all over the floor.

"How do they do that? How did Inky get the cellophane off?" Sister put her hands on her hips.

"Foxes work magic." Betty laughed, then looked at her silver-haired friend. "Jane, I love you. I could have lost you." She hugged Sister.

"I love you too." Sister hugged Betty back. "But by God, Betty, we would have died game."

ACKNOWLEDGMENTS

Marion Maggiolo and Wendy Saunders helped enormously by fighting their way through a first draft, correcting mistakes and making good suggestions.

For the record, the information regarding Horse Country's security system is false for obvious reasons. The John Barton Payne massive trophy, owned by the Warrenton Horse Show, is housed there because Marion's security system is second only to the bank's. The bank did not have a large enough space to house this incredible bowl, ladle, and tray, known affectionately as "Big John."

The Warrenton Horse Show, an outdoor show held at summer's end, is a delightful spectacle, well run and worth a visit.

For those of you not able to make the trip to Warrenton, you can visit Horse Country at www.HorseCountryLife.com. The phone is 1-800-882-4868. You always meet people you know there even if you've never met them before.

Special thanks to Danielle Durkin, my former editor, and good luck writing her own novels.

Man does not live by bread alone but this woman does when she's writing. Were it not for Mrs. Ryan Schilling and her soda bread, Mrs. Robert Satterfield and her banana bread, Mrs. William Stevenson III and her corn bread, I'd perish. Emily, Sue, and Lynn, respectively, are also members of Oak Ridge Hunt

Club. Sue leads first flight and is bold as brass. Emily is training as a whipper-in and helps me in the kennels, and Lynn is our hunt secretary, a task I wouldn't wish on a dog and she performs it with aplomb.

I note here the passing of my glorious, huge, old Plott hound, Punch. He was eighteen, had all his faculties, but age caught up with him May 1, 2007. Born to hunt bear, he did so without my contrivance. When he finally realized we hunt foxes around here, he declined smaller game and took up hunting thunderstorms. This had to be seen to be believed. He was a dear friend and I will miss him. Even my cats miss him, which is a testimony to his personality.

On another note, four hunt books equal one year. I have not clearly stated this before but thought perhaps I should. Each book represents a season: spring, summer, fall, winter. If I didn't do this, Sister would be one hundred before you know it. Yes, she has to grow older, as do I, but let's not rush it.

Center Point Publishing

600 Brooks Road • PO Box 1
Thorndike ME 04986-0001 USA

(207) 568-3717

US & Canada:
1 800 929-9108
www.centerpointlargeprint.com